WHAT THE WIFE KNEW

Also by Darby Kane

Pretty Little Wife
The Replacement Wife
The Last Invitation
The Engagement Party

WHAT THE WIFE KNEW

A Novel

DARBY KANE

wm
WILLIAM MORROW
An Imprint of HarperCollins*Publishers*

This is a work of fiction. Names, characters, places, and incidents are products of the author's imagination or are used fictitiously and are not to be construed as real. Any resemblance to actual events, locales, organizations, or persons, living or dead, is entirely coincidental.

WHAT THE WIFE KNEW. Copyright © 2024 by HelenKay Dimon. All rights reserved. Printed in the United States of America. No part of this book may be used or reproduced in any manner whatsoever without written permission except in the case of brief quotations embodied in critical articles and reviews. For information, address HarperCollins Publishers, 195 Broadway, New York, NY 10007.

HarperCollins books may be purchased for educational, business, or sales promotional use. For information, please email the Special Markets Department at SPsales@harpercollins.com.

FIRST EDITION

Interior text design by Diahann Sturge-Campbell

Library of Congress Cataloging-in-Publication Data has been applied for.

ISBN 978-0-06-335196-7
ISBN 978-0-06-335200-1 (hardcover library edition)

24 25 26 27 28 LBC 5 4 3 2 1

To all the survivors of family dysfunction who vowed not to pass the mess on to the next generation. You are society's silent heroes.

To my mom, who is nothing like the moms in this book. I swear this is fiction.

I will hurt you for this. I don't know how yet, but give me time. A day will come when you think yourself safe and happy, and suddenly your joy will turn to ashes in your mouth, and you'll know the debt is paid.

—George R. R. Martin, *A Clash of Kings*

WHAT THE WIFE KNEW

Chapter One

HER

Present Day

I'd never attended a funeral before, but I needed to be in the room for this one, mostly to make sure the jackass in the casket stayed dead. I now understood why people dreaded these things. The weeping. The somber music. The recounting of stories no one cared about. The pregame week of casseroles.

Richmond Dougherty. Make that Dr. Richmond Dougherty. Renowned pediatric surgeon. Childhood hero. Infamous tragedy survivor. He deserved to be in a box. He should have been in a box decades ago, but some things took time.

The dramatic music swelled and the minister, or whatever his official title was, finished what felt like the twentieth prayer of the hourlong service. When everyone stood, I turned, ready to bolt outside for some fresh air. Then the line started.

The audience queued in the center aisle, headed toward the casket. With a low rumble of uncomfortable conversation, the mourners and gawkers filed up, one by one, and paid homage to the now-boxed Richmond. Some people peeked inside before moving on. Others stopped. A few talked to the dead body.

My stomach growled, making me regret leaving half a bagel on the kitchen counter before this shindig started.

Minutes dragged by, slow enough for the prolonged genuflecting to turn comical. Finally, Kathryn Dougherty, high school sweetheart and mother to Richmond's two perfectly educated, perfectly dressed children, wandered up to take her turn. With unsteady steps, she passed the cascade of blue and yellow bouquets, colors said to be Richmond's favorites. She plunged headfirst into the drama with teary nods to a few people on her right and the reach of a consoling hand toward someone in the pews to her left, fingers never quite touching.

An expert level display of grief and ego. The woman was on fire.

Her son, Wyatt, twenty and doing an admirable job of hiding his panic because Daddy's death touched off a tectonic shift in the handling of family assets, slipped in beside his mother and half dragged, half carried the wilting woman to the front of the room. Neither paid much attention to fifteen-year-old Portia, who tagged along. She walked with hesitant steps, sniffling in her flowing black dress, likely wishing she were back in the safe arms of her swanky boarding school.

The organist marked the somber family death march by pounding out chords in such an exaggerated manner that more than one person winced at the harsh melody. The scene was quite the mesmerizing display. Just as Kathryn intended.

I fought the urge to glance at my cellphone as Kathryn finally arrived at the casket. A heart-wrenching sob echoed throughout the church before she flung her body over Richmond's. Her arms disappeared inside the casket. Her hair somehow didn't move, but kudos to her for playing the role to the very end. That kind of commitment deserved a round of applause to accompany the stunned gasps floating through the room.

"This can't be happening." Kathryn choked out the words through a new bout of uncontrolled crying. "I can't lose you."

Too late.

Wyatt rushed to fish his mother out of the casket and knocked against the flower spray resting on top, sending loose petals spilling onto Kathryn and whatever else was in the box.

"Noooo." Kathryn broke into a full-throated wail this time.

Shouting *yes!* seemed like too much, so I refrained.

"Mom. It's okay. Come on." Wyatt hovered over Kathryn's convulsing body, trying to lift her off his dead father.

Stark whispers bounced around the back of the room. I ignored them, transfixed by the acting master class in front of me. Portia didn't appear as impressed. She walked away from her mother in a gloomy cloud of teenage despair just as the minister swooped in to assist Wyatt. Kathryn's legs barely held her as they pulled her out and dropped her sobbing form into a nearby pew.

This bitch knew how to work a room.

With a deep inhale, the minister dragged his attention away from all the weeping and waved his hand in my direction. "Mrs. Dougherty?"

Oh, shit. Right. Me. Mrs. Addison Dougherty. Dear dead Richmond's much younger second wife. A recent addition to this dysfunctional family. Town pariah. The person most people blamed for Richmond being in that box.

They weren't totally wrong. I wanted to kill him.

Someone beat me to it.

Chapter Two

HER

Married, Day Sixteen

The bedroom lights flickered on and off as music blared through all three stories of the large colonial house. An early morning unwanted wake-up call. The screen saver on my cellphone said it wasn't yet three. The pounding near my temples would likely last all day.

Richmond was consistent. A jackass, but a consistent one. He'd been playing this game for four days now. He'd weaponized the smart-home devices, sending the house into a downward spiral of flashing lights, spiking temperatures, and malfunctioning alarms.

So much for thinking he'd get bored. He'd ratcheted up his nonsense and added music from the whole-house speakers this round. The only solace came from knowing messing with me meant messing up his own sleep. But his behavior begged for a harsh lesson. The kind of metaphorical beating that would make him hesitate before unleashing his next bright idea.

Like most men in his I-deserve-expensive-things circle, he craved power, but he failed to understand how to harness it. Real power grew out of a festering anger that fought any form of healing. Match fury with rigid determination and a bone-deep sense of *I don't care what you think about me,* and you win.

Richmond didn't have the nerve. Behind the toothy grin and love of shiny objects, he needed to be liked. To be praised and honored. To believe the masses existed to bask in his glory. That misplaced hubris would be his downfall. Because all the male posturing in the world couldn't defeat a ticked-off woman on a mission.

Richmond had tricks and nighttime maneuvers. An array of covert actions to prove he reigned as top bully in the household. I had leverage. And a bat.

Throwing off the covers, I slid out of bed and into my slippers. The night-light from the attached bathroom showed the way. After a quick check in the mirror to make sure my loose pajamas still covered what needed to remain covered, I grabbed the end of the bat from its resting place next to my side of the bed.

There was no need to rush because revenge should be savored. By the time I reached my bedroom door, my sole goal and deepest desire turned to making Richmond wet himself with fear.

Undoing the bolt lock took a second then into the hallway, ready to go and swinging the weapon I'd bought for added security a week ago. The walk to his bedroom door took a dramatically long time. The moonlight streaming through the window lit my path. I marched past a series of closed doors until I got to his end of the second-floor hallway. The space under the closed door leading to this suite remained dark, as if he were pretending to be asleep.

Nice try.

He started this battle. Tonight, I would end it.

I turned the knob but the door didn't move. He'd locked it. Unlucky for him, I'd predicted another night of household harassment and loosened the screws to his simple chain lock. Why? Because I played this game better than he did. I created the fucking game.

One well-placed shoulder shove nearly knocked the door off its hinges.

"What the hell?" The light beside his bed clicked on. Richmond sat there, wide-eyed and gawking.

A good start.

"You've been a very bad boy, my dear husband."

He reached for his cellphone and did something to make the music clanging through the house stop. Next came the removal of his earplugs. Then he shot me his best *outraged man* expression. "What are you doing?"

Such unimpressive huffing and puffing. I aimed the end of the bat in the direction of his head. "I warned you to behave."

"Get the hell out of my bedroom."

"That doesn't sound like an apology." Time to swing and that stupid plaque hanging on the wall looked like the perfect target. The award naming him as a top doctor in New York State. It used to hang on the wall in the primary bedroom, but he took it with him when he relocated like it was his prized possession and not some nonsense way for a magazine to sell ads.

The *crack* split through the quiet room as wood slammed into the plaster with enough force to vibrate up my arms and put a dent in the wall. The award landed with a thud. The lamp on the chest of drawers beneath it teetered then fell, crashing and ripping a hole in the shade.

Perfect.

He stood up. "You stupid—"

"No." A slight pivot and now the bat hovered between us. "You don't get to create chaos then belittle me with nasty names when I call you out on your bullshit."

Standing six feet away, he stared at the end of the bat, clearly weighing the chance of grabbing it before I could land another swing.

"I dare you." Part of me ached for him to push me too far. "Please give me an excuse to beat you to death with this."

His eyes darted left then right as he performed what looked like a mental countdown. Probably giving himself a *you can do it* rah-rah speech like the psychopath he was.

He'd been showered with years of fawning press. Sycophantic fans prattled on about his courage and good looks. The black hair with silver streaks. The deep blue eyes. His admirers missed his rotting heart. The one I dreamed about tearing out of his chest, throwing on the floor, and stomping into a pulverized puddle of slush.

He took a deep breath. "What are you doing in here, Addison?"

An interesting change in tone. He sounded calm and reassuring. Refocused and carefully tuned to suggest I was the unhinged one. When he talked like this my paranoia about the presence of listening devices spiked. He was supposed to be a genius, after all. But I repeatedly checked and used a bug sweeper and never found anything, so I didn't edit my words when we were alone.

Smart or not he deserved the hellfire I'd been using to douse his once-storybook adult life. And I was only getting started.

"I told you to stop playing with the smart-home features." I'd been pretty clear on that point. Warned him more than once that he was wandering down a dangerous path. One that could blow up what was left of his carefully structured life.

He shook his head. "And I reminded you this is my house."

Oh, come on. This fight didn't require much energy at all. He could do better. "Not anymore."

A nerve in his cheek twitched. "I wanted to listen to music."

I refused to give him the satisfaction of calling out the blatant lie. Not when the bat could speak for me. The second swing lacked the star power of the first, but it was more targeted. The end smacked into the small case on his dresser that housed his prized watch. The crystal shattered and pieces pinged against the hardwood floor.

He dove as if he could catch the parts and magically put the timepiece back together in midair. When he looked up again he was on his knees in the middle of the guest room floor, cradling his beloved and now destroyed watch. "One of these days you're going to go too far."

An empty threat. How adorable. "Then what will happen?"

For a few seconds he stared, silently seething as hatred oozed out of him. Those priceless surgeon's hands cradled the broken and once very expensive watch. His thumb brushed over what had been its face. "You win this round."

He gave in quicker than expected. That couldn't be good. "Tomorrow we'll change the passwords."

He hadn't blinked since I stalked into the room. He was a man accustomed to getting his way. He bullied and harassed. Plotted without regard for anyone else. He was the type to force people to squeal then complain about the noise they made.

Those days were over.

"We'll change the passwords if you get rid of the bat." He stood up, looming over me and using every inch of his six-one frame to intimidate.

Dark energy swirled around us. A toxic mix of contempt and mistrust. I sucked it in and used it as fuel. "This isn't a negotiation."

"I can't spend my nights worrying that you'll get pissed off and kill me in my sleep. My job is too demanding. I need focus and rest."

Always the victim. "I'm impressed you got this far into the conversation before reminding me about how important you are."

"Some of us worked hard to earn the life we have." He nodded in my direction. "Some of us just take."

This asshole. He acted as if I didn't know what I knew. "Do you really want to have that discussion, dearest husband?"

He finally looked away to stare at the window and acres of quiet night beyond. "Don't call me that."

"Then let me be clear, *Richmond*." I waited until he looked at me again. "If I wanted to kill you, you'd be dead. So stop tempting me."

Chapter Three

HER

Present Day

Elias Zimmer showed up at the front door two days after Richmond and his box were dumped in the ground. After the initial flurry of activity and accusations following Richmond's death, my life had returned to its usual quiet. *Usual* in the sense of life without Richmond. So, happier.

At the time of his death we'd been married for ninety-seven days. A minister performed the very private ceremony in the family room of a house. No kids. No relatives. No friends, except for Elias, Richmond's personal lawyer.

Less than four months had passed since I took on the last name I loathed and married the man I ached to kill. Now I lived in the six-million-dollar house the original Mrs. Dougherty, Kathryn, handpicked but never occupied because Richmond divorced her first. A seven-bedroom house in Rye, New York, ridiculously oversized for the two people who were supposed to reside in it full-time.

Kathryn, who everyone agreed had impeccable taste—except for her taste in men, which could only be described as questionable—picked the place because of the lush grounds, the high-end appointments, and the close-in commute to Richmond's work at New York–Presbyterian Hospital in upper Manhattan. As part of the divorce, she got "stuck" with the older family home nearby, where she'd raised the kids. A mini mansion she now viewed as a hovel. Never mind that Kathryn's hovel actually was beautiful, still big, and expensive, just less enormous and less expensive than the one I'd snagged. Mine was also closer to the water, which made Kathryn wail about the unfairness.

What-*the-fuck*-ever.

The house and Richmond's will and the trust, and all the related money stuff, were the reasons Elias sat at my breakfast bar, sipping a latte I made with that fancy coffeemaker that took two days and an online video to learn to use.

"How are you?" he asked.

A seemingly innocuous question. My get-ready-for-a-shitstorm shield went up. "Fine."

Elias eyed me over the cup.

I eyed him back.

Elias was a lawyer, which meant he wasn't necessarily a narcissist or a psychopath but probably. Unclear at the moment which way he'd tip.

He definitely fell into the attorney category of *should be ashamed of his outrageous hourly rate but wasn't.* All pressed in his dark blue suit. Attractive and chiseled enough to win over a jury. Not too attractive or chiseled to piss them off or cheer for him to lose. Brown hair, graying at the temples. Dark eyes, like a shark lurking in shallow water. Always watching, assessing, judging.

Various online searches touted his self-made-man status. A guy who went from dockworker's son to big-time partner in a big-time New York City law firm. In his early fifties and divorced in a *we're still best friends* sort of way where he dragged the ex, Jessica or Jenny or something with a *J* sound, to all of his social events.

That last part suggested he might have something to hide, and I'd dug around to find out. Good to have leverage and all that, but unlike many in his social class who could best be summed up as *new money and very questionable,* Elias seemed to be exactly as presented. A successful, very smart attorney.

Call me skeptical.

In past meetings, formal and informal, he'd spoken with an economy of words and glanced at his phone every few seconds. He'd been in the house for more than ten minutes and had yet to pull his cell out of his suit jacket. That could mean anything.

"There are a few papers I need you to sign." He plunked down a stack on the kitchen counter in front of him.

"Uh-huh." Not signing those.

He smiled as if he knew the direction of my thoughts. "Technically, I'm your attorney now."

"Not technically or otherwise."

"This is a statement signed by Richmond." He pulled out a sheet from the top of the pile, as if he'd expected my screw-you response and prepared for it, then laid the document in front of me. "He was quite clear that if anything happened to him I was to step in, secure your rights, and represent your interests in his estate. He said I was to make sure you were happy."

That didn't sound like Richmond. "Why?"

Elias laughed. "Honestly? I have no idea. Even though what Richmond told me was confidential due to attorney-client privilege, he refused to tell me why the two of you married so quickly, or at all, and why it was so important to him that you got whatever you wanted even after his death."

There it was. The backhanded question I had no intention of answering. But kudos to the counselor for trying to pry open that bolted door.

"A love match?" Not sure how I got that vomit-inducing phrase out. Especially when the real answer was that Richmond wanted to preserve his unearned hero status after death and believed our Faustian bargain would ensure his legacy. Well, he miscalculated because I always intended to ruin him—dead or alive—and keep the money.

"You slept in separate bedrooms." Elias hesitated after dropping that insight. "You never said a decent word to or about each other, and that includes on your wedding day a short time ago."

"A hundred and eleven days." But it felt longer because every day of being the second Mrs. Dougherty dragged on like the countdown in a long prison sentence.

"I think you had something on him. Something very bad."

"That sounds like blackmail." And it was, which made me the blackmailed-him-into-marriage type. A crown I wore with pride.

Elias shrugged. "That's between the two of you . . . or was. My only concern now is to ensure your rights to the house and the assets, even if that means battling Kathryn and the kids."

"Ah, yes. Them." A few of my many outstanding problems. "But isn't it a conflict for you to represent Richmond then represent me?"

"He signed a waiver."

This felt like a trap. "I'm not sure what there is to handle since Richmond and Kathryn had a divorce agreement."

"True, but the divorce, his remarriage to you, and his death all happened within a very short time. Some might question the timing."

The whole damn town questioned it. "*Some* should mind their own business."

"You are my priority."

That sounded wrong. "So I'm stuck paying your outrageous hourly fee now?"

Elias downed the rest of his latte. "Yes, but you're welcome to obtain your own counsel. If you do, I will work with that person to protect your interests."

And that sounded too easy. "What are you doing right now?"

He reshuffled the papers into a tight, orderly bundle. "Lawyering."

"Yeah, I get that. I mean the *being decent* part." The concepts of decency and niceness always stumped me. I wasn't raised with either. I grew up in a household driven by petty grievances . . . and some not so petty. You schemed and looked for an advantage to win every battle, and everything was a battle. The steps were clear. Study. Wait. Attack. That was on the good days. "You're not name-calling or looking at me like I'm beneath you."

"Sounds like you've known some awful people."

"Your social set excels at that sort of thing."

He smiled. "It's also your social set now."

"I dare you to tell the neighbors that."

He sighed in the way older wealthy dudes did when they wanted to bring a conversation to a close on their terms. "Despite your reservations, which are understandable under the circumstances, Richmond did provide for you but there's a significant chance of Kathryn contesting the agreement now that he's dead."

Annoying but not a surprise. "She's the gift that keeps on giving."

"I believe she would say the same thing about you."

The distinctive *bong* of the doorbell echoed through the house in a deep, rich tone that could only be described as overly dramatic. Less drama would be a nice change.

I made a mental note to disconnect it as I picked up my cellphone and clicked on the security system app. The house sat behind a gate and that gate should be locked, sending a big *keep out* warning to anyone who wandered by, including anyone with the last name of Dougherty.

The video filled my screen. "Oh, shit."

"Kathryn?"

"Worse." I flipped the phone around to show Elias the image.

"Ah, yes. Detective Sessions. The other reason I'm here." Elias nodded. "He has news about the preliminary findings relating to Richmond's death."

"Funny how you forgot to mention that interesting tidbit before now."

"I did say that I consider myself your attorney, and you will need an attorney for the next few minutes. So, since I'm here . . ." Elias ended his speech with a shrug.

Asshole. "Why exactly do I need your services this fine morning?"

"They believe Richmond's death was not due to an accidental fall. It looks more like he was hit with something first." Elias's stare grew more intense. "Possibly a bat."

Chapter Four

HER

Present Day

Detective Dominick Sessions's stomping footsteps signaled his entry before he appeared in the doorway of the wood-paneled library. With a long stride and his chin up, he stalked into the room and stopped next to the intricately carved floor-to-ceiling fireplace.

The stale stench of *trying too hard* wound around him in an invisible cloud. He wore gray dress pants and a blazer in a slightly different shade of gray. The outfit said a lot about the wealth he tried to portray versus the wealth he actually possessed. A forty-something hometown boy who gave off a whiff of *not in my town* as he looked around the room.

Outmaneuvering him shouldn't be a problem. Dodging Elias's haunting "bat" reference might not be so easy.

As Elias suggested, I sat on the cream-colored couch positioned in the center of the room. Letting Elias play fetch and welcome the detective into the house gave me a few minutes to think, and now that reprieve had ended.

The detective nodded in my general direction. "Mrs. Dougherty."

Still hated that name. "Did you need something, Detective?"

Elias didn't sit. Didn't shuffle or fidget. He stood, holding a pen. He somehow commanded the room even though the taller, bulkier detective outweighed Elias's runner's frame by at least forty pounds.

Elias jumped right in. "You said you have news."

The detective frowned. "I'm confused about why you're here."

Now the unannounced appearance made sense. The detective had treated Elias to a good-ole-boy head's-up, not realizing Elias would be present as my attorney. Understandable. Elias being here confused me, too, but I crossed my legs and settled in for the show.

"I'm acting as Mrs. Dougherty's attorney," Elias continued.

Acting. The word seemed problematic. Probably just lawyer-speak, but who knew.

This time the detective's eyes narrowed. "Isn't that a conflict of interest?"

Looked like I wasn't the only one with that question.

"No," Elias said.

If I trusted Elias, I might enjoy the abruptness of his answer. But I didn't so . . . "Is there a problem, Detective?"

"Your interests and your late husband's might not, uh . . . completely, uh . . ." The detective winced instead of finishing his sentence.

"Align?" Elias asked, filling in the blank. "That's not a problem. Mr. and Mrs. Dougherty were completely in sync. They shared a loving marriage and a life view as well as their assets. I represent both the estate and Mrs. Dougherty."

Fascinating how he could just say wild shit and pull it off.

"That might not always be the case." The detective shot Elias one of those man-to-man looks. "Certain issues could arise."

Okay, enough of the coded doublespeak. "Just say whatever you're trying to dance around, hoping Elias will decipher it. Why are you here?"

"Mrs. Dougherty has been through a lot of unexpected turmoil over the last few weeks." Elias took a step closer to the couch. "It might be better if you outlined your concerns, Nick."

Nick?

The detective nodded. "There's a question about Richmond's manner of death. It would be helpful if Mrs. Dougherty came with me to answer some questions."

A perp walk. Not happening.

"I'm not—" I stopped because Elias held up his hand. At some point he'd need a lecture about that gesture being annoying and to never do it again, but the middle of this conversation didn't seem like the right time.

"I see." Elias nodded.

"Right." The detective took a slight step back, as if clearing the way for me to walk out of the house with him. "If you would just—"

"No," Elias said again.

The detective frowned. "Excuse me?"

"She's in mourning, Nick."

The detective shot a quick glance in my direction. "Clearly."

"I'm concerned you're digging for something without having any basis to do so. Investigating is your job, of course, but she isn't going to undergo hours of useless questioning in the hope that you can discover a crumb of information that's not there." Elias pocketed the pen he'd been holding. "You can run requests through me. If it becomes necessary to speak with her, then, of course, we will comply. But until that time, no."

I heard the unspoken *fuck you* in Elias's response. He treated police questioning like an invitation to a Fourth of July family barbecue with that one wacky uncle who could talk for hours about the government putting listening devices in food.

Who knew declining was an option?

The detective sighed. "There's no need to make this combative."

Elias nodded. "I agree."

Testosterone battles weren't my thing. Nothing about a fight filled with metaphorical chest pumping and dick measuring impressed me, but Elias holding his ground without trouble turned out to be the unexpected highlight of my day.

Still didn't trust him as far as I could drop-kick him.

"Look, we both know you're getting a lot of pressure from above to find a problem. To put my client on the defensive," Elias said. "*Someone* is whispering in your ear about Addison."

That whispering someone being Kathryn. She should be careful because I could do some whispering about her.

Elias continued as if he knew I wanted to say the comment out loud. "Richmond fell down the stairs. A tragic situation but end of story."

"The fall that led to his death was his third supposed accident in a span of two months. Those accidents all coming once he moved into the same house with your client." The detective shot me a questioning look. "Have anything to say about that?"

Nope.

"She's grieving. Richmond's accidents, so soon after their marriage, were a concern for her, as well." Elias shot me a look that said *stay quiet* before focusing on the detective again. "I can show you out."

Elias gestured toward the hallway behind the detective, giving the man no choice but to leave, but not before the detective offered a final parting shot. "The medical examiner changed the preliminary cause of death from 'accident' to 'undetermined.' Once she has the toxicology results we'll know more and we will have a conversation, Mrs. Dougherty."

Lucky me. "I'll look forward to that."

Elias escorted the detective out and returned in record time to meet me back in the kitchen. "Maybe ratchet down the sarcasm when dealing with Detective Sessions or anyone from his office. Local law enforcement wade through a lot of social nonsense and don't have a great deal of experience with murder cases, so let's not actively antagonize them."

"You're asking a lot." Then there was this part. "And you're hired, at least until I figure out what game you're playing. If it's follow-the-biggest-paycheck, then fine. I can appreciate wanting to get paid. But if you're messing with me to benefit Kathryn or—"

"I'd get disbarred."

"Right. Because all attorneys are so honorable."

He picked up his empty coffee cup and placed it in the sink. "The police, with Kathryn's pushing, are going to be all over this."

"She's the angry former spouse. They should question her." Seemed logical to me.

"My point is that I expect the police will get a search warrant for the house and for Richmond's office."

Not the best news but the way Elias kept standing there suggested something worse was coming. "What are you not saying?"

"I'm not saying anything because I can't." Elias took out his cell and glanced at the screen for the first time since he'd arrived. "If, hypothetically, you had a bat and I took it and hid it for you, I'd get in serious trouble. Similarly, I can't tell you to hide a bat that may or may not be in the house because that, too, would be problematic."

So many hypotheticals. "I didn't kill Richmond."

"I didn't ask."

It sounded like someone hoped to set me up for Richmond's death. That meant my new focus was figuring out who wiped out the scumbag and why they thought coming for me was a good idea. But I did have one nagging question. "You don't care? I thought Richmond was your friend."

"He wasn't but I didn't kill him."

"I didn't ask." But now I wondered.

Elias just became a lot more interesting.

Chapter Five

HER

Seven Months Earlier

Richmond Dougherty was not a hard man to find. He hid in plain sight. His face had been splashed all over the news, on gossip sites, and in true crime forums on and off for the past twenty-seven years. His place in history firmly established eleven days before his eighteenth birthday, when he appeared before the cameras teary and dazed, covered in blood and shaking. A victim and a hero.

Since then, he'd crafted his image. Packaged, shined, and sold it. A survivor on a mission. A young man who'd refused to cower. A person who did the right thing. A savior surgeon who continued to put others first and gave hope to countless parents.

The truth was he craved attention, sucked it in like oxygen. He gathered up every scrap of praise, breathed life into it, and thrived off of it. Some saw his surgical skills as a calling. A gift from God. People could believe what they wanted, what they needed, but deifying Richmond was like putting a golden crown on the devil himself.

I knew him. From a distance, but I saw the real him. The lies.

The deceit. I'd been briefed and weaponized. I'd heard about him since birth. My life's goal had been spelled out and hammered into me for more than a decade: destroy Richmond Dougherty. Unmask him. Tell his secrets. Shred his reputation.

Watching him now, sitting in a dark corner of a nondescript bar just outside Philadelphia, I could see every flaw etched on his face. The shadows under the supposed handsome charm. A lurking darkness that poisoned every decent act.

He leaned in and smiled as he played with the fingers of the pretty blonde sitting next to him in the circular booth. He was forty-four. She was far too young for him. Miles better than him. A woman who should run.

She was also not his wife.

While Kathryn wiled away at home, putting the final touches on a charity luncheon scheduled for next week, Richmond was here, at his pretend conference in another state, screwing his weekend conquest. The woman crossed her legs and dipped her head to one side. She flirted, unaware that she'd bought into a PR image. A shimmer of a man.

She deserved better. So did Richmond's mistress back home. The one who worked in his medical office. So did his wife. So did all of the people unlucky enough to stray into his path.

I'd studied his string of women because I'd been looking for the best way to wiggle into his life. I'd followed him and paid for information, all to discover he was a mediocre man who liked to stockpile pretty women.

Adultery. How original.

His pathetic weakness created a perfect and obvious angle of attack. His voice made my fury spike, so the idea of letting him touch me, even a brush of his hand on my arm, made me gag. Still, a few seconds playing the role of a needy, breathless fan and he'd be panting to get me out of my underwear. Then I'd stab him. Metaphorically, of course, but a killing blow.

Today was the beginning of the end of Richard Dougherty.

Chapter Six

HER

Present Day

Getting rid of a bat with the whole town watching turned out to be a tougher task than expected. Mostly because I couldn't find the damn thing. With Richmond dead, I didn't need it or think about it, so I missed the fact it was no longer near my bed.

The search warrant countdown clock ticked in my head as I debated where the person who actually did kill Richmond might have hidden it. The idea clearly was to point a flashing *she's guilty* arrow at my head, which meant the bat had to be on the property. That left three acres and more than six thousand square feet of house to cover.

Annoyed didn't begin to describe my rancid mood.

I started my room-to-room search in the bedroom Richmond had used after I kicked him out of the primary suite. Investigating led to a bone-deep need to rid the house of any evidence he'd ever existed. His clothes sat in piles on the upstairs floor. Knickknacks, collected items, and the shrine he'd created of all his awards and acknowledgments filled two boxes.

I'd dragged some of the crap downstairs and dumped it on the kitchen counter then circled back, intending to return to the second floor but only got as far as his personal office next to the staircase. A room I was now searching. Supposed to be searching.

The leather chair proved to be a distraction. While I swiveled back and forth my gaze wandered over every inch of the office. Photos, some with the kids. Most with colleagues or at speaking engagements. His medical school diploma from Columbia University. A framed article about his residency at Johns Hopkins University in Baltimore.

Maryland. That's where Richmond's story began. Where he became a hero. Annapolis, Maryland, to be exact. Home of the U.S. Naval Academy, sailing, seafood, and the infamous Richmond Dougherty. The first three things lived up to the hype.

One last spin and . . . *what the hell?*

The late September sun beamed over the grass, highlighting a figure as he sprinted around the bottom of the U-shaped driveway and down the line of trees outlining the side of the property. Doubled over and running. A man sneaking across the lawn.

Where was a killer guard dog when you needed one?

I didn't call the police or rush around because there was no need. Richmond's son, Wyatt, was lurking about, further proving the asshole gene ran deep in the male side of the Dougherty clan.

A quick text to Elias seemed in order. If I had to beat the crap out of Wyatt I wanted it to be clear the kid came for me first. That done, I looked up again. Wyatt had disappeared from view. The squirrelly little—

Beep

The house security app on my phone. The one letting me know someone had opened a door and used the code to keep the alarm from squealing. The side door. Looked like Wyatt had let himself into *my* house through the mudroom off the kitchen.

A crystal lamp with a heavy base qualified as the closest makeshift weapon. I grabbed it as I tiptoed into the foyer toward the kitchen.

"You should know I called the police." Threats felt right, so I kept going. "I have a gun and New York allows me to shoot an intruder on sight." No idea if that was true but it sounded good.

Wyatt's voice wound through the downstairs. "What the hell is this?"

Not the reaction I expected. Lowering the lamp, I stepped into the kitchen. The cellphone in my pocket buzzed as Wyatt pawed through a box of his dad's treasures.

"What are you doing with all of this?" Wyatt's mouth dropped open. "These aren't yours."

I set the lamp on the kitchen island. "Which is why the items are in boxes."

"Dad has been gone for less than two weeks and you're getting rid of his stuff?"

Wyatt's broken expression hinted at the epic battle waging inside him. Whether or not Richmond's shitty personality defined the sum total of his parenting skills wasn't clear but probably didn't matter. Wyatt would feel whatever he felt about losing his dad. No one else owned that. Any apology or accounting he might have needed from Richmond disappeared forever. The fights, the guilt, the happy times, the failures, the comments left unspoken, all dissipated into memories, good and bad, without the sweet satisfaction of having the last word.

Hate and empathy bounced off each other as I struggled to regain my ambivalence. Part of me felt for the kid. I knew all too well how hard it was to walk a safe path with a shockingly dysfunctional parent.

"Wyatt, listen—"

"It's not bad enough you killed him. Now you're going to erase him?"

The latter sounded appealing. I had to wade through the former first. "I didn't kill him."

"He had two accidents. Then the third one . . ."

"Do you understand what *accident* means?" Assessing the incidents, who had access to Richmond and the will to end him, played nonstop in my head. Putting those pieces together would take time, and quiet, which meant Wyatt needed to leave.

"He hated you." Wyatt practically sneered as he said the words. Like he'd spilled some deep secret in a moment of triumph.

Sorry, kid. No surprise.

"We were married." Saying that out loud always stung a bit.

"He told me . . ." Wyatt traded talking for fidgeting. He shifted his weight and glanced around. Generally looked ready to bolt.

"What did your father say?" Not the truth. Richmond had an allergy to honesty. But something. "Please explain."

Wyatt's head shot up again, giving full eye contact. "He said he would take care of this—of you—and fix everything, but now he's dead."

In addition to sucking in general it appeared Richmond sucked at protecting his kids from news they shouldn't know. No setting of appropriate boundaries here. *Shocking.* "You're saying he threatened me?"

Wyatt took a step back. "Don't twist my words."

A mix of twentysomething self-righteousness and bad judgment choked the room. I'd been practicing de-escalation for most of my life and put those skills into action now. "Let's calm down and have an adult conversation."

Wyatt shoulders fell in a look of total defeat. "Why are you throwing away Dad's things?"

Pivot to a lie. That always worked. "I was packing them up for you and your sister."

Wyatt's hands clenched and unclenched as he stood there, clearly battling the crash of emotions inside him. He'd gone for full drama today, wearing black jeans and a black tee. If he had a weapon, he hid it well. But that led to more questions. Why not come to the door? Why was he really here? Was he planting evidence?

That last one kept my guard up.

"Let's start over." I maneuvered to stand on the opposite side of the kitchen island, the safe side next to the drawer with a hammer in it. "How did you get in the house?"

He stared at me.

I returned the stare, daring him to speak. "Say something. Preferably the truth. I didn't call the police on you, so just tell me."

"Dad gave me a key and the alarm code."

"I changed the alarm code after he died. And I'm changing the locks as soon as I can get someone who does that out here. Just so you know." I hadn't gotten around to nailing down the security issues and wrongly believed the alarm would be sufficient. Lesson learned.

"He had a secondary code set up. One for me."

Wyatt's words cleared away the haze. Forget the twinge of compassion. Someone had gotten into the house and killed Richmond. Someone took my bat and made me a potential suspect. That *someone* could be Wyatt. "How convenient."

Wyatt looked around the kitchen before falling back on staring again. "Why marry him at all? You didn't love him."

Answering that seemed risky. "He married me, Wyatt. Did he tell you why?"

"He said he had no choice."

The first, and possibly only, honest thing Richmond had ever said. But that created a new problem. One thing Richmond could be counted on to do was save his own ass. Tattling about our arrangement put my ass on the line.

One more reason to hate the guy, dead or not.

Chapter Seven

HER

Present Day

The back door off the kitchen slammed open. Elias blew in half out of breath. He wore a suit but no tie. His hands went up in the air as if he were refereeing some sort of sporting event. "I'm here. Stop. I'm here."

Apparently no one used the front door or knew how to ring a doorbell in this ridiculously overpriced town. But that entrance. Wow. I glanced at Wyatt, who had not stopped glaring at me. "In case you missed it, Elias is here."

"You . . ." Wyatt stammered and stopped. His usual recently-been-yachting tanned skin turned blotchy as his mouth stretched into a thin line. "Are you pregnant?"

"What?" All that bluster and that was his question? "How did you jump to that conclusion?"

"The timeline. Dad dumping Mom. All that crap about them being separated for months just so he could get a faster divorce. The rushed agreement that made Mom furious. The fights over this house. The quickie secret marriage to you." Wyatt counted out all of my perceived sins on his fingers. "Why do all of that and turn his life upside down unless it was for a baby?"

The question was a lot, so I ignored him and focused on Elias. "How did you get here so fast?"

"I live two streets away and was working from home today."

"In a suit?" And a fancy watch that looked more expensive than some cars. Not the cars in Rye but cars in other towns. "Your hourly rate is too high."

Elias sighed. "Is this relevant?"

"I guess not." Back to the annoying man-child standing in my kitchen. "Wyatt, here, has been practicing his trespassing skills."

But Wyatt refused to let go of the worry in his head. "Answer my question."

I drew my hand up and down in front of me and over the non-existent baby bump. "If I were pregnant, you'd know."

If I were pregnant it would be both horrifying and a miracle since I never had sex with Richmond. The idea of him touching me was so repugnant I almost heaved.

"Not if you faked a pregnancy to trick him." Wyatt started nodding as if he'd come to some sort of higher understanding. "That's it, right? You pretended to be pregnant to force him into marrying you. He was like that. A good man . . . or he was before he met you."

My heart rate kicked up until the pressure thumped in my ears. "Your father was not . . ." Elias's throat-clearing stopped me from tumbling over the verbal edge. A few deep breaths and I tried again. "Okay, look. Not pregnant. Never pretended to be pregnant."

Wyatt's jaw still clenched. "He would have cared enough about a kid to agree to get stuck with you."

Wrong. Richmond only cared about himself. Telling Wyatt that harsh truth might be a service that saved him years of anguish, guilt, and therapy. He'd only experience freedom once he realized he was a victim in his family's story. Parenthood wasn't a magic pill that turned empty people into loving beings. Viciousness seeped out. Scheming became a habit. Acts that minimized and disregarded hit like a slap until the sorry reality that biology didn't guarantee unconditional love settled in.

I lived that truth, but Wyatt wasn't ready to heed my advice. His deep wounds hadn't had time to scab over. A willingness to learn waited in a distant future . . . if at all.

"Why are you here?" Elias asked.

Wyatt's anger still burned and it came out in his harsh voice. "This is my father's house. I have every right to be here."

"That's actually not correct." Elias flipped into serious lawyer mode. "You never lived here, your name isn't on the deed, and you did not inherit the property. This house belongs to your stepmother."

Wyatt made a face. "Don't call her that."

Hard agree. "Yeah, don't."

We all stood in silence for a few seconds. Wyatt was about to launch into what was likely another round of unhelpful whining, so I took over. "Did you forget something the last time you were here?"

The question seemed to snap Wyatt out of his fury. He blinked as his expression morphed from surprise to carefully blank. "What are you talking about?"

Wyatt had a tell. A brief moment when his gaze darted up and to the left right before he lied. Good to know. "Let's talk about all the times you let yourself in the house when I wasn't here. When you came to snoop around or, maybe, meet with your dad. Did that happen, Wyatt?"

"I'm leaving and taking these." Wyatt grabbed the nearest box and dragged it off the counter. "Dad was right. You're nothing but a disgusting—"

"No," Elias warned.

"Yeah, watch it." Looked like all of the Dougherty men liked to throw nasty words around. "I can still call the police and have you hauled out of here."

"He's out of line but let's cut him a break," Elias said. "He's a kid."

Wyatt didn't need more coddling. Mommy and Daddy had shielded him from enough harsh reality already. "I'm only seven years older than he is."

"I'm going to figure out what you did to Dad." Wyatt nodded, as if he was buying into his own argument. "He married you for a specific reason and I'll bet he died for the same reason."

"Wyatt, that's enough," Elias said.

Wyatt kept right on talking and issuing empty threats. "You're not going to get away with this. I'm going to stop you."

"Go back to college and let the grown-ups handle your father's estate." Condescending, yes, but Wyatt deserved a verbal smackdown. An actual smackdown wouldn't hurt either.

Wyatt shook his head. "You should watch your back."

Without another word, he marched out of the room. He left a box behind and didn't bother to look inside the one he took. He probably knew what the contents were. If he'd been visiting covertly as I suspected, he wouldn't need an inventory to figure out what to take.

I waited for the back door to slam shut with his exit. A quick check of the security app showed him stomping across the lawn. "Kathryn and Richmond did well with him. He's a charmer."

Elias leaned against the counter, much more relaxed now. "In his defense, you were provoking him."

"You should know I'm not a fan of the whole devil's advocate thing. I'm also impervious to guilt. Find another tactic."

"Noted." Elias glanced at the remaining box. "As a general rule, getting rid of your dead husband's personal items only a few weeks after his potential murder makes it seem like you're happy he's gone. The police will be looking for moves like this."

Elias wasn't wrong. Despite my need to purge it was too soon to pack up and unload Richmond's things even though that was the end goal. Sell everything, cash out, move on. Out of New York. Far away from the stench of the Dougherty name and as soon as possible.

But all of that missed the point. "Wyatt broke into my house."

"Are you really afraid of Wyatt? Do you want him arrested? Because his father gave him a key, which makes things cloudy."

Cloudy. Richmond. That conniving asshole. Of course he roped his son into the mess by providing an open door to my private space. The man had no boundaries . . . well, he did now because he was in a box. "No to both questions."

"But?"

Elias read the situation right. My mind kept whirling, racing through the possibilities and problems waiting in the future. "Wyatt got nervous and defensive when I asked him questions. That wasn't just about being caught sneaking in. It felt like he was looking for something or maybe looking to plant evidence."

"Don't jump to conclusions."

Too late. "All of this tells me one thing. Wyatt has something to hide."

Elias let out a long sigh. "Sounds like he thinks the same thing about you."

"The difference is I'm going to figure out his secret. He's not touching mine."

Chapter Eight
HER

Six Months Earlier

I waited for Richmond to return to the table with a fancy drink I had no intention of tasting. Three weeks of following him led me to this Brooklyn neighborhood and a dark-walled bar with a speakeasy vibe. He'd been nearby giving some sort of speech at a conference and stopped off here, likely to troll for a new woman to sleep with, which turned out to be perfect timing for me.

After a bit of flirting from across the room, he made his move. All smiles and deep voice, and now we sat in a dark corner, a few hours before rush hour.

Target acquired. Connection made.

He slipped into the booth, bringing his body close enough that his expensive cologne clashed with my drugstore vanilla bath gel. A vision of stabbing him with the toothpick holding the olive in my drink floated through my mind, but I refrained.

"You don't look like a Janet." His smile suggested he thought that was a good line.

"Who do I look like?"

"Oh, I don't know." His finger slipped over the back of my hand as he leaned in. His breath blew across my ear. "What do you want me to call you? And how will it sound when I whisper it in bed?"

Much closer and he'd be on my lap, and I would lose it on him. Forget timing and practice, this guy made me want to smash his face in. "You'll know soon enough, Dr. Dougherty."

"Call me Richmond."

Asshole.

"I love a woman who goes after what she wants." He took another peek down the deep V of my neckline. "I'm imagining how good you'll look naked on white sheets."

No way that line worked on any woman. He sounded like a serial killer.

"You don't have to be somewhere, like the hospital?" Continuing the *aren't you that important doctor?* ruse to stroke his ego would make the fall even harder. "Your time must be in huge demand."

He laughed. "I can take a break to see what you're hiding under that beautiful dress."

That called for an eye roll but I held it in. "What if I said *nothing*?"

"I think we should go somewhere and talk about that." He trailed his fingers up my thigh and under the hem of my skirt. "You can show me."

Yeah, time to wrap this up.

My hand covered his, stopping its upward climb. "Your wife won't come after me, will she?"

He winked. "We have an understanding."

Sure, they did. "Did you have an understanding when you were in high school?"

His body stilled before he pulled back. "What?"

"The school shooting. The stories about you being a hero." I did the winking this time. "We both know that's bullshit. Does your wife know and did she back then? You were high school sweethearts, so it's a valid question."

"What the hell is this?" His flirty tone and sly smile disappeared in a flash of anger. "I don't know what you think—"

"Your tough guy posturing doesn't impress me. It won't scare me off." I moved the drink to the side and out of spilling range since I planned on returning the expensive dress. "I know better."

"Listen, you little bitch." He bent forward, closing the distance between us until his body almost surrounded mine. His voice didn't rise but his demeanor switched from inviting to threatening. Fury thrummed off him.

The bartender shot me a look of concern, but I shook my head before turning back to the hovering doctor and his intimidation tactics. "I thought you wanted to see me naked."

"I don't know who you think you're talking to."

"A liar." I waited to see how that would land, but he stayed quiet. "Oh, did you think your *do you know who I am* garbage would work on me?"

To be fair, it worked on a lot of people. He'd scammed and lied his way into a prominent position and sterling reputation, neither of which he deserved.

His hand balled into a fist on the table. "I'll play along. What's the goal here?"

"I know what you did back then. What really happened."

"I saved my high school from a massacre. I was the hero that day." He shoved away from me and started to stand up. "So why don't you slither back to whatever street corner you usually work. You're losing money in here."

A typical response and not a very original one. Instead of continuing the argument, I slipped a piece of paper out of my purse and placed it on the table. "That's a map. A map you drew twenty-seven years ago."

He glanced at it but his expression didn't change. "I've never seen that before."

Very cool. Impressive, but then he'd had a lot of practice perfecting his lying game. "It's a map of the high school you attended. All part of the plan you created then put in motion when you were a senior. Just seventeen and already ruthless."

He slid back into the booth but not as close to me this time. "You should write fiction."

"It's your list of *things to do* that day." I pointed to the notes on the side then to the stick figures and where they stood on the crude floor plan. "Your drawing."

His expression didn't communicate anything. If he heard the gallop of his demented past catching up with him, he hid it well.

"Did you dream up this little scam all on your own?"

So charming. "Being a condescending asshole isn't going to stop this conversation or what's about to happen to you."

"You're pathetic." He let out a dramatic sigh. "You have some big fantasy in your head about hitting the jackpot by besting someone far superior to you."

I looked around. "Is this mythical person in the room with us now?"

"This is quite a con." He shook his head in a gesture designed to dismiss me. "But the free ride you're hoping for? Not going to happen, honey."

"Well, *sweetie*." I used the tip of my finger to circle the first-floor lockers on the map, a location that played a prominent role in his heroic fable. "This area should look familiar. Should I read the list to you? *Enter building through door closest to the gym at—*"

"I can read." No hitch to his voice. Only a slight uptick in anger.

"The staging of a scheme this big must have been difficult. Pretty sinister stuff for a high school kid. People died."

"I know what happened."

"Do you? Because this is one of several items, all debunking your hero story." I pushed the map closer to him. "Every single one of those items is in my possession. Put together, they show what a twisted fuck you really are."

"Someone sold you a wild story. Sorry to spoil your hoped-for payday but this document is fake." He picked up the paper, crumpled it in his fist, and stuffed it in his suit jacket pocket.

"You know it's a copy, right? I have the original. All the originals."

"What's the goal here, Janet . . . or whoever you are?"

"To dismantle your life." Destroy everything he had and everything he cared about, ruin his reputation, take what I could get, leave him begging for relief . . . then end him.

Fury radiated off him now and threaded through his voice. "This is asinine."

His eyes narrowed and I almost laughed at how the scowl fit the real him better than those phony smiles. "I can see you mentally plotting, thinking maybe you'll threaten me or hurt me. Dig up my past. Dispose of me. To be fair, doc, you excel at that sort of thing."

"You seem to think I'll write you a big check to keep you from spewing lies." He scoffed as if he had leverage. "You don't have the balls for this game, hon. You're way out of your league. You can't beat me. I will bury you. I have lawyers. Clout. Respect. Resources. What do you have? Nothing. A piece of paper anyone could have drawn."

The look in his eyes didn't match the strength of his mocking tone. Maybe not fear. Not yet. But interest. His mind likely raced, trying to remember what evidence could be out there. What pieces of the truth he thought he'd buried long ago still lingered.

"Imagine how your reputation will crumble when people learn the truth. Your job. Your family. All that money. Those articles about you being a brave little hero." I made an exploding gesture with my hand. "All gone."

"Would anyone even care if you disappeared?"

There it was. Gloves off. The last of the pseudo-hero shimmer gone. The Mr. Nice Guy façade replaced by an empty shell. And that's how I thought of him. Vacant, hollow, and vicious.

"You should know you're not the only one who can plan a spectacle. I took precautions. Hurting me, messing with me in any way guarantees the information you fear most and probably believed no longer existed, up until a few minutes ago, will be released to the public. So your sole job should be keeping me safe and happy."

He shook his head. "This is all about money. For your kind, it always is."

"You think you can call me names and I'll slink away. You're wrong." So close to the final attack now. My smile refused to dim. "Don't misunderstand me. I'm definitely going to take your money. A lot of it. But that's just a side benefit."

"You're insane if you think I'm going to let you drag me along on this fairy tale."

"Unfortunately for you, very sane." I picked up my glass and put it in front of him. "Drink up. We have a schedule to plan if you hope to win my silence."

Chapter Nine

HER

Present Day

Having the whole town think you offed your famous husband made it tough to sneak out for coffee. After two days of rattling around in that big house and hours spent searching for the bat, I needed a break.

A simple plan. Pick a small place on a side street. Outside of rush hour. Quick in and out. It didn't work because the entire café patronage of eight stilled when I walked inside. The air. The people. The talking. It all stopped. Only the sound of dishes clanking in the back room and the hiss of the espresso machine greeted me. A group of women at one table openly stared. One pointed and shook her head.

Such a welcoming town. Kathryn's town. News of my venturing out in public likely ricocheted around the country club set via text right now.

The choking tension of the room clashed with the welcoming smiley faces drawn on the chalkboard menu, announcing the daily specials. The guy behind the counter glanced around as if he needed someone to tell him what to do.

Fine. I'd do it.

He greeted my order with a nod then gestured for me to step

back and wait. Not wanting spit in my cup, I hovered on the other side of the counter and watched him make the drink.

What felt like an hour passed before he handed me the to-go cup. A quick tip, the kind I wish I would have gotten back when I waited tables and washed other people's dishes, then out. Not one to linger but not one to run from a problem either, I greeted every nosy patron with eye contact and a smile as I took sure, confident steps to the door. No bolting in shame here.

Once outside, I gulped in fresh air to decelerate my racing heartbeat. But the drink would need to wait. The new problem was the man leaning against the driver's side door of my SUV.

An unwanted confrontation. On the street where everyone could see and report back to the police and Kathryn. The fine people of this town had been whispering and gossiping since I landed here as the new Mrs. Dougherty. Only the touching of my car was new.

"Yes?" I figured that greeting covered most things.

The man had a jumpy, uncomfortable-in-his-own-skin look about him. He wore khakis and an oxford shirt hidden behind a light jacket. The ensemble said *Dad picking up the kids from middle school.* Not threatening but this could flip in a minute. It always amazed me how fast a man could move when he led with a punch. But this guy's hands were fisted at his sides. Every now and then I heard a jingle, which probably meant he was holding a set of keys. No weapon made that sound . . . I hoped.

"You're Mrs. Dougherty."

Were we going to fight on the street? "I am."

"Your husband's death won't stop this."

Cryptic and unhelpful but intriguing. "Clue me in here. What are you talking about?"

He finally blinked, breaking the charged staring contest between us. "I thought he faked it at first."

That sounded like something Richmond would do. "He's very dead. I assure you."

His untimely demise had been all over the news and in screaming headlines and retrospectives on his life. Avoiding his face and the overly flattering stories had been impossible. I know because I'd tried.

"Was the possibility of bad publicity too much? With his ego I bet he couldn't stand to see his secrets dragged out in public," the man said.

This was an odd game, but the guy had my attention. Not just mine. The ladies sitting at the café window openly gawked. A man a few parking spaces away took an unusually long time shutting his car door.

"Richmond fell down the stairs at the house. It was an accident." I almost screamed that last part for our unwanted audience before lowering my voice again. "What publicity?"

"He tried to pay me off, you know."

I didn't because I had no idea what we were talking about, but Richmond's tactics weren't new. He'd tried that with me, too. Eventually. His answer to every problem: throw money at it. He'd threatened and puffed up his chest, but I won and now had to deal with whatever fallout the guy leaning on my car had in mind. "Sir, I don't—"

"You can't avoid the truth." His eyes narrowed as he looked me up and down. Not in a sexual way. Assessing, like sizing up an opponent. "You're his wife. You know. His attorney knows."

Ah, yes. Elias. Of course. Drill down and there he was. Knee-deep in all the trouble.

"We're not done. I'm not letting this go." The guy talked in some sort of code and nothing about the conversation made sense. "I made a promise to my son."

A clue. Richmond had been a pediatric surgeon. A highly specialized field that paid well. There were fewer than two hundred specialists in New York State, and only a couple thousand in the entire country, and none of them was as well-known as Richmond. The notoriety fed his ego. It also sounded like he'd landed in a pile of crap.

I wanted to ask the man if his son was okay but dreaded the answer. An innocuous question seemed safer. "What's your name?"

"Did your husband have so many enemies that you don't even know who I am?"

Possibly? "Humor me and fill me in."

"Peter Cullen. My son's name was Ben."

Was. Shit. The worst word. "I honestly don't know anything about you or your son, or whatever beef you had with Richmond, but I can talk to the attorney and—"

"I know I should be celebrating. Karma finally got your husband and now he can't hurt anyone else. But it's not enough. People need to know."

Amen to that. "If you're owed money, I'll make sure you get it."

"It's not about the money. It's about making sure people know who Dr. Dougherty, dead or alive, truly was."

Sounded like I could get to like this Peter guy.

He pushed off from the car and walked away without saying anything else. I didn't try to stop him because he deserved to have the last word. More details would have been good, but now I had a hint about where to look next in the *who killed Richmond* saga. Not Peter, unless this was some sort of deflection to throw the scent off him. If he had done the deed, good for him. He'd get a pass and a warning to not implicate me.

One of those documents back at the house might explain the issue with the Cullen family. Elias had to know. People at the hospital must have a clue.

Time to shake the truth loose.

Chapter Ten

HER

Present Day

My cellphone buzzed on the drive home from the coffee place. I hadn't bothered to plug it in, thinking a few quick turns and I'd be in the driveway. A glance at the screen showed missed calls from the alarm company. Amazing how fast people moved when you scanned your husband's death certificate and sent it over, confirming he could no longer pay the bill.

Wyatt could kiss that special code goodbye.

The last turn into my driveway and . . . an open gate. A police car. Elias. Detective Sessions. This couldn't be good. Hiding wasn't an option. That left standing there while the police pawed through everything in the house and located that damn bat.

I got out of the car and met Elias and the detective by the bottom step leading to the front door. Two policemen passed me and went into the house without saying a word. "I guess you got a search warrant."

"The alarm went off," Detective Sessions said. "You should have received a call."

Wyatt. Again. Had to be. "And you brought the entire department over to check on the house?"

The detective frowned. "We respond to alarms. I'm assuming you support that."

Elias did a quick cellphone check then slipped it into his suit pocket. "I'm an emergency contact for your system. When you didn't respond, I got the call. I can be here in a few minutes from my house, so I came to check on you. The police were already here."

Sounded convenient, as did all the work Elias did from home lately. "We're going to have a talk about that what else of mine you're listed on."

Elias shot me a *not now* look.

One person seemed to be missing from this scene. "Where's Wyatt?"

"Why would your stepson be here?" Detective Sessions asked.

Elias jumped right in. "He wouldn't set off the alarm. He has a code."

But someone broke in, or tried to. *What if I had been here?* The question ran through my head, and I blinked it out. Wyatt had to be the answer. His misdirected anger made sense. Someone else breaking in, stranger or not, opened up a world of new worries . . . and revived a few dormant fears. The ones I'd buried and ignored as soon as I got old enough to fight back.

Before marrying Richmond, I didn't own anything of value. I kept the lights on. I could guard a studio apartment without moving. Sit in a chair and see every wall. No one could hide and jump out at me. This house was one big hiding place.

Someone killed Richmond. I assumed that was about *him.* I'd blocked any thought about me being a target or in danger, but now I wasn't so sure. "So, where are we on the thief-in-my-house question right now?"

The detective nodded toward the front door. "The officers looked inside and—"

"Wait. Is this some sort of scam to avoid getting the search warrant? Like, a bait-and-switch kind of thing." That would suck but it was an answer I could live with. The detective playing games meant danger, but not the type that would keep me up at night, huddled in a corner, listening for every noise.

"It looks like someone entered the house through the back French doors off the breakfast room. The glass is broken. They likely smashed it to open the lock." The detective walked through the facts in a monotone voice. "The hit was enough to trip the motion sensor on the door. The silent alarm went off. The alarm company called you. You ignored the call. The company then called us, which is standard procedure. We got in the house through the broken door."

He used all those words to make it sound like the situation was my fault.

"I was getting coffee." I held up the almost empty cup as evidence.

"In this town?" Elias whistled. "Brave."

"You have no idea." I grabbed my cell out of my bag and brought up the security system app. "There are cameras. Richmond had a thing about being able to watch the entire property from the privacy of his office."

Elias and the detective crowded in while I hit the video playback for the short time while I was out. The system cycled through different camera angles without showing much of anything. Detective Sessions took the phone and tried again.

"I'll need a copy of this, but I'm seeing flashes of movement only." He glanced up at the house to the obvious camera by the front door. "It looks like the person knew where the video blind spots were and stuck to them."

That fast my suspicions about Wyatt returned then expanded to add Kathryn. She exercised a lot of control over her kids. Maybe that extended to secret alarm codes. "Someone familiar with the property did this."

The detective sent me a questioning look. "Do you have a name in mind?"

Not yet. Saying anything would play into the stereotypical idea of a cat fight between Richmond's women, and that wasn't going to happen. "Just thinking out loud."

"We'll need you to do a walk-through and tell us if anything is missing."

"Are we sure the person who broke in left?" I asked. "It's a big place. Lots of rooms and doors. So many hiding places."

"I'll go with her," Elias said. "We can provide you with a list of missing items."

The detective nodded. "I'm sure you will."

Chapter Eleven

HER

Married, Day Twenty

Changing the alarm passcodes bought me some breathing room from the unnecessary household hijinks. Richmond thrived on nasty games. I'd been on a constant state of alert and barely sleeping, trying to anticipate what new form of torture his tiny mind would dream up.

My blackmail threat slowed him down, but it wouldn't stop him. He wasn't the type to back down. His ego wouldn't allow for the possibility of defeat. He'd keep pushing, convinced he could beat me, and at some point I'd have to follow through on my ultimatum. But I wasn't ready yet. To avoid suspicion and gather all the intel I could, I needed to play along with this fake marriage thing for a little while and be on guard the whole time.

My usual late-night routine consisted of grabbing a drink of water and hunkering down in my room to ride it out until morning. Not the best marital honeymoon period a woman ever had but probably not the worst.

Even something as simple as hydration came with potential pitfalls with Richmond roaming around. I picked my glass. After thoroughly cleaning it, I poured the water. I locked my bedroom door. Richmond never got near anything that went on or in my body. The guy had access to drugs and no boundaries. A dangerous combination.

Tonight I forgot to bring the drink with me, which meant a trip downstairs to the kitchen. Flashlight in hand, I stepped into the hall and let the silence envelope me. I'd become an expert at using denial as a bandage for a lifetime of inflicted wounds. Pulling back from the edge, punching down, confining my fear to the waiting darkness and out of my head, was my specialty. None of those shields worked tonight. I employed every trick and learned behavior to force my legs to move.

Calm down.

Time for common sense. My stuttered breathing was a reaction to the house . . . and Richmond's nonsense . . . and the ridiculous marriage that threw us together. Anyone would be twitchy. I was fine.

Thanks to the placement of the window and security lights outside, the upstairs was suspended in a sort of twilight. I could see around me and make out the top of the staircase without trouble. Being quick and quiet was the goal here.

Darkness welled up around me as I started to descend. The small lamp on the entry table was supposed to turn on automatically once the sun went down. I'd programmed several lamps around the house to stay lit . . . just in case. Tonight, only bleak nothingness greeted me.

Could silence grow louder? Because it thundered in my ears.

I slowed my steps and hit the light switch, expecting the chandelier to light up the entryway like a Christmas parade. I flipped it up and down and nothing happened.

I balanced my back against the wall and stood there, restless but still. Nervous to go up and terrified to finish going down. The night closed in as I fumbled with the flashlight.

Click. Click.

More nothing.

I shook it. Turned it around. Weighed it in my palm. It was lighter than it should be.

Where the hell were the batteries?

My knees buckled and my body started to slide. No. I could not fall. I could not sit on the step in a stagnant puddle of dread. I needed to race back up the stairs and lock myself in my bedroom, where I'd be safe with my bat.

But my bare feet stayed where they were. My heartbeat bonged like an old-fashioned grandfather clock and vibrated through every part of my body—head, ears, thighs. The blood pounded through me, rushing faster as the screaming ramped up in my head. My nerves tingled on the edge of pain. A full-body crash waited in the shadows, and I fought it with what little energy I had left.

Plastered against the wall, unmoving, I tried to slow my breathing. Willed my body to regain control from the strangling panic. I could handle this. I thought the words as I slammed my body harder against the protective barrier behind me.

No one could sneak up on me. No one could touch me.

The lights blinked on. All of them. The entire first floor burst to life. My eyes clamped shut to avoid the sudden brightness.

That's when I felt it. That creeping sensation that said I wasn't alone.

I opened my eyes again and there he was. Richmond, standing

at the bottom of the steps in lounge pants and a sweater. Only a few feet away. Watching me.

His mouth broke into a smile. "You're afraid of the dark."

Shit.

He laughed. "Isn't that interesting."

Chapter Twelve

HER

Present Day

I'd spent the entire marriage, short as it was, hating this house. It stood as a symbol of Richmond's wealth and reputation. As fake, empty, and cold as he was. Burning it down wasn't an option, so I stayed in it with the intention of selling once enough time had passed to avoid inviting further suspicion.

Walking inside after the break-in, a different sort of weight crashed down on me. A whisper of unease ratcheted up to a deafening roar. The sense that while I was busy setting up my game, someone had hatched a plan that made me a target.

My presence in town shielded Richmond's real killer. My lack of control over the situation pissed me off. The alarm had provided some security and now that bit of safety had been blown apart.

"You're scowling." Elias made the comment as he checked the den closet.

"Someone broke into my house. Since I'm almost always here, I have to assume they intended to find me." Saying the words out loud made them suck even more.

"You might be jumping to conclusions."

"Annoying me is never the right answer, Elias."

He closed the door and treated me to eye contact. "Will you be okay here by yourself?"

With Richmond dead I should be. "I have no idea. Yesterday I would have said yes. Today, no clue."

"Do you have a friend you can call to come and stay with you?"

"No." Literally, no. None. Friendships, genuine relationships of any kind, were the first casualties of the life choices I'd made.

"Maybe a hotel?"

That veered close to admitting defeat. No thank you.

"I'll call and get the window fixed and be fine." Definitely time to switch gears. "But while you're here we should talk about Peter Cullen."

A sudden silence buzzed around us. Elias's mouth opened and closed before he spoke again. "This is the first time you've mentioned him. Do you think he's involved in the break-in?"

No, and that was the only thing I was sure of at the moment. "Peter was at the café with me when this happened."

"You met him for coffee?" Elias sounded stunned.

Interesting. "Did I say that?"

"Sort of." He frowned. "How do you even know Peter Cullen?"

The man was so hard to read. I strained to hear or see any changes in his voice or demeanor. Elias had stiffened a bit across the shoulders but otherwise, nothing. That level of practiced non-reaction was impressive.

"You go first." It was worth a try.

He shook his head. "Attorney-client privilege continues even after Richmond's death."

"But it can be waived." See, I owned a computer and could search things, too.

"The law is a bit more nuanced than that. The executor of the estate can waive privilege in certain circumstances. In this case, still me."

Blah, blah, blah. Always a legal loophole that favored his argument over mine. "Figures you'd find a way to avoid gossiping about what you know."

"Is the Peter Cullen issue the reason you and Richmond got married so quickly? Is that the secret you held over him?"

So, Elias really didn't know the reason behind my marriage blackmail. He was in for a jolt if he figured it out. "Maybe."

Elias tried to hide it, but a smile crept out. "I'm not going to accidentally spill what I know."

But now I knew there was something to spill. *The Peter Cullen issue.* One more secret Richmond hid. This time with Elias's assistance. "We'll see."

Chapter Thirteen

HER

Present Day

Today sucked.

Detective Sessions promised to "have a word" with Wyatt about dropping in at the house, but that didn't ease the haunting sensation of being outplayed. It was almost two in the morning. I'd spent hours after the police left cleaning up, getting the broken glass fixed, and checking every room and every closet for potential attackers. My shower consisted of standing in the far corner, staring at the glass door so no one could slip in behind me while the water circled the drain.

Welcoming soft sheets and dragging exhaustion couldn't wipe out the memory of the horrors that waited in the dark. Being a kid with a mother who went out at night and didn't believe in wasting money she needed for groceries on babysitters made me a target. No amount of crying or begging had stopped her. She'd shake her head, then call out a reminder to lock the door behind her as she left whatever rundown apartment we were living in at the time.

I learned early to sleep with a weapon. Back then, a knife. When I was ten I had to use it. Doing so trapped me in the mess

I lived in now, ceding control over my choices and paying a lifetime of penance for the sin of slicing first.

With my bat missing, I improvised and grabbed a screwdriver and a hammer and tucked them under the pillow next to mine. A knife made more sense, but flashes of being drenched in blood stopped me. A blade was always my weapon of last resort.

The fluffed-up pillows piled behind me meant sleeping sitting up. The position sucked but it was better than dying lying down. I held my flashlight and strained to hear the sound of footsteps coming down the hall, but the big house stayed silent.

A company representative walked me through resetting the house alarm and deleting Wyatt's code. I kept Elias as my emergency contact. We had a mutually beneficial relationship. I liked how fast he could get to the house and he would want me alive long enough to pay his bill.

After quiet minutes scanning the room and glancing at the night outside, I felt some of my jumpiness fade. Enough remained to keep me careful.

"Go to sleep." I reached over and turned off the light closest to the bed, leaving the bathroom one on.

A flash. Something flickered in the corner of my eye. A tick of a warning set off a siren in my head. My heart felt like it exploded as I grabbed for the hammer and pushed my back deeper into the pillows.

Before I could turn on the flashlight, I saw it. The scrawl of what looked like glowing fluorescent-yellow paint on the wall across from me. Scribbled over the bedroom wallpaper and the mirror. Invisible in the light but clear now.

YOU WILL PAY

The sound of my labored breathing echoed through the quiet room. My palm ached from the tight grip on the hammer. I read the words then reread them.

The truth settled in my brain. The break-in hadn't been about stealing anything or looking for something. It had been a warning. A show that they—whoever "they" were—could get to me at any time.

Go ahead and try.

I'd killed before. I could kill again.

Chapter Fourteen

HER

Present Day

After a night without sleep the *bong* of the doorbell was not a welcome wake-up call. The gate should be locked, so anyone getting to the front door would need special access of some type. Probably Wyatt. Possibly Elias. Both options reminded me I needed to change the gate code as well as every other security code in the house.

With a groan I lifted my head off the kitchen island. Not the best place to take a nap but the location had the benefit of being near the coffeemaker. This was going to be a three-cup day.

I shuffled to the front door as I brought up the security app on my cellphone. The face peering into the outside camera made me stop.

Kathryn. At my house.

Pretending not to be home was an option. That came in second to installing a trapdoor right by the entrance to eliminate unwanted guests. One push of the button and—*whoosh*—they'd be gone.

Back in reality, I opened the door. Kathryn stood there, dressed like she was on her way to one of her fancy literary luncheons. She pulled off a cream-colored pantsuit and matching blouse. The kind of outfit most people would have stained with a pen mark ten seconds after they put it on.

Not a mark on it and, as usual, not a blond hair out of place. She wore it in a bob just above her shoulders. Straight, smooth, and expensive. The style matched her jewelry. A thin gold chain with diamonds and a bracelet with more diamonds. The woman reeked of wealth.

She also wasn't invited. "How did you get past the gate?"

Kathryn tucked her clutch bag under her right arm and sighed, as if she was the one barely tolerating this visit. "I know my way around the property. This used to be my house."

"We both know you never lived here. If I remember correctly it was being painted pre-move-in when Richmond asked for a divorce." I kept my hand on the door, blocking any chance of her wandering inside.

"Thanks to you." Kathryn's mouth twisted in a frown as she looked me up and down. The expression of distaste ruined her otherwise impressively smooth skin and pretty face. "What in the world are you wearing?"

Lounge pants, a frayed T-shirt, and pink bunny slippers. My favorite outfit. "My Tuesday ballgown is in the washing machine."

Kathryn made a huffing sound and waved her hand in the air. "Let me in."

Oh, come on. Did people really jump at her barking commands? "Uh, no."

"We need to talk. This is the kind of information that should remain private."

Intriguing. Knowing I'd regret it, I conceded and stepped

back so she could slither inside. "Go directly to the kitchen. I don't need you skulking around."

"I assure you I do not *skulk*." Her heels clicked on the marble entry as she walked straight through to the kitchen as ordered. She scanned the room, taking in every inch, before standing next to the breakfast bar. Perfect posture on full display.

I couldn't figure her out, and I'd tried. I watched her for weeks before I moved in on Richmond. She greeted everyone with a smile. Remembered names and little details about them. An impressive skill, actually. When the spotlight shifted off her, her expression changed. Hardened, void of emotion.

My initial reaction was she'd been playing the role of Mrs. Dougherty for so long, tolerating his cheating and dismissal, that she'd lost herself. Then I watched her with him during a flower show gala she chaired. An event I didn't even know existed. They presented as a couple more in sync than in love. Fake, driven, and unconcerned about the victims they left in their wake.

That day she'd fought with two patrons who dared to question her, resorting to a *do you know who I am* argument to get her way. Kathryn wasn't one to fade into the background. She thrived off Richmond's reputation. Used it, threw it around, and demanded respect just because of her name. His perfect wife. Ruthless on the inside with an attractive exterior.

The close-in gala view killed most of the sympathy I might have had for her. "What do you want, Kathryn?"

"It's time for you to leave."

Honestly, this bitch could not stop. Entitlement thrummed off her. "My house, this town, or the state?"

"All of the above." She made the comment without a hint of self-awareness, standing there like she owned the place.

I borrowed a terse answer from Elias's playbook. "No."

"We both know you forced my husband into marriage—"

"*My* husband." That was the only time saying the phrase didn't make me cringe.

"He gave in to you and look what happened." Kathryn lifted her hands in the air as if she'd spilled some big secret. "I warned him."

I refused to make this ridiculous conversation easy on her. She stormed into my house before noon making demands. She deserved what she got.

"He's dead. Likely by your hand," she said.

Another cup of coffee. That was the answer.

"You have the benefit of his last name." She set her leather clutch on top of the breakfast bar but wisely didn't sit. "There is nothing more for you in this town."

I poured a cup, not bothering to offer her one. She wasn't staying. "But everyone is so nice and welcoming here."

"Your sarcasm isn't appreciated."

"That's a shame because sarcasm makes up a large portion of my personality."

Kathryn kept right on talking. "Your experience at the café yesterday was only a peek into the resounding dismissal you can expect without Richmond to protect you."

"Funny how you know about my trip."

"Despite your prestigious last name, which you should surrender, no restaurant will take your reservation. No store will accommodate you. I'm not sure where you're getting your groceries, but I'll stop that, too."

That was quite the list of threats. "Are you done talking yet?"

"You should take this seriously. I can and will make your life difficult. No allies. No friends." She made *a tsk-tsk* sound. "If you think your days are dreary now, just wait. One word from me and no one will accept you or your stolen money."

Stolen. Interesting word choice.

"Addison, hear me when I promise that you're finished in this town." She smiled. "Now I'm done."

Chapter Fifteen

HER

Present Day

Kathryn turned in her usual fine performance. Haughty with just a hint of real emotion. Unfortunately for her, I wasn't in the mood for fake or genuine Kathryn today.

"*You're not wanted here* should be the town motto." After her big speech, the lingering question was if she knew about my run-in with Peter Cullen or the details of his battle with Richmond. Not that I was going to give her the satisfaction of asking for her help in any way.

"We will come to an understanding," she said.

"I should probably sit down for this." But I didn't.

"You should be in jail. One word from me to the press and everyone will know Richmond didn't fall. That his scheming, greedy wife inherited far too much when he died and that made him an unwitting target. The conclusion will be clear. You killed him." She stopped to take a deep breath. "You do not deserve it, but I will refrain from pulling every string and calling in every favor to make sure you're arrested and fully disgraced in exchange for a few items."

I braced for what promised to be a spectacular list of ridiculous demands.

"I will regain ownership of this house and all the contents in it, including anything that belonged to Richmond. You may keep whatever clothing you brought with you, though if this outfit is an example you would be wise to throw the contents of your closet away."

She couldn't help herself. That was the only explanation for this nonsense. "You're really selling this plan."

"Further, all accounts and investments will be returned to my name. That includes transferring the proceeds from the trust Richmond inherited from his parents. Elias can figure out those details. In the meantime, we will agree to a sum to pay you for your time. A hundred thousand should be more than adequate for the few months you insinuated yourself into our lives. I'll have Elias write up whatever agreement is needed to make all of these arrangements happen."

The mention of the trust pissed me off more than her unwanted visit. Blood money, pure and simple. "Is that your entire offer?"

Her sour expression suggested she didn't like being questioned. "It's not an offer. It's the deal. The only deal I will make with you to keep you free so you can run off and destroy the next family."

"First, and I can't stress this enough, I don't want anything to do with the money Richmond inherited from his parents." The account, all twelve million and change, was separate and untouched by me and would stay that way until I figured out which worthy charity Richmond would have despised the most and donated it there. "Second, you can shove that offer or deal or whatever you want to call it up your ass."

Kathryn frowned. "That language is unnecessary."

"You don't have any leverage here. You already received all you're going to get in the divorce settlement." An impressive sum because I'd demanded Richmond assume responsibility for the kids' reasonable expenses, give Kathryn the house she lived in, pay alimony, and divide the non-inheritance liquid accounts, with her getting a higher percentage. Kathryn had been married to the jackass, so she'd earned it.

"You don't belong here. More importantly, you don't deserve to be here." Kathryn looked around as if she were talking about the house, but she obviously meant *in New York*.

"Yet my name is on the house title, not yours." A fact she liked to forget.

"Richmond made it clear your marriage was a joke." Some of the stiffness left Kathryn's shoulders. "He intended to divorce you as soon as possible, but your actions made that impossible."

Now, that was interesting. How did Richmond intend to make that happen? Bigger question . . . what did Kathryn know about my blackmail and what really happened twenty-seven years ago? "I didn't kill him."

She snorted. "No one believes that."

Fair enough. "Are you still in mourning? Because that funeral display was impressive."

"My grief was very real."

Was. She appeared fine and in fighting form now. "Uh-huh."

"I'm not going to debate this with you, Addison. Detective Sessions is a friend. He knows Richmond's death was not an accident. With the right amount of pressure everything you schemed to take from me will be lost, along with your freedom. You belong in a prison cell, but I'm giving you one chance to avoid that, but you have to walk away now and stay away."

She couldn't possibly think this posturing would work, which made me wonder if her impromptu visit was really some sort of scouting expedition. Subterfuge. She seemed obsessed with regaining entry to this house. No clue but this visit had my mind spinning and not in the way she'd planned.

"Here's my counter." Kathryn started to interrupt me, but I cut her off. "No, listen. I want to make sure you hear me. I'll keep everything, and you'll get out of my house and never come back. In exchange, I won't immediately start spilling your messed-up family secrets."

Her body stilled. "What does that mean?"

"I think we both know." Well, I knew. I had no idea what she knew but she'd stepped over a line. "I could remind Detective Sessions and his boss, and whoever else will listen, that if someone killed Richmond the most likely suspect is his bitter ex-wife."

"You're a pathetic, low-class, opportunistic bitch."

She sounded just like her ex. "I've been called worse."

She grabbed her clutch and stuck it under her arm again. "You'll regret this."

"I doubt it."

Chapter Sixteen

HER

Married, Day Fifty-Four

My run ended too soon. Fearing some Kathryn-supporting neighbor might mow me down in an expensive sedan made getting fresh air and burning off tension risky. But I refused to hide in the house every minute of the day. I'm not the family member who should be ashamed. That person sat at the breakfast bar, eating a sandwich. Unfortunately, he didn't choke on it.

Without saying a word, I slipped into the kitchen and refilled my water bottle while Richmond lectured Wyatt about his grades. Never mind that it was summer, long before the kid returned to college for his junior year.

"We will not have a repeat of last year's embarrassing effort." Richmond finished the comment then took another bite of his sandwich.

Wyatt, fully flustered and running his hand through his hair, fidgeted on the barstool. "I swear I did the best I could."

"Bullshit." Richmond finally lowered the sandwich and gave his son eye contact. "You can't spend all your time drinking and going out with friends and expect I'll fix it for you when you miss your classes and fail out."

"I didn't fail. My grade point average—"

"You're an adult now. Act like it." Richmond's angry tone echoed through the kitchen. So did the harsh coughing that followed.

For a few seconds Wyatt just sat there in the eye of the suffocating tension. Part of me wanted to leave. The other part wanted to stay in case Richmond's rant got out of hand. Protecting Wyatt from his father's wrath wasn't my job, but I still felt bad for the kid. Being Richmond Dougherty's son couldn't have been an easy ride, especially because behind closed doors Richmond's demanding nature was second only to his lack of empathy.

Father of the Year.

Wyatt didn't say anything for a few minutes. He gnawed on his bottom lip and generally looked like he was winding up the courage to contradict his father. "I'm not sure biology is the right major for me."

"You need that foundation if you're going to be a doctor." Richmond's coughing died down, but his voice sounded scratchy.

"Is that what he wants?" The question slipped out. It was the obvious one that Richmond should have asked, but he didn't, so I tried.

Richmond didn't look at me, but his hands tightened into fists. "I don't need your help, Addison."

"I'm talking to my dad." Wyatt's rough tone matched his scowl.

The kid needed to learn when to accept a lifeline. That was a lesson someone else could teach him. I tagged out. "Right. Continue."

Richmond went back to eating and talking. "You have to be

realistic. You're accustomed to a certain lifestyle. One I don't intend to provide forever. That means you need to be able to support yourself, and I'm not talking about just getting by."

"I could do a lot of other things."

"You need a career. Medicine is the most obvious option." Richmond's coughing returned. He picked up his empty mug and moved it closer to my side of the breakfast bar. "Coffee."

He had to be kidding. "You can make it yourself."

Richmond gave me his full attention this time. "You don't need to be in here for this discussion. It's between me and my son."

That guaranteed I was staying. "I wouldn't want to miss any of your wisdom."

"Hey." Wyatt stood up. "Don't talk to him like that."

A wheezing sound cut off whatever other gem the kid intended to say. Richmond coughed until he gasped. It sounded like he couldn't draw in enough air.

"Dad?" Wyatt looked from his father to me. "Do something."

Such as? I didn't know what the hell was happening.

Richmond tugged at the neckline of his polo shirt. "Can't breathe."

I stopped lounging against the sink. He had my full attention now.

"Are you choking?" That was the only thing that made sense. But he could talk. That was good, right?

Richmond slid off the stool as if his bones had disintegrated. His body went into free fall and slammed to the floor without him bracing for impact.

"Dad!" Wyatt tried to pick Richmond up. When that didn't

work, Wyatt sat on the floor and gathered his father's limp body on his lap.

"Help me." Richmond grabbed Wyatt's arm as he gasped. His breath came out as a mix of a cough and rough panting.

The color drained from Wyatt's face as he looked up. "Addison?"

My body refused to move. Scattered thoughts filled my brain. Saving Richmond now could provide cover for what I had planned for him later . . . or I could end this now and be done. Thoughts about letting Richmond die on the floor battled with the pain and confusion in Wyatt's voice. Hating Richmond and making Wyatt hold his father while he died were two different things. I could only live with one of them.

My legs finally worked. I pushed away from the counter and joined Wyatt on the floor, issuing orders as I took over. "Call 911."

Wyatt rocked back and forth, cradling his father's convulsing body.

I could not handle this alone. "Wyatt, do it now."

The wheezing grew louder. Richmond struggled to breathe and talk. Finally, the mumbling made sense. "Pen."

"He means his adrenaline pen." Wyatt stood up. His hands shook as reached for his cellphone.

Right. Whatever. "Make the call, Wyatt."

"He has a severe shellfish allergy. You know that, right?"

So? "He was eating a turkey sandwich."

Wyatt and I shouted back and forth at each other. Energy surged through me as tension pinged around the room. Every minute felt frantic and out of control. The walls closed in until it was just the three of us in this tiny bit of space. Claustrophobic and frenetic. Sounds and smells crashed together, heightening the chaos.

Richmond rolled on his side, facing me. "Can't . . ."

Wyatt yelled into the phone about needing an ambulance. I could barely hear him say the address over Richmond's desperate attempts to inhale. His chests rose and fell as he fought for air.

"Where's his adrenaline pen?" Wyatt was asking me.

Richmond's wallet. His keys. I knew where he kept those but not a pen. "I have no idea."

"How can you not know?" Wyatt screamed the question before talking to the person on the other end of the phone again.

I jumped when Richmond grabbed my hand. "Addison . . ."

Wyatt kept shouting and crying. "Help him!"

Get up. The order filtered through the white noise fogging my brain. I scrambled to my feet then stopped. Looking around the kitchen didn't help. I couldn't focus on anything.

That bag he carried around. The messenger bag. There had to be an adrenaline pen in there. I maneuvered around Wyatt and headed for the foyer.

"Where are you going?" he cried out.

"I'm getting the pen." I grabbed the bag and brought it into the kitchen. Turned it upside down and shook it. A stethoscope fell out and hit the counter with a crack. A blood pressure cuff. Bandages. A bunch of stuff I couldn't identify.

There, stuck in the side compartment, the needed adrenaline pen. That fast the crescendo of noise bouncing around my brain clicked off. My heart pounded but my mind cleared.

Wyatt was pacing, not looking at me. I glanced at Richmond. His body shifted and jerked as if he was having a seizure, but his gaze locked with mine in a look of terror. Of fury.

"Don't," he choked out.

Yes, do it. Let him die. End it right here.

My fingers brushed over the one thing that should end Richmond's torment and save him. But there was another choice. A much darker one. Temptation pulled at me.

Three words thundered in my brain: *He deserves it.*

Chapter Seventeen

HER

Married, Day Fifty-Four

Richmond's coughing ratcheted up and his body curled into a tight ball. The combination broke the spell.

"Got it." I grabbed the needed pen and kneeled next to Richmond.

His face was red and blotchy. Those objectively handsome features hidden under a mask of writhing pain and clenched teeth. "My leg."

One shot into his thigh and the rocking and flailing immediately eased. The harsh panting subsided a minute later as he rolled onto his back and gulped in air.

"You were going to let me die." Richmond's condemnation came out as a whisper.

"What did he say?" Wyatt asked.

There was enough paranoia flying around the kitchen without adding more. "Is the ambulance on the way?"

"Yes." The fear still hadn't left Wyatt's eyes. "Is he breathing?"

"Yeah." I grabbed the half-eaten sandwich off the counter. "I don't get it. It's turkey."

Wyatt kept talking with the person on the phone. "He still looks gray."

I sniffed the sandwich but only smelled the turkey. "Maybe it went bad."

Richmond tried to lift his head then let it fall back against the floor. "You poisoned me."

Wyatt stepped closer. "What?"

"You need to get the gate." Richmond let out a long exhale, this one not as labored. "Let the ambulance crew in."

Wyatt obeyed, leaving me stuck with Richmond. Seething had replaced coughing.

I slipped the sandwich back on the counter, not wanting to touch it. Just in case. "It was probably some sort of cross-contamination thing. You should talk to the guy at the deli counter."

"You did this." Richmond didn't whisper this time. He pushed up on his elbows. "You put shellfish in there."

An interesting idea, but no. "How would I do that?"

A siren wailed in the distance and grew louder with each second. When Richmond Dougherty needed help everyone rushed to his side in record time.

"You hesitated." His voice dripped with disdain. "You debated letting me die. I saw you."

He finally understood the intensity of my hate. He knew now that I *could*. He didn't realize how easy it would be. The only thing that saved him was Wyatt being there. I couldn't let the kid watch his dad die and be tormented forever by not being able to save him.

That was a weakness. One I hoped to bury. "If that truly was a reaction to shellfish, you should be asking how the contaminant got in your sandwich. Who else have you screwed, metaphorically or otherwise?"

"Dad?" Wyatt called out but didn't return to the kitchen. "They're here."

Had I known about his allergy and that I could trigger it, maybe I would have tried. Not sure, but now I couldn't think of much else, except one thing.

I leaned in closer to Richmond so Wyatt wouldn't overhear. "It looks like I'm not the only person in this town who hates you. Which means I have an ally and you should be very careful."

Chapter Eighteen

HER

Present Day

The waiting area outside Richmond's medical office had a sterile, artwork-in-hotels look to it. Beige walls with a yellow tint. Blue chairs and matching blue carpet that felt squishy when you walked on it. No way Kathryn designed this place . . . or ever stepped in here.

The offices were in a separate building adjacent to the hospital where Richmond had performed most of his surgeries. The practice consisted of several doctors I'd met only briefly and didn't intend to get to know now, but Thomas Linfield had other ideas. He was the pediatric neurosurgeon who ran the office and Richmond's former business partner. When I called about coming to clean out Richmond's office, Linfield insisted on having a meeting. A meeting that was supposed to start a half hour ago.

If the delay was a power move, I wasn't impressed.

Just as I started calling Elias to enlist his expensive help, Dr. Linfield rushed around the corner and stopped in front of me. Fit in a fancy dark suit. Squinty eyes behind glasses. He was a yacht club guy, and his gray hair had that permanent windblown look to it.

"I'm sorry I kept you waiting," he said.

Uh-huh. Sure, he was.

He clasped his hands in front of him as if he were going to start praying. "Please accept my condolences about Richmond. I meant to talk with you sooner. He was a great man."

He wasn't. "Thanks."

Thomas had been to the house a few times while Richmond was still alive, and we'd exchanged mundane greetings. The office also threw a party to celebrate our sham of a marriage. I had no interest in going out to dinner or playing the role for an extended period of time, but I needed that one party to publicly establish myself as his wife and learn about who mattered to Richmond or might have intel on him.

We managed to be civil and pretend to be married for two hours, delivering virtuoso acting performances as the music played and the waitstaff passed hors d'oeuvres. Him to shore up his reputation after dumping his wife for a younger woman. Me to study the crowd.

Once it was over, I vowed never to repeat the evening. Richmond squawked at first about needing to keep up appearances. His reputation mattered and all that. None of it swayed me. I was content to play the reclusive new wife as I plotted his downfall. But it did mean that to get answers to questions now I had to talk with some of the same people I'd avoided for months.

Thomas shook his head. "I saw you at the service but everything was so chaotic and difficult. It seemed like the wrong place to talk."

Because Kathryn was there. Thomas had chatted with her. Huddled together, whispering back and forth. Kathryn had worked the entire funeral, making sure to remind everyone she was the first Mrs. Dougherty and the only one who mattered.

I didn't care then or now because I had no desire to make friends with anyone attached to Richmond. I was here for other reasons. "I'm not sure why you had to come and meet me. I don't need an escort into Richmond's office."

"Actually, you do." Thomas settled in the chair next to mine. "I know this is a surprise but I'm afraid I can't let you—"

"I'm going to stop you." Not in the mood for a power move by this guy. "I'm Richmond's wife. Richmond was a partner in this venture and some of his property is here. Plus, there are partnership payouts that you and my attorney need to work out and I want to be ready."

That sounded right. The threat made Thomas go pale, so it must have been.

"Mrs. Dougherty said—"

"I'm Mrs. Dougherty." Sometimes throwing the name around shifted the conversation in my direction.

"The other . . . she said . . ." He stopped for a few seconds, as if searching for a coherent argument.

Another Kathryn roadblock. Of course. "Whatever Kathryn said or didn't say is irrelevant. She and Richmond were divorced. She has no interest in his estate or this practice. Sharing information with her would be inappropriate."

Thomas looked rattled. "I wasn't privy to the divorce arrangements."

Not buying it. Men talked. They shared *my wife is so awful* stories. His business partners would know the settlement terms because they had a financial interest in Richmond and Kathryn's divorce.

Then it hit me. "Has Kathryn been in his office since he died?"

"No, of course not." Thomas's voice didn't waver that time.

"She asked to, but no. There are confidential records in the office."

"Dr. Linfield—"

"Thomas."

Not Tom. He wanted the full Thomas. Might be a rich-guy thing. Same with why Richmond was never Rich. "I don't want to fight with you."

"I don't want that either."

"You're welcome to join me in the office while I sift through Richmond's things, but I'm sure you have better things to do." This seemed like the right time for a full-throated bluff. "Or we can call Elias Zimmer and he can explain my rights to you as Richmond's spouse."

"Elias?"

Throwing Elias's name around worked, too. Good to know. "My attorney."

"I didn't realize." Thomas stood up and pulled a set of keys out of his pants pocket. "But you're correct. I don't have the time to sit in here all afternoon."

He was a man who made people wait and never apologized for it. The medical industry thrived on that sort of thing. He had a *big, important air* about him just like Richmond. That hadn't turned out so great for Richmond.

Thomas opened the door and gestured for me to go inside. The office had a very different look from the waiting area. A massive mahogany desk filled the far end of the room. Bookshelves and filing cabinets lined two walls. This room did bear Kathryn's mark. The soothing medium blue paint and fancy charcoal drawings of what looked like the kids when they were younger gave the space a more refined, high-end look. That likely made it easier to charge the rates Richmond did . . . or had.

"Is there something specific you're looking for?" Thomas asked.

Good question. This likely amounted to a wasted enterprise. Richmond wouldn't store his secrets somewhere so obvious. The best way to get information stood in front of me.

"We, of course, removed all of the patient files," he continued.

That answered that. "The safe."

Thomas didn't act shocked at the suggestion. "I don't have the key."

"I do." I held it up. At least I assumed it was a safe key. It had been in one of Richmond's dresser drawers and had a label that said "safe," so I took a shot. The lack of a safe at the house pointed me here.

"Bottom left drawer." Thomas sounded resigned to let my fishing expedition happen.

The red leather desk chair had an *I'm the boss* feel to it. I could almost imagine Richmond lounging there, dreaming up new ways to be an asshole.

I opened the drawer in question, hoping the safe required a key and not a code because I had no idea what Richmond's secret password might be. A black box was hidden inside. One turn and it opened. *Jackpot.* This might be the first time my luck held in months.

I tried to pull the safe out but the damn thing seemed to be attached to the wood. What I really wanted to do was load the contents of the office on a truck—all of it—and take it back to the house to sift through in private. Thomas didn't strike me as a guy who would let that happen.

A quick visual inventory turned up some personal items. A few envelopes I didn't want to open in front of Thomas. Assorted files, including one marked with each kid's name. A binder with clippings from articles about Richmond. Of course he kept them here, where he could read them every day. Narcissistic jackass.

No matter what was in there it was all going home with me. I scooped out the contents and dumped it all on the desk. "Do you have a box?"

"I need to look through every item. There could be confidential information in there."

"We both know it would have been reckless to keep patient information locked away where no one else could find it. This is clearly personal material, right?"

Thomas wore the frown of a man not accustomed to being told no. "I have to insist—"

Enough of this. "I talked with Peter Cullen the other day."

Now Thomas looked horrified. All wide-eyed with his mouth hanging open. "Why would you do that? What about the litigation?"

Legal proceedings. Elias needed a lecture about his gatekeeping tendencies.

"I know about the issues between Peter and my husband." I didn't. And if I had to say "husband" one more time I was going to lose it.

Thomas frowned. "That's unfortunate."

I leaned back in the big chair. "I would have to know, wouldn't I?"

"Well, yes."

It had been a guess but an educated one. If Richmond's assets had been in peril that meant mine were now on shaky ground. "Where is the paperwork relating to the Cullens?"

"With the attorneys." Thomas seemed to compose himself. His voice returned to normal after a few minutes of being louder and higher. "Mr. Cullen is very upset, understandably so, but his accusations are without basis."

Someone needed to start spilling the information on these allegations. "That's not what Peter thinks."

"The man lost his son. A devastating and unfortunate reality in surgeries of that type."

The stink of cover-up was all over this. "I'm taking everything on this desk and everything not nailed down in this office home with me."

Thomas shook his head. "It would be better—"

"That wasn't a request. As the person who may end up being at least partially financially responsible if Richmond did screw up, I get to decide." Then just for fun: "Fetch me that box."

Chapter Nineteen

HER

Present Day

I arrived back at the house to another unexpected visit from Elias. Impeccable timing. I was just about to contact him and demand information about this possible lawsuit and threaten not to pay his bill if he said no.

After a quick look at the safe contents while in the car, nothing struck me as very interesting. The kids' files contained receipts for expenses Richmond had paid on their behalf. Knowing him, he probably intended to present them with a bill for reimbursement when each graduated from college.

Elias sat down across from me with Richmond's home office desk between us. "I hear Kathryn visited yesterday morning."

Of course he knew. He seemed to be connected to everyone and everything in this town. "It didn't go so great."

"She made that clear." Elias pocketed his cellphone and gave me his full attention. "She tracked me down to rant while I was in the middle of a business dinner last night."

"And here I thought I'd won her over with my obvious charm."

Elias sighed. "Kathryn is not a woman you want as an enemy. She has a lot of power in this town."

"Do you hear yourself?"

"She's raised money for police-related charities. She can call in favors."

"Unless she plans on manufacturing evidence"—and that was my worry—"I should be fine. Now, why are you here?"

"About that . . ." Elias was not one to hesitate but he came to a full stop.

I prepared to be annoyed. "This sounds promising."

"Yes, well. I have a . . . let's call it a request." He cleared his throat. "From Kathryn, actually."

"The same woman who's whining about me all over town?"

Another Elias sigh. "Admittedly, her timing is not ideal."

I was starting to hate hearing her name. Yeah, she was the first Mrs. Dougherty and very pissed that there was a second Mrs. Dougherty, but she sure grabbed that divorce settlement agreement without any hesitation. She even went along with the fake separation timeline Richmond needed in order to get a quick divorce from her and marry me.

The series of events had been too easy. That never felt right. Still didn't. It was like a hole I needed to fill, but I wasn't sure how. Her acquiescence might have meant she'd been looking for a way to parachute out of the marriage to Richmond. That, I could admire.

"Is this the same offer where I give her everything and skip town?"

Elias frowned. "What?"

Thought so. "She showed up. She threatened. Told me all the money and property should be hers. I think she called me trash, or something similar."

"She didn't mention any of that."

"Of course not." Remembering the conversation with Kathryn made whatever residual guilt I'd harbored for upending her life vanish. Her sense of entitlement killed my tolerance for her. "Let's get this over with so I can say no. What's her request?"

"Money."

The Dougherty family's favorite topic. How to get it. How to hoard it. "She has money."

Elias hesitated for a second time, which was scary. "She wants to use Richmond's money. The money that goes to you now that he's dead. Specifically, she wants you to pay for Portia's school expenses and for the remainder of Wyatt's college expenses, including the payment for next semester, which is now due and should have already been paid by Richmond."

I swiveled the chair back and forth. Not a big swing but enough to signal I didn't take this conversation seriously. "Okay, I'll play along. Why does she think I would do any of that?"

"Under the divorce agreement Richmond was to pay those expenses and alimony. You were instrumental in securing those provisions for Kathryn, even though she doesn't know that."

"I'm regretting helping her now." I actually wasn't. Screwing Richmond didn't mean I wanted to give him ammunition to financially screw Kathryn and the kids. He was my target, not them.

"She says Richmond promised, outside of their written divorce settlement agreement, to secure his monetary obligations to her by taking out life insurance, payable to Kathryn if anything happened to him."

"Let me guess. He didn't." Once an asshole, always an asshole.

"It was an oral agreement."

I stopped swiveling. "Did you hear this magical agreement or know about it before now?"

"No. It's a standard clause but it wasn't in the signed agreement."

"So, we're talking about a top-secret understanding only Kathryn knows about, which benefits Kathryn. Convenient." I had to give her credit. She knew how to play this game.

"Richmond and Kathryn made a lot of private side deals over the objections of their attorneys. Kathryn's divorce counsel was furious she consented to the settlement terms after meeting alone with Richmond. The attorney advised her against signing."

"I bet. How much money are we talking about?" Because I wasn't a total bitch. I could share for the kids' sakes.

"Portia's school, including boarding, costs about seventy thousand dollars a year."

No fucking way. "Did she switch to one in Paris? Does she get there by private jet?"

"Hackley. It's in Tarrytown."

"I'm betting the public schools in Rye are perfectly fine. They're also free."

Elias kept going, obviously missing my tone. "With all the fees and his student apartment, the cost for Wyatt to attend Tufts is a little over eighty thousand dollars per year."

Elias was messing with me. He had to be. "You're spouting off these numbers like they make sense."

"And then there's money for Kathryn."

"No."

"She believes—"

"I said no." After her performance in the kitchen? Absolutely not.

"As the administrator of the estate, I have oversight of all the accounts. You never accessed any of the money in the joint accounts while the two of you were married. The separate account he set up for you, yes, but even then, not much."

"Kind of kills the whole *she married him for his money* theory, right?"

"Technically, you do, or will soon, have access to all of his assets and property and be a rich woman, so your argument is not as compelling as you might think."

"Killjoy."

"You recently paid household and funeral expenses. Nothing unusual except one six-thousand-dollar withdrawal for you, which is inconsequential compared to the multimillion-dollar estate."

Nosy bastard. "And?"

"Paying for the children's expenses would go a long way to smoothing some of the rough feelings between you and Kathryn."

"I'm actually not interested in smoothing Kathryn."

"She is threatening to sue Richmond's estate. That doesn't mean she'd win. She very likely wouldn't because of the divorce agreement, but a lawsuit takes time and money." He leaned back in his chair. "As you've pointed out, my hourly rate is not inconsequential."

"Happy you finally admit that."

"Keep in mind, to Kathryn you're the other woman. The mistress who stole her husband of over twenty years and turned her life upside down. She views herself as your victim."

"Clearly." What the hell. Why not? What else would I do with that much money? "Fine. You can pay the kids' school expenses from whatever joint or Richmond account works best. Mostly because I believe the kids are better off being away from this town and their father's overblown reputation. And if they're gone they can't drop in and visit me."

"Good, I'll tell—"

"On one condition."

Elias let out a woe-is-me exhale. "I'm listening."

"Peter Cullen. I want info. Talk."

Chapter Twenty

HER

Present Day

Elias groaned and shifted in his chair. Even took a minute to stare out the window, deliberately prolonging his response. "I heard you went to Richmond's medical office this morning."

So that was it. The gossip had found its way back to him. "People in this town are very chatty. Funny how they all chat to you."

"Thomas contacted me because he was trying to figure out what obligation he had to share information with you."

Squirrelly bastard. "Are you his attorney, too?"

"No."

"Then I hope you told him to open the verbal vault and answer my questions."

"Since it's possible you'll need to deal with the collateral damage, I'll answer questions, if I can." Elias brushed a piece of lint, or something visible only to him, off his navy dress pants. "What do you want to know?"

Every last thing. "What were Peter and Richmond fighting about?"

"Peter blames Richmond for the death of his son, Ben. He died during a complex surgery. A radical neuroblastoma excision."

I regretted starting with that question. "One of those words sounds like cancer."

"Yes. The procedure was made more difficult due to Ben's age and the tumor's location in his abdomen." Elias stopped and took in a long breath, as if he dreaded the rest of what he intended to say. "There were complications. Ben lost a lot of blood and then went into cardiac arrest. He was six when he died."

My conversation with Peter outside the café hinted at a horror but hearing it spelled out in detail was so much worse. Traumatic, shitty, and unfair. "Now I understand why Ben's father is a mess. He's claiming this is a case of medical malpractice?"

Elias winced. "Yes and no. There were several accusations, some of which were unexpected."

More legal vomit. "You used a lot of words to avoid saying anything interesting."

"Mr. Cullen insists Richmond wasn't the one who actually performed the surgery."

"What? I don't get it."

"Peter received an anonymous tip that Richmond had someone step in for him during surgery. Allegedly, that person didn't have the necessary oversight and surgical skills, which caused Ben's death." Elias started to take out his cell when it buzzed but then stopped. Even he must have realized prioritizing anything else above this conversation was a bad idea. "This source claimed to work at the hospital and contends Richmond frequently relied on other people to perform his surgeries for him."

The allegation didn't make sense. "I know there are teaching hospitals. Is that what we're talking about?"

"No. Richmond and everyone in the room insist Richmond

was the one in control during the entire eight-hour operation and that he did everything possible to save Ben."

Richmond insists was a bad start to any defense. "Were these other professionals in the room employed by Richmond or the hospital?"

"They were handpicked by Richmond." Elias quickly pivoted, not leaving room for questions. "Mr. Cullen is convinced Richmond had a drinking problem or some other issue that drove him out of surgery and that the hospital and members of the surgical team are conspiring to cover it up."

"I didn't see any signs of drug or alcohol use." I supported any question anyone had about Richmond without much convincing or any evidence. But this? "Richmond wasn't a total dumbass. Why would he take the risk of handing off the surgery?"

"He wouldn't. He shouldn't need to with his expertise."

Hmmm. Too quick. Too practiced. Too sure. "What aren't you saying?"

"Mr. Cullen obtained a lawyer and was threatening to sue Richmond before his death. The hospital is involved."

Not a surprise. But, no, there was something else. Some nugget of ugly information Elias was dancing around to avoid spitting it out. If I couldn't get it from him, I'd find someone else. "What's the name of the person who supposedly performed the surgery? Was it Thomas? That guy seems like a problem."

"August Christopher. He's a doctor who frequently assisted Richmond during complex surgeries."

An unusual jumpiness radiated off Elias. It made me nervous. "What does August say about all of this? Where is he?"

"He separated from the hospital and the medical practice and left town right after Richmond died. There's been an issue with finding him."

Bingo. "You mean he's gone."

"He's been difficult to locate."

Elias sure did like to have the last word. He'd learn I did, too. "Let's skip the verbal gymnastics. You're saying a person who could have ruined Richmond's reputation is missing."

"What are you implying?"

That Richmond might have killed again.

Chapter Twenty-One

HER

Present Day

The steady stream of alarm-ignoring unwanted drop-in visitors and the threat of an impending police search made me twitchy. A walk of the property seemed in order. Not that it was a quick process. Three acres filled with lots of bushes and flower beds perfect for hiding a potentially incriminating bat took more than a few minutes to search.

The temperature had finally dropped as New York started its march into fall. A patchwork of red and orange foliage lit up the yard and lined the town's streets. The fiery colors contrasted with the early October gray clouds. I'd slipped an oversized sweater over my T-shirt to ward off the chill as I checked for obvious signs of evidence planting.

The most likely place had been the three-car garage or one of Richmond's two vehicles sitting untouched in there. The area had the benefit of nooks and shelves and cabinets. Someone could hide the bat, even stick it under a car seat, where it would be found but not easily. One of those clever hiding places the police would think to check but the person framing me might believe I wasn't smart enough to avoid.

I didn't find anything. Before I tore apart the house for a second time, I headed for the two outbuildings on the property. Neither sat near the house. Both provided ample opportunities to hide shit.

One building was a fancy-looking shed that housed the garden equipment. The other was a greenhouse. It was in pristine shape but empty because Richmond didn't care about flowers and Kathryn never had the chance to move in and fill it.

A tour of the shed didn't turn up much. I now knew I'd inherited a riding lawn mower and lots of shiny probably-never-used tools, but neither of those things pointed me toward the bat.

The greenhouse had a pitched roof and tinted glass walls. Glass everything. Benches outlined the internal space and an empty table ran down the middle of the twenty-foot-long structure. Some empty pots and heaters. Nothing too exciting. Still, the cabinets around the sink at the far end of the building needed a quick check.

I walked along the wooden floor, scanning the area for hidden spaces. Buckets, a watering can, and assorted sprays and bottles under the sink were the only sign there was once life in here.

Frustrated and hungry, I spun around to leave and glanced up to see if the sun had bothered to come out. All the vents on the ceiling were closed. A hanging shelf about five feet off the ground ran down each of the long sides of the greenhouse. After a few steps I saw it. A sliver of something peeking above the shelf lip on the right.

I balanced on the bench and stretched up. The second my hand touched the wood I knew what it was. The bat.

One look at it and I saw the bloodstains.

Chapter Twenty-Two

HER

Present Day

Finding the bat and knowing what to do with it were two different things. I should have thought this through. My cellphone buzzed in my pocket, and I ignored it. Hiding evidence came first. Make that destroying evidence. Burning the evidence might be a possibility.

My mind raced with solutions and warnings. I'm not sure how long I stood on the bench, but my cell buzzed twice more. Now wasn't the time for alarm companies or scam calls. I needed to think.

The weight of the bat felt familiar. The brown splashes and dots on it were new.

Think.

The answer came in a flash. Rinse off the bat, scrub off any stains, then hide it in a place, not at the house, where one might find a bat. A Little League baseball field came to mind. There were a thousand of them in the area.

If a kid found it, though . . . Enough people had been traumatized by Richmond. I didn't want to add anyone else, especially not an innocent child.

Then there was the other problem. The police or Kathryn or

even Kathryn with the police's help could be watching. Leading them straight to what seemed to be the murder weapon was not a great plan. Not that I had another one.

I jumped down. As soon as my feet hit the floor I saw movement outside. People in my yard. More unwanted company. The worst unwanted company—Elias and Detective Sessions.

"Is there no other crime in this town?"

They stood at the back of the house. They looked up. They looked around. They stared at the greenhouse. The damn door was open. Could they see me from that far away? Could they see the bat in my hand? I hid it behind my back as if that would help.

Holy shit.

When they started walking toward me, they weren't rushing. But they weren't going away either.

Clean. Clean. Clean.

I raced to the sink, trying to duck and stay out of sight, which was not an easy task in a building made of glass. My heartbeat thundered in my ears. Panicked, my brain started to shut down. That could not happen. I did a mental kick start as I reached into the cabinets and dragged out a bucket. A bottle tipped over and a can of bug spray rolled around, making more noise than I wanted, but I kept moving.

The men marched at a steady pace. I never appreciated the size of the three-acre property as much as I did right now. Fingers crossed that the greenhouse was too far from them to get a good look at my scrambling inside.

My breathing grew labored, almost staccato, as I alternated between reading labels on the bottles and cans under the sink and peeking behind me to see how close I was to being arrested. Insecticide. Liquid dish soap. A disinfectant with bleach. The last one. That should work. Actually, I had no idea if it would work. They didn't teach me how to destroy DNA in that one community college English class I took.

I stood up, taking the bottle with me and dunked the stained end of the bat in the bucket. Cold water rushed over my hands as I poured a healthy portion of the hoped-for DNA killer over the bat then rinsed. The slight sting on my skin didn't stop me from sloshing the mix of water and disinfectant around and wiping down the bat. But I still held the damn thing, which meant fingerprints. I scanned the sink and immediate area for the sponge or towel. No luck.

My T-shirt. The only choice. Without taking my sweater off, I slipped my arms out of the sleeves and then out of the shirt underneath and ripped the tee over my head. As an awkward preteen, I'd perfected the technique for removing a bra from under my clothes. The skill worked here, too.

The voices drew closer. I couldn't hear the actual words. Only the low rumble of men locked in a discussion.

I soaked the T-shirt and rubbed it over the bat. Scrubbing, cleaning, and possibly erasing. The burning sensation from the disinfectant made my hands ache and the air catch in my throat. Another pour of the liquid and I'd rubbed down the entire bat.

The harsh stench of disinfectant filled the greenhouse. There was no way to hide that smell or the damp bat. The goal was to minimize the damage.

Elias laughed over something the detective said. The topic sounded sports related. I didn't have time to stop and listen. Rinsing then wringing out the T-shirt as well as I could, I slipped it back on under my sweater and tucked the soaked edges into my yoga pants. Getting dressed was harder than undressing. Arms flailed. My sweater nearly strangled me.

"Oh, shit." The cold wet shirt stuck to bare skin, knocking the breath right out of me. My internal temperature took a nosedive. A scalding shower could happen later . . . unless I was in jail.

I ran around in circles, or it felt that way. I'd seen a television show, one of those FBI dramas, about collecting evidence from pipes, so I splashed the disinfectant in the sink and poured some down the drain. Maybe that would kill any hope for DNA recovery.

Now for a cover story. I dropped the bucket on the closest bench. Water spilled over the rim and onto the wood. The renewed smell of chlorine hit like a punch. On the bench. On my sweater. On my skin. In my hair.

The plan was to pretend I was cleaning. Using the underside of my sweater, I wiped the bat down, getting it as dry as possible, then threw it under the sink. Forget removing it from the property. There wasn't even time to hide it now.

A last-minute kick and the cabinet door slammed shut just as the detective stepped inside the greenhouse.

Chapter Twenty-Three

HER

Seventeen Years Earlier

The blood wouldn't wash off.

I scrubbed with the same sponge I usually used to clean the frying pan. Tried twisting my hands together under the hot water until my fingers burned and my skin turned a weird pinkish red. The color matched the bubbles of soap filling the sink.

No matter how hard I rubbed, the red stain under my fingernails wouldn't go away. I could still see it. Feel it.

No. No. No.

My body rocked back and forth from the force of the scraping and washing. I brushed hard, tearing at the skin around my nails as a strange buzzing filled my head.

I could take the pain. What scared me was my mom.

My mind wandered to another place. One with sunshine and a playground. A big grassy space like the field where I used to play soccer. My time on the team only lasted for a few weeks before Mom yanked me out, saying the sport took up too much of her time. A kid at school made fun of me until I lied and told him I was playing on another team. A better team.

I lied a lot. To get things. To get out of things. To avoid the yelling.

The memory of my mom's voice rang in my ears. She'd yawn and lie on the couch. *You need to start doing something around here. I can't do everything.*

My mind snapped back to the sink. Tears fell. I sniffed them back, but they turned into a wild hiccup I couldn't control. I stared at the curtains. The small blue flowers on the once-white background that had turned a gross yellow.

I tried to pretend I was somewhere else. Anywhere else.

The water swirled down the drain. Any sign of blood was gone now except for the droplets hanging from my hair. My pajamas were soaked. My favorites with the pink and white stripes. The ones I begged Mom to buy. They were my only birthday present this year.

The shorts were just a little bit long but that meant they hid more of my skin and would fit me for longer. Once they got too small, Mom wouldn't buy me another set. She said they were too babyish for a ten-year-old.

The thick red splotch across the front of my top felt wet and sticky against my skin. Red dots covered me like a fine mist down to my knees. I curled my bare toes into the floor so I wouldn't see the wash of red covering my right foot.

I'd stepped in the blood and almost slipped but grabbed the counter for balance. The move left a scary handprint on the tile countertop. Mine. I stared at it, willing it away.

Mom was going to kill me.

It was my job to keep the apartment clean. To stay quiet so she could sleep. To make my breakfast and get myself to school so she could rest from her jobs.

I messed up. The knife under my pillow was supposed to scare him. He put his hand over my mouth, and I lashed out before I even woke up. The rest was a blur. I didn't remember stabbing or stumbling to the kitchen. He must have followed me, bleeding and injured.

My gaze shifted from my foot to the floor. Blood formed a puddle under his still body. It slowly spread out as if it were reaching for me, ready to drag me down with him.

He didn't move. I knew he couldn't.

I killed him.

Chapter Twenty-Four

HER

Present Day

Detective Sessions's gaze traveled from me to the greenhouse sink and back again. "It looks like I'm an hour too late with the search warrant."

Elias winced. "I tried to call and text."

That explained the buzzing in my pocket. Next time, I'd answer my damn cell. "I was cleaning."

"I wonder why."

From the smart-ass tone the detective didn't expect an answer, but I tried to make one up anyway. "I read that before I can plant anything in the greenhouse I needed to disinfect it. Something about mold and mildew."

The explanation sounded somewhat plausible in my head. Not so much out loud. Elias frowned, so he wasn't convinced.

His suit today was black. The red tie didn't break up the bleakness. "Detective Sessions has a search warrant for the house, the vehicles, and the grounds," Elias said.

Of course. I knew this was coming but had hoped for a bit more time.

I'd removed the locks on the bedroom doors, though the police probably saw them the night Richmond died. That problem waited for me at some future time. I had enough to worry about right now without taking that on.

Any other sign of the battle that waged in the house should be gone. I even managed to get the threatening note off my bedroom wall . . . mostly. It now was an undecipherable smear that showed up when the lights were off. That's why I hung a picture in front of it.

The detective walked down the aisle toward me. "I gave your attorney here a courtesy heads-up, which I now regret."

Elias shook his head. "Come on, Nick. You were with me the whole time. You watched me try to call her."

"Was that for show?" The detective stalked as if tracking down prey. His gaze scanned ceiling to floor, skimming along the empty tables and benches. "Because this little scene looks like you'd already warned her to destroy evidence."

Elias walked down the opposite side of the long middle table separating the room. "You sound paranoid. You know me better than that."

The detective finally reached me. Elias got there a second later. Water ran down the inside of my leg. If I moved it would drip into my sneaker then onto the floor. A dead giveaway.

The detective pointed at the bucket. "What are you doing?"

This felt like a trap. I'd already mentioned cleaning. "Vacuuming."

Elias sighed. "Addison, don't."

The detective seemed even less impressed with my sarcasm. "This isn't a joke, Mrs. Dougherty. Your husband is dead."

As if I didn't know that. "I'm trying to take my mind off my grief. To keep my hands and mind busy."

"Sure, you are." The detective looked in the sink. "You look heartbroken."

Apparently it was fine for the detective to dish out sarcasm.

"Nick, that's enough."

The detective looked on the floor around the sink before stepping back to the bench and the bucket. "Sorry, Elias. I can't hear you over the smell of bleach."

Turned out the detective was pretty good at sarcasm. But the longer we stood there the wetter my pants got. The dizzier the fumes made me. The chance of messing up, saying the wrong thing, making the wrong move, increased with every passing minute.

"I'm going to need you to step out of the greenhouse, Mrs. Dougherty."

I regretted putting the wet shirt back on. "I should shower and—"

"You're not to enter the house or walk around the yard until my people are done conducting the search." The detective nodded in Elias's direction. "You can wait with your attorney or leave the premises, but the cars stay here."

That didn't leave many options. I picked up the bucket. "I'll dump—"

"No." The detective stopped me. "That stays here as well."

He was serious about this. His belief I'd killed Richmond had become entrenched. He was all in. Even if I did succeed in destroying all of the DNA evidence, which was doubtful, I couldn't get around the presence of the bat. The detective or someone who worked for him would stumble over the probable murder weapon. If they missed it, they should be fired.

"Once we're done here, she'll need to come in and answer questions," Detective Sessions said.

Elias nodded. "We'll see if you still want that once the search is complete."

Oh, he would. But I did appreciate the thrust and parry these two were engaged in. Detective Sessions clearly thought he'd gained the upper hand. Elias still didn't back down. I was stuck in the middle with no obvious way out of this.

The person trying to frame me won this round. They'd gotten on the property weeks ago without breaking in, suggesting Richmond knew them and welcomed them in. The killer had known about my bat and had time to go into my bedroom and take it on the day Richmond died. That meant the killer didn't bring a weapon with them, and the murder might not have been planned. After killing Richmond, they'd hid the makeshift murder weapon where I would be compromised. And they'd accomplished all of that during one of the few times I ventured out of the house during my fake marriage.

That amounted to a lot of well-thought-out and skilled moves. The series of events also suggested the real killer had been on the property repeatedly. Gaining access, hanging around. Only a few people could pull that off. One of them was Elias. The rest of the suspects had the last name of Dougherty or worked with Richmond.

"Addison?"

From the look on Elias's face he'd called my name more than once.

"We need to go outside and let Detective Sessions and his people work."

That was the last thing I wanted to do but I did it anyway. I got to the doorway of the greenhouse before the detective piped up again.

"Mrs. Dougherty?"

My feet sloshed around in my now-wet shoes. Had the wetness soaked through my sweater?

"Tell me again where you were around the time of your husband's death."

Not around. At the time. My alibi, and a good one. I was in Deer Park. An hour away. "Olympic Diner. Getting lost in a plate of french fries. Why?"

"And you'd been there before. Several times."

Not a question, which hinted at a potential problem.

"What are you after here, Nick?" Elias asked.

"I'm trying to firm up the alibi she gave on the scene."

The "scene" being the house on the day Richmond was killed. I'd driven home, walked in, and saw Richmond in a pool of red at the bottom of the stairs. Blood streaked across the floor. Sprayed on the walls. I almost bolted.

That's what I'd done the last time I was in a room with a dead body, and I'd paid for that choice every day since. This time I stayed and called for an ambulance.

The detective stared at me, clearly expecting an actual answer. Since Elias didn't shut the conversation down, I repeated the alibi I'd provided that day. "Richmond said he had work to do, so I went for a drive and stopped at the diner."

Out of habit, paid cash. I was depending on the memory of the waitress and security camera footage to corroborate my presence.

The detective smiled. "We'll talk soon."

"What was that about?" Elias asked as the two of us crossed the yard on the way back to the house.

"I'm not sure." The possibilities swirled in my head.

"I'm guessing they're going to find something incriminating in this greenhouse search?"

"Yes." But I was more concerned about what the detective already knew about the diner and how that intel would kick my ass.

Chapter Twenty-Five

HER

Present Day

The last twenty-four hours crawled by without the expected knock on the door by Detective Sessions and his minions. I didn't know if he'd actually be the one to come and arrest me. Probably, since I think it was a fantasy of his. Elias warned me about questioning and forensic testing and a whole bunch of nonsense I barely remember because I was wearing a disinfectant-soaked T-shirt at the time.

After I finally got permission to return to the house I used the rest of last night to put everything the police ripped apart back together. The crime scene cleaners had already been here once to remove any sign of Richmond's demise. I didn't want a repeat of that experience.

My nosy neighbors spent most of the search warrant time standing outside in their driveways, straining for a better look. By now, the news of what had happened likely ping-ponged around the country club set. The idea of walking into a beehive of angry Richmond supporters kept me at home. I could make my own coffee.

Three showers and the smell of disinfectant still clung to my hair. I needed industrial-strength shampoo to kill the scent.

Searching for it would be risky but maybe there was a way. I'd barely swiped my finger across the cellphone screen when I heard the deep *bong* from the front gate and my security app lit up.

I checked the video. "Sweet hell."

A Kathryn and Portia visit this time. Looked like news about the search warrant had made its way across town to the other Dougherty household. Last thing I needed was a showdown and I really didn't want to engage in a yelling match in front of Richmond's kid.

Bong

The noise turned into one long moan. I could see from the camera that Kathryn held her finger on the intercom button. The woman was endlessly annoying.

Fine. I'd play along. The app let me respond without leaving the kitchen.

"What do you want?" Nothing in my tone said *welcome.*

"Let us in." Kathryn's clipped voice echoed through the kitchen.

A snide response about her having her own house seemed in order. Only the panicked look on Portia's face stopped me. The kid wanted to be anywhere else. I empathized because I once was that age and wanted to escape a messy mother-daughter relationship.

I blew out a long breath and prepared for another unwanted round with Kathryn. Five minutes after I buzzed them in the doorbell rang. Two minutes after that we were standing in my kitchen. The goal was to confine Kathryn to one room of the house. Not let her wander around and cause trouble.

"You changed the gate code."

Kathryn barely let me walk into the room before launching that one. I ignored her and focused on Portia, whom I'd spoken to exactly twice in my life for a total of less than five minutes. "Do you want something to drink?"

Portia shook her head.

She looked less severe today than she had at her father's funeral. Still dressed all in black. Black pants and a black sweater. The latest in sullen teenage fashion. But her choice of outfit didn't explain why she was here.

"Is your school on some kind of break?"

Kathryn held up her hand to stop Portia from answering. "She's staying with me for a few days to get her bearings."

"My school is about twenty minutes away. It's easy to go back and forth. I only board five days a week anyway," Portia said.

"It's what?" Why in the world was I paying for her to live and sleep at a spa-like adventure camp that was close enough to home for her to bike to it? I should have listened closer when Elias brought this subject up and I agreed to pay. Kathryn and Richmond really wanted to offload this poor girl.

"Thanks, by the way." Portia's voice came out like a whisper this time.

The kid stumped me. "For what?"

Portia shrugged. "Mom said you're paying for my school through college graduation."

Is that what I agreed to? She was fifteen. That meant years of being connected to this family in some way.

"I didn't *tell* you. You were snooping around my desk and saw the confirming email I sent to the school about the payment responsibility change."

Kathryn made it very hard to like her even a little bit. Treat me like shit, sure. That was to be expected. Snapping at her grieving kid was an asshole move. "You've already notified the school they should forward the bill to me?"

"Of course. The boarding fees were due, so I couldn't wait. The school needed to know about the new arrangements."

Yeah, of course. Silly me.

"And it's all of the school bills, not just tuition. Housing. Meals. Uniforms. Activity fees." Kathryn had the nerve to smile. One of pure satisfaction.

This conversation kept rolling downhill. Time to end it. "I appreciate the gratitude but—"

"Look." Kathryn let out a long sigh as she plopped her expensive bag on the counter next to her and wrapped her fingers around the edge of the counter. "I'm here about a retrospective."

That sounded like rich people code for something. I had no idea what. "Excuse me?"

"A celebration of Richmond's life."

Hell no. "Wasn't that what the funeral was for?"

Kathryn ignored the question. "We're thinking about a party of his closest friends and colleagues."

I waited for the punch line.

"As his widow that is something you should organize and pay for," Kathryn added.

I finally sat down on the stool because I didn't see a quick end to this conversation. Kathryn was fired up. I wouldn't have been surprised if she handed me a stack of bills for her personal expenses. "Is there anything you don't think I should pay for?"

"Oh, you're going to pay." Kathryn dropped that nugget as if it were some sort of *gotcha*.

Portia rolled her eyes. "Mom."

But that didn't stop Kathryn. "I heard the police were here."

And there it was. The real reason for the visit.

"They searched the house and grounds. It's standard procedure in a case like this." At least that's what Elias told me. This was actually the second search. The police took a good look around, collected forensic evidence, and snapped photos on the day of Richmond's death. This was their second shot. The one that telegraphed a *we're closing in* message to me.

"You mean in a murder case. Richmond was murdered," Kathryn said.

Portia winced. Kathryn didn't notice. I did. "Maybe now isn't the time to discuss this."

"My children deserve answers. Closure." Kathryn put a supportive hand on Portia's back. Ran a hand over Portia's hair.

The gesture looked affectionate. Genuine. Motherly. I was more familiar with maternal touching as part of a ruse. A setup for a scam. Kathryn's sudden care and attention for her daughter surprised me. It didn't logically follow the conversation and her seething up until now. It also stopped me from telling Kathryn to shut up.

I went with a more neutral comment. "I thought you were here about a party."

"The police fumbled the investigation from the beginning. You should have been arrested that first night before you could destroy evidence. I made demands but Nick insisted he couldn't storm in here without probable cause. I guess he has it now." Kathryn's voice stayed calm and steady. "You should have taken my deal."

Portia shirked away from her mom's hold. "Mom, we should go."

This kid might be the only family member I liked. "Listen to your daughter."

Kathryn had her agenda and was not ready to abandon it. "On second thought, it might make sense to postpone the party. You can't exactly organize it from jail."

The woman didn't have an *off* button. "I treasure our visits."

"Mom, you promised," Portia said.

"We'll leave." Kathryn didn't try to hide her big smile. "Don't make any major changes to the house. You won't have it for long."

Chapter Twenty-Six

HER

Present Day

Finding out who was framing me before I was arrested was my number one goal. Figuring out Richmond's surgery mess and his role in Ben Cullen's death was a close second since the two could be related.

Elias still didn't offer as many details as I wanted, so I pivoted to a weaker target. Dr. Thomas Linfield. He thought he was coming over to pick up confidential files I claimed to have found in the box I took from the office. We both agreed they should be handled with care, so he volunteered.

For a guy with a fancy medical degree and decades of practice convincing people about how smart he was, he was easy to fool. He sat on the couch in the library, sipping the coffee I made for him, without a clue he was being played.

I sat down, leaving plenty of room between us in case this conversation went sideways. *Always be prepared for the worst when it came to dealing with men.* That was one of my life rules, and I had no intention of abandoning it now.

I set my untouched coffee down on the table and dove in. "We have a mutual interest."

Thomas's eyebrow lifted as he stared at me over the rim of his mug. "Oh?"

"August Christopher."

With that name and his specific medical credentials, August should have been an easy man to find but that wasn't the case. I'd done some computer searches, mindful of the fact the police were likely watching. They were welcome to look into the surgery issue and Richmond's lies and save me from having to do it, but I doubted I'd get that lucky.

Every lead turned into a dead end. This August guy wasn't reachable or locatable at any of the places the internet searches suggested he might be.

"How do you know about August?" Thomas asked.

"Richmond and I were married. We talked about important issues." That sounded like something a real married woman might say, so I went with it.

Thomas set his mug down. "Is August mentioned in the files you called me about?"

Not at all, actually. "He's integral to Peter Cullen's allegations about the death of his son."

Thomas exhaled and managed to make it sound condescending. "I can't discuss this topic with you."

"You can tell me how many times August filled in for Richmond during surgery." The idea still didn't make sense. The one thing Richmond valued was his reputation. He'd need a significant reason to take that risk, and none came to me.

"That's only an allegation."

Not the adamant denial I expected. Not an *it didn't happen* or *that's ridiculous* but a much more careful response.

"August is missing. I want to know why." I had theories, all of which centered on Richmond sucking.

Thomas sat up straight now, fully alert. Every word mentally dissected and measured before saying them out loud. "August left our practice for another position."

Fine. We could do this the hard way. "Where?"

"I'm not at liberty to—"

"Where he works can't be top secret. Surely, his patients would know."

"There are privacy concerns."

That had to be a made-up thing. Elias threw that kind of sentence out there whenever he didn't want to share information. Sounded like Thomas knew the same trick.

"You do understand that a detective is looking into Richmond's life, right? That includes Richmond's medical practice. Detective Sessions is going to rip every piece of this story apart." Probably not true, but I needed leverage.

"My understanding is there's no need for further investigation." Thomas seemed to hesitate for maximum impact. "They have a suspect in Richmond's murder."

The entire town had weighed the nonexistent evidence and found me guilty. "I didn't kill my husband, which means someone else did and that person better hope they covered their tracks."

"I wouldn't know anything about that."

But he'd tensed. A slight movement, but I saw it. "You and your medical practice can't hide from this."

"You would be wise to stop digging around, Mrs. Dougherty."

Empty threats seemed to be second nature to rich people.

They threw out words and tried to make others scared, but none of them had the stomach to get really dirty. I'd spent most of my twenty-seven years learning how to read people, and Thomas didn't have the stamina for this game.

He continued. "Do you really want *your* life dissected and pulled apart? Every secret revealed? Your marriage to Richmond examined?"

Score one for the doc for trying to walk down a road that would turn him into roadkill. "You're welcome to try, but if you're going to take a shot I'd suggest you perfect your aim first."

"I didn't mean—"

Yeah, he did. "The hospital and your medical group are about to be sued. It would be easier to shift the blame away from your group and solely onto Richmond if his wife was on board."

"What's in it for you? Why would you help the practice?"

Because I wanted to destroy Richmond even though he was dead. If he hadn't gotten himself killed I'd be destroying him right now. His being in a box changed my methods, not my focus. "You don't need to worry about that."

Thomas sat there in silence for a few minutes then stood up. "I'll show myself out."

He feared blowback on his livelihood. That's how his type acted—in their own best interest. Always.

I followed him to the entry hall without saying a word.

He was the one to restart the conversation. "I worked with Richmond for years. Excellent references. Supremely talented. Respected. A significant moneymaker who could rally support."

"That sounds like his self-written bio. What did you really think?" People buried their skepticism when it came to Richmond. They lapped up every word he uttered until the line between fantasy and reality blurred.

"I'm not denying that the real Richmond Dougherty behind all the hype was . . ." Thomas visibly searched for the right word. "Difficult."

An interesting place to land. "Understatement."

"I don't know you and I don't trust you."

That was the first smart thing Thomas had said since he entered the house. "The feeling is mutual but not relevant to our respective interests. You want to avoid liability."

Thomas shook his head. "I want to set the record straight."

Trifling nonsense. It sounded like Thomas lied so often about his concerns that he now bought his own bullshit. "I'd think you'd want to bury the truth because as Richmond's partner you could easily become collateral damage in his mess."

"Our lawyers—"

"We both know that some secrets are both too dangerous to share and too big to hide . . . without help."

Thomas fell silent again. He didn't move for the door. He stood in the middle of the foyer with his hands fisted at his sides and his mouth locked in an unreadable expression.

When he started talking again his voice had dropped lower. "Sticking your nose into this situation could lead to a very dark place."

"Richmond is dead, Thomas. There's no need to protect him."

Thomas's eyes narrowed. "I'd think you'd want to preserve his legacy."

"You were right earlier. You don't know me at all." And I needed to find August and fast.

Chapter Twenty-Seven

HER

Married, Day Twenty-Seven

Parties weren't my thing. Elaborate wedding celebrations complete with cake and decorations were even less my thing. Richmond's business partners threw this one for us. That didn't make it any easier to take seriously despite the fancy dress that cost more than I used to earn in a week.

A sizable engagement ring and matching wedding band sparkled on my finger. Someone else's rings. No idea who they belonged to. Richmond threw the set at me before we left the house and warned I could have them for one night only then it was back to the cheap band he bought for when I ventured out in public.

As the guest of honor, one of the two, I had to look and act a certain way. Grateful and in love. I was neither.

The restless mood of the crowd resulted in an abundance of awkward small talk. Dodging whispers and pretending not to hear some of the more inventive gossip bouncing around about me had me wishing I were anywhere else.

I married Richmond. The town loved Kathryn. The party highlighted that she was out as wife, and I was in. After a few hours it was clear everyone in the room hated my new title as much as I did.

The whirl of music, forced smiles, and food finally died down, leaving a few stragglers in the parking lot. They huddled around Richmond and soaked in his . . . what? Brilliance? Ego? Unrelenting bullshit? I'd had enough of him for one day, so I didn't bother to find out. Exhaustion outran my annoyance as I leaned against the car, ready to climb in and wishing I'd grabbed the keys from Richmond on the way out.

The spectacle could go on for hours. Tonight he was *on*. He laughed and joked. Traded stories as he worked the room and now the car lot. Every person he spoke with got his full attention for the short period of time he spent with them. Their faces lit up and they hung on every word. He nodded, looked interested, asked questions. He had a gift for making people feel special, if only for a few minutes.

The public Richmond differed greatly from the one I battled on a daily basis. He charmed his audience. They thanked him with their rapt attention. His big smile hadn't faltered all night. Until right now.

He crossed the lot toward me with his back to his adoring fans and friends. The ever-present scowl he reserved for me firmly back in place. The door lock chirped. I slid inside without saying a word, mostly to dispel any idea he might have about giving me a kiss or showing affection to please the crowd.

Arriving together at this shindig was his idea. He insisted and even I could admit it would look odd for us to show up separately to a party thrown in our honor. That meant leaving together.

We drove home in silence, which I preferred, letting the steady thump of the wheels against the road serve as the only background noise. I closed my eyes for a second and dreamed of plunging into a warm bath. The heated leather seat lulled me into a daze.

My whole body jerked. The seat belt pulled tight at the sudden movement. I wasn't sure how much time had passed. No way I dozed off. I'd been so careful not to give Richmond the upper hand. But the car had stopped.

Richmond turned off the engine, leaving us trapped together in a suffocating fishbowl. I looked for lights, buildings, people, even nighttime joggers, but all around us darkness waited. Silence wrapped around the car as I struggled to sit up straight and be ready for whatever came next.

Forget that. Escape was the right answer.

My muddled mind cleared long enough for me to grab the door handle. I didn't want to be out there, but I couldn't be in here.

"Don't bother." Richmond pointed in the direction of my lap. "Seat belt lock."

Wasn't he an enterprising psychopath. "You just happen to carry around a seat belt lock?"

He tapped his fingers against the wheel. "You're a fan of games. I thought we'd play one. Out here. In the dark. You don't mind the dark, do you, Addison?"

The amusement in his voice sent my anxiety spiking. My breath came in pants and the air in the car felt sticky and humid.

Get it together.

I stopped fidgeting and tried to bury my rising fear. He would not see me lose it. But where the hell were we? Trees towered over the car. Shrubs lined my side. I struggled to see white or yellow lines indicating a two-way road. This looked more like an unpaved service path.

He liked issuing orders. It was time for him to obey one. "Open the door. Now."

"And leave my new wife alone in the woods?" Even his humming sounded sarcastic. "What kind of husband would I be?"

"You suck as a husband and a human." I pulled and tugged but the seat belt lock stayed latched.

"So you've said."

"Give me the key for the seat belt." Did it have a key? I shifted around, looking for one. "Take this off."

"I told some people at the party how upset you've been. Never leaving the house. Feeling inferior and out of place. Threatening to leave." He nodded. "I'm sure they wouldn't be surprised if you just . . . disappeared."

His memory seemed to be failing. "Will they be surprised when they find out you're a fraud?"

He laughed. "Should we go for a walk? Get some fresh air and enjoy the moonlight?"

"Take me home." My voice stayed steady. I had no clue how because my insides were bouncing and swirling. My mind wouldn't clear long enough for me to dream up a solid plan.

"Do you have any idea what I could do to you right now? Out here. Alone." He finally looked at me. The flat tone matched his empty expression. All the life from the party had been sucked out of him, leaving an empty shell. A dangerous, angry empty shell. "You're not so tough without your bat."

My bat. My flashlight. The night-lights I used to stave off the shadows. I missed all of that. My throat closed and my fingers clenched against the armrest.

"You put on a show at the beginning of the night, but you couldn't keep up the act. You started frowning and made it clear you wanted to leave. I should thank you for that because the attitude change supports my story. *You saw her mood swing. She's jealous of Kathryn. She kept spiraling then she stormed out of the house.*" He said the last part in a mocking tone.

"You have your phone and car GPS. They would give you away." I had no idea if that was true. I couldn't think or reason through any words before they popped out. The night kept pressing in, stealing the air.

Again he hummed, sounding very impressed with his maneuvering. "Good point. I wouldn't want to leave any evidence behind."

"Then what are you doing?"

"Taking my new wife for a drive." Satisfaction thrummed off him. "This is a beautiful forty-seven acres of woods, ponds, and rocks. Anything could happen out here."

"Here" likely being the nature center. It should be closed at this time of night, but could you really close the outdoors?

I tried to swallow the thick lump of fear clogging my throat. I could outrun him in other conditions. The paralyzing panic that sprang up when the darkness fell threatened any plans of escape. His advantage in size foreclosed fighting back.

He looked out the windowshield. "I like the dark."

Fucker. "You would."

He smiled, clearly enjoying my vulnerability. "I wanted to bring you out here to remind you."

Word games. Great. “Have you forgotten about the evidence I have?”

“I remember but you need to know I intend to fight back.” He opened his hand to reveal a small key. He dropped it in my lap. “You think you’ve won, but the war between us is just getting started.”

Chapter Twenty-Eight

HER

Present Day

Most lawyers probably refused to make house calls. Understandably so, but Elias was not one of them. The risk of social ruin that came with people seeing us in public together explained why he volunteered to commute between our properties instead. No matter how or why, he showed up at a respectable hour on Saturday morning with take-out coffees and earned my temporary gratitude.

Now to drop the reason for my invitation. "I need you to do a favor for me."

He froze with a cup halfway to his mouth. "You understand I'm your attorney and not your personal assistant, right?"

"Unfortunately, but this will benefit you, too." We sat across from each other at the kitchen table. This close I could see what he was thinking as he thought it, which might not be a great thing. "You said your good pal, Detective Nick, was likely going through my phone records and bank accounts and having me followed."

"He's not my—"

"You two are very chummy. It's unsettling."

Elias slowly lowered his coffee cup to the table and leaned

back in his chair. "I came to talk to you about the bat and you being found in the greenhouse with said bat, and the disinfectant you clearly used right before we found you trying to hide said bat."

So many *said* references. "I was looking for *said* offending item so I could get rid of it."

Elias exhaled and made a lot of noise doing it. "Don't say that to anyone else."

He was missing the point, so I highlighted it for him. "I just happened to find the hidden bat when you and the detective just happened to step into my yard. Convenient, right?"

"Are you saying Detective Sessions hid the bat to frame you?"

"I wasn't but I won't think of anything else now." It made sense. Detective Sessions wasn't my biggest fan and solving Richmond's murder in a way that painted me as evil would buy him a lot of goodwill in this town. "Don't look so shocked. If you were being framed, wouldn't you do everything you could to throw the scent off you?"

"When the forensic testing comes back—"

"We'll deal with that nightmare later." Thinking about everything that could go wrong would paralyze me. I needed to stay nimble. "In the meantime, I can't go out and investigate. Not without drawing even more attention to myself."

Elias frowned because that's what Elias did when we talked. It fit with the *disappointed dad* way he had of dealing with me. "Investigate what?"

"Who killed Richmond, what happened to that missing doctor who's alleged to have conducted Richmond's surgeries, that August guy, and if the two events are related." Elias stared at me, so I stared back. "You have to admit August being missing isn't normal. People who spend years of their lives and tons of money becoming a doctor don't just walk away from it."

This time Elias moved the coffee cup off to the side, as if he feared knocking it over. "A boy died. It's not that surprising August might want time off to deal with the loss."

I preferred my version of events. "Or Richmond was trying to hide the truth by either paying August off or threatening him or, worse, killing him. All those options would explain why August is missing now."

"Killing him? You're adding one plus one and getting fifty-seven."

"That's a good line." Back to the reason I invited him over. "We need to find August."

"We?"

"You need to know where he is and what he knows before Peter Cullen's lawsuit heats up. There are limits on what I can do even in terms of computer searches with the detective lurking around." Being the subject of a murder investigation made conducting an investigation of my own tough. "That means the footwork falls to you."

"I don't agree with your premise or your conclusion."

"Talk like a normal person."

He sighed again. Bigger this time. "It would be best if you stayed out of this and let the detective and his team do their jobs."

"The bat had blood on it. It was hidden in my greenhouse. I touched it when I found it."

"You're sure it was blood?"

"It was my bat and there were new stains on it, so yeah, I'm pretty sure." I saw the brownish streaks every time I closed my eyes. After years of blocking the memory of blood on my hands, I had a haunting new one.

"So, you want to find August to take your mind off the bat?" Elias asked.

"No. I want to make sure August is still alive and see what he knows because that answer could relate to Richmond's murder."

"I don't see the connection."

I finished off my coffee before diving in. "Unless the alarm malfunctioned, no one broke into this house that day, which means Richmond let his attacker walk right in. He was a safety guy. He kept the property locked up and the alarm on. We know from the security logs that he disabled both an hour before his death as if he was expecting someone."

"The security video doesn't show anyone entering the property."

"So what? The same thing happened the other day when the alarm went off." I sat forward in my chair, trying to telegraph the urgency of this topic. "Look, there are only a few people Richmond would have invited in without question. You, his ex and their kids, Thomas, and possibly this August guy."

Elias's eyebrow lifted. "And you."

"I'm the only one I know is innocent."

Elias snorted. "Thanks for the vote of confidence."

I never invited friends over for tea. Neither did Richmond. That was one benefit of a fake marriage. There was no need to make fake small talk. We counted on the false belief that we, as newlyweds, wanted privacy. Then we retreated to our respective parts of the house and ignored each other . . . except when we didn't.

"Richmond could have lured August to the house and then August was forced to protect himself," I said.

"I think we've officially crossed the line from nonfiction to fiction." Elias's eye roll meant he didn't understand Richmond was a killer.

I knew better. "You don't think Richmond could do something intentional and so awful?"

"As homicide? No."

To tell or not to tell. The options spun around in my head. The inclination was to keep my secrets close and under wraps, but I needed Elias as an ally. Even if he was the one who killed Richmond, which seemed like a stretch, he could at least make sure I didn't get framed for the deed. That required we reach some sort of understanding.

Rather than rushing in, I tried wading in. "What if I told you everything you know about Richmond is a lie?"

"Be more specific."

Fucking lawyers. "Okay. What if I told you the whole story about Richmond stopping the shooting at his high school when he was seventeen was fake?"

Elias stared at me for a few tense seconds in silence. "I'd remind you that we know what happened that day. There's school security video. A redacted version ran for years on true crime shows and in that documentary. The footage still shows up now and then on the anniversary of the thwarted shooting."

"What did you really see?"

"Two kids shot in a school hallway. One was an innocent bystander."

I knew the death toll better than anyone. "Zach Bryant. Hit

by a stray bullet when Richmond and his baby brother, Cooper, wrestled for the gun."

"You're forgetting the part where Richmond tackled Cooper and shot him to stop him from conducting a school massacre. Richmond picked the safety of the entire school over his brother."

Elias was wrong. I hadn't forgotten a damn thing. I remembered every second of that video. "That's such a great hero story. It's a shame it's not true."

"What?" Elias leaned in as confusion took over his tone. "How can you know that?"

I studied Richmond. Knew him. Lived with his lies. "I have evidence. Richmond married me to keep me from releasing it."

The truth sat between us, burrowing a hole in the long-told fantasy Richmond had concocted and the public bought without question. Every word I uttered, tearing the bonds holding the lie together.

"If you do have something like—"

"I do." I was in it now and didn't see any reason to play coy.

Elias's frown deepened. "If true, you could have exposed Richmond without getting near him. Why go through the sham of a wedding and all that came after?"

Because I wanted to rip Richmond's life apart, make him feel helpless and under siege, and the best way to do that was from the inside. But, in the end, I made my choices because of my mother, her vengeance, and her inability to tell the truth. "I had my reasons."

Elias seemed to turn the new information over in his mind, dissecting it and trying to push it aside. "Look, I'll admit Richmond could be an asshole but—"

"You help me locate August and figure out who other than me wanted Richmond dead and I'll tell you every sordid detail, starting with what really happened at the Dougherty house that morning twenty-seven years ago."

That was the deal. One I never intended to offer, but I also never intended to go to jail, so it was time to adapt.

"You're saying the entire hero story is a lie."

"Yes." Four people died that day. It was time people knew why. "Deal?"

"Deal."

Chapter Twenty-Nine

HER

Present Day

Two days had passed since Elias promised to look into August's whereabouts. I'd appealed to his sense of curiosity. From a subtle hint here and a stray comment there, it was clear Elias didn't worship Richmond like so many others did. But believing Richmond would kill his own brother might be a stretch. I couldn't blame Elias for the skepticism. The entire country suffered from a collective brainwashing about the tragedy. But I had Elias's attention and right now that's all I needed.

I checked my quiet cellphone. No answers yet. I'd give Elias a few more hours before I started a nonstop texting spree. We were in a race against whatever the detective might find or make up. There was little chance my panicked cleanup job wiped the bat clean of all DNA evidence. I missed something. I could feel it.

No news and a lingering sense of dread kept me at the house. I didn't have anywhere to go anyway, but a drive or a sandwich at the diner would have been nice. I liked that place, and the detective was right. I'd been there several times. I just hadn't been totally truthful about why.

Right now, I had to clear my head. A walk to the mailbox at

the end of the long driveway might be enough to burn off some nervous energy. Probably not, but it was worth a try.

A sunny fall day greeted me when I stepped outside. The wind blew through the trees, sending yellow and red leaves swirling to the ground. With each step, I got lost in a round-robin of over-thinking, worrying, and second-guessing. Richmond's killer. Richmond's lies. Richmond's antics. They pinged off each other in my mind.

The guy was as much of a pain in the ass dead as he'd been alive.

I arrived at the front gate and tested the lock to make sure it worked. There'd been too many unwanted visitors lately. I no longer trusted the gate, fancy alarms, or a wall of tall trees to keep me hidden and safe.

For once the neighbors across the street weren't loitering in their driveway, waiting to catch a glimpse of something juicy at my gate. I didn't know their names. Didn't care. Most of the time I couldn't even see their house from mine. I only knew they were FOKs, Friends of Kathryn, and she visited often.

I opened the mailbox door on my side of the fence. The other side had a lock on it that, in theory, prevented nosy people from being extra nosy and sorting through my mail. Three days of mail had collected. It consisted of Richmond's alumni magazine, which he clearly wouldn't be reading from now on. A few cards addressed to Mrs. Dougherty, likely obligatory condolence nonsense. A new bill in my name from the alarm company and a few random flyers.

The last thing was a brown envelope. There was no scenario where a plain brown envelope with my name scribbled across the front signaled good news. I debated leaving it in the box but grabbed it instead. The temptation to rip it open tugged at me. I made it the whole way to the front door before I gave in. The contents spilled out. Another terse note with the same message as the one written on my wall in super-secret paint.

YOU WILL PAY

Photos of me. All recent. All at the house. Me in the driveway with Elias. Me on the back deck, looking out over the yard. Me walking to the greenhouse, wearing what I now thought of as my disinfectant outfit. The detective had taken it with him in the search.

My gaze zipped from the front gate to the trees outlining the property. Even with the dropping leaves they provided cover. Houses sat on either side of my property but not close enough to peer into their living rooms.

The photos were a bit blurry, as if the person who took them did so from a distance and then zoomed in. I had no idea how the stalking photographer managed to get the shots and print them out. Worse, I couldn't figure out where the person stood to get the pictures.

I studied each one. They all came from one side of the house. From a higher angle off to my left. I held my middle finger up in the air just in case the amateur photographer was there and looking for a show.

Inside. I needed to get inside and spend some time with the pictures and the security footage to see if the cameras had caught anyone or any movement. The motion sensors should have gone off, but if the person stayed outside the fence, maybe not.

The only thing I knew for sure was that someone was watching. And they wanted me to know it.

Chapter Thirty

HER

Present Day

Wyatt showed up at the security gate before ten the next morning. So much for the idea that paying his school bills would buy me some distance from his simmering rage.

I took a photo off the security feed and sent it to Elias with a *can we do something about him?* text before ushering Wyatt into the house. A fight on the street wouldn't work because I hated the idea of lingering outside. Too many eyes. Too many covert opportunities to spy on me and launch a new round of threats.

Once in the house, Wyatt followed me through to the kitchen. He watched me make a latte then a second one for him.

"What do you want?" I didn't have the patience for, or any interest in, a more tactful opening. That one would have to do.

"I needed to see you."

The entire family excelled at unnecessary drama. "I'm concerned about your definition of *need*."

He fidgeted on the stool at the kitchen island. "I've heard things."

Rumors. The town's favorite pastime. "You're going to have to be more specific."

"Mom says you agreed to pay for stuff." He hesitated as if expecting me to jump in. When I didn't, he rambled on. "For me and for Portia."

"Your school. That's it." If he wanted a car or a trip to Europe he could beg his mother.

"What's your game?"

I sighed because *come on*. "Wyatt, I'm going to be honest with you. I'm sick of everyone with the last name of Dougherty, so you would be wise to jump ahead to your point."

"Dad made it clear you were after his money, which he figured out too late to stop you."

It wasn't a surprise that Richmond painted himself as an innocent victim in our marriage, but that didn't make the lie any less annoying. "It's possible your family—not me—has an obsession with money."

Wyatt blew right by the comment. "I don't get it. You worked hard to screw him financially. You fucked over my mom. Yet you're turning around and agreeing to pay for stuff? I doubt you feel bad about what you did, so handing out money now makes no sense."

"I can see where you'd think that."

"Do you believe we'll feel grateful and rush to support you when you're arrested? Because we won't. So what do you expect to get out of this?"

Quid pro quo. A lesson Wyatt learned directly from Richmond. Every act, no matter how seemingly benevolent, came with a price tag. Life amounted to a back-and-forth lobbying for a superior position. Nothing, including parental love, was unconditional in this family.

I understood because I'd grown up that way, too. But I recognized the game. Wyatt still didn't.

"There's no agenda here. I'm trying to work my way through what happens now that your dad is dead." The desperate need to cash out and run grew stronger every single day.

"You're not who he said you were . . . unless you killed him. Mom thinks you did." Wyatt's head dropped and he ran his fingers through his hair. "I can't stand not knowing."

Wyatt looked every inch of an emotionally embattled son locked in a mire of confusion and despair. Richmond never suffered from a guilty conscience. Maybe Wyatt wasn't that lucky.

Killer. Victim. I couldn't tell where he fell.

"Dad was so pissed off. He convinced me to . . ." Wyatt shook his head as his hand clamped down on the coffee mug in front of him.

Oh . . . "To what?"

Wyatt continued to shake his head. "Never mind."

Not likely to happen. Not when he was so close to cracking and telling me what he knew. The truth clawed at him. I could see the words trying to punch their way out.

"What did your father tell you to do to me?" It was a guess. An educated one, but I couldn't see the full picture without more of a hint.

Richmond had messed up this kid. Told him too much about some things and lied about others until Wyatt's common sense got choked out in his dad's stranglehold. Freeing Wyatt from Richmond's suffocating shadow wasn't my job but watching the kid bounce from angry to confused to lost in the span of a minute proved difficult.

Wyatt wasn't Richmond. My life would have been easier if I could have drawn the parallel and written both father and son off as mirror gene pool disasters. But Wyatt lacked the obvious killer instinct and drive. The mix of bloodlust and greed that shaped so many of Richmond's actions didn't seem to have passed to the son.

"I didn't have a choice." Wyatt whispered the comment without giving away more.

Fucking Richmond. "Wyatt, I can't help you unless I know what you're talking about and, believe it or not, I do want to help."

The knock at the back door made us both jump. Elias walked in, seemingly oblivious to the starkness of the mood and the blunting impact of his intrusion.

"The gate was open." Elias stared at Wyatt. "I guess you didn't close it on the way in."

Interesting. Wyatt might be more like his old man than I thought. Was this some new ploy? Get into the house, lure me into a false sense of security, then mess with the security system. The kid's sad face and haunted eyes may have tricked me, making me think whatever gibberish fell out of his mouth sounded genuine.

Elias didn't wait for a response. "I need to talk with your stepmom."

"Oh." Wyatt slipped off the stool. "Right."

The conversation ended on an unsatisfactory note. "We didn't finish our talk."

He made it to the back door without making eye contact. "Forget I came."

Then he was gone. I opened the security app and confirmed he got into his car and headed for the front gate.

"Did you invite him over? Actually, forget that." Elias put Wyatt's abandoned mug in the sink. "Detective Sessions needs to see us."

My world tilted. "I thought you refused a meeting."

"He made it clear we don't have a choice this time."

Chapter Thirty-One

HER

Present Day

Police headquarters sat on the edge of the main part of town, not far from the rail station. It consisted of a nondescript grayish stone building connected to the local courthouse. For a fancy real estate area, the inside of the building was decidedly not fancy. Except for the bulletproof glass and uniformed police officers, it looked like a typical older building with an open area carved out in front and offices behind.

The space buzzed with activity. All of that stopped when I walked inside. The sudden silence unnerved me. "Am I going to be arrested?"

Elias answered my whisper with one of his own. "Probably not."

"You're not very comforting."

"Elias. Mrs. Dougherty." Detective Sessions gestured for us to join him on the other side of the room.

A few officers stepped out of the way, letting us pass. The second we reached Detective Sessions the mumble of conversation in the room restarted.

We stood in front of a closed door. Elias immediately resorted to his usual lawyer-questioning mode. "What's going on, Nick?"

"Your client didn't do a very good job of hiding the bat. The presumed murder weapon." The detective smiled as he said the words. His face beamed with self-satisfaction.

"*She* didn't try to hide it." Only because I didn't have time, but still. I was standing right there. *Talk to me or at least use my name.*

"But hiding things is what you do, right?" Detective Sessions clearly didn't want an answer to his rhetorical question. He was too busy enjoying the sound of his own voice. "I'm referring to your trips to that diner and the substantial recent withdrawal of funds from your bank account."

Elias had called the sum insignificant. The detective thought it was a big deal. Neither of them knew what they were talking about, but my job wasn't to cough up answers and make the questioning easier. Elias made that much clear during the car ride over here.

"The fact she didn't lie about the diner or the money suggests she has nothing to hide," Elias said.

"Or it could mean she's not as smart as she thinks she is. She wouldn't be the first person to get tripped up by their ego."

Did they even need me for this conversation?

Elias stepped closer to the detective, cutting off visual access to any nearby gawkers. "What exactly are we talking about? You know she has an alibi for the time of Richmond's fall."

"His murder." The detective stopped talking to Elias and aimed his comments directly at me. "We're waiting on the tests on the bat and other items collected from your house. Standard procedure but I think we all know the bat ties to Richmond's death and to you."

I didn't say a word. Denying any of this had the potential to bite me in the ass later.

"Mrs. Dougherty should consider this her opportunity to step up and be the first one to talk," the detective said.

First? A chilling word.

The detective shook his head. "I warned you about the conflict of interest, Elias."

"I haven't heard anything that makes me rethink my legal position."

The detective hadn't said much of substance. He was too busy preening. But I could feel the boom hovering over my head, waiting to fall.

"We tracked that checking account withdrawal. It took some time because your client got it in cash, but the videos we collected from the diner led us to the recipient. She used a debit card, making her easy to find. A woman with a pretty sordid history and more than one dead husband in her past. The kind of woman someone might pay to kill a spouse."

Boom. The verbal hit vibrated through every part of me.

The only thing more annoying than the detective's broad smile was his cocky stance. Both signaled trouble. The kind of trouble I'd been running from my entire life.

"You think she hired someone to kill Richmond?" Elias asked.

"Answer this, Mrs. Dougherty. How quickly do you think your accomplice will turn on you when she realizes she's caught and is looking for a way to lessen her prison time?"

The detective didn't offer more of an explanation or wait for a response. He opened the door behind him. His big *ta-da* moment consisted of showing off a woman sitting at a table in what looked like a small office.

The detective's eyebrow lifted. "I believe you two know each other."

Unfortunately, yes. "Hi, Mom."

Chapter Thirty-Two

HER

Present Day

Detective Sessions looked the exact opposite of cocky now. His mouth had drawn into a tight, thin line. His swagger was long gone.

He'd closed the door on Mom, trapping her inside the suffocating space, and ushered Elias and me into the windowless room next door. Detective Sessions barely waited until we sat down before launching into the jumble of thoughts in his head. "There's no way that woman is your mother. She's far too young. I might believe sister but not mother."

The groan escaped before I could stop it. "Please don't say that to her."

The detective kept frowning. "You're almost the same age."

He thought she'd told the truth about her age. Adorable. He better up his game or Mom would have him running in circles. That might be interesting to watch if it didn't mean I also had to deal with her.

No matter how good Mom looked, she was never as young as she claimed to be. She hadn't lived an easy life but none of the strife or deceit showed on her face. She hid her underlying deviousness and murky morality behind big brown eyes and a body toned from years of dancing. Pretty with a bright smile and killer legs, she could pass for far younger. And she did. All the time.

The detective opened a file in front of him. He'd probably been carrying it earlier, but I'd missed it until now. "I've seen her driver's license and the birth date on it makes her thirty-nine. You're twenty-seven. You're saying she gave birth to you when she was twelve?"

"It sounds like Mom *accidentally* wrote the wrong birth date down. Again." She'd been knocking off time every birthday over the last decade. In another few years Mom would claim to be younger than I was and have the fake documents to prove it.

"You're saying she lied when she got her license?"

I almost felt sorry for the detective for moving into Lizzy's orbit.

"I'm betting she'll be stunned—positively shocked—that the wrong birth date is on there." More like stunned she got caught. "Then she'll explain that some sort of operator or computer error must have caused the problem and she missed it."

She loved to mess with people. She got off on being noticed and hit her stride whenever anyone praised her hotness. She reeled men in and played flirty games until they showered her with gifts and money.

She wasn't a grifter. She was more of a serial girlfriend and sometime wife who lavished attention on the men she targeted to get what she wanted in return. Dating was nothing more to her than an acceptable way to obtain goods—meals, televisions, apartments, checks—in exchange for sex.

I judged her for many things but not that. People were too precious about sex. She recognized it as a persuasive tool and used it. She knew her talents and capitalized on them, which I admired. If a man had done the same thing he'd be viewed as a player. Why should Mom be held to a different standard? She insisted on being paid. What other people saw as relationships, she saw as work, and she'd been working hard for a long time.

"My mom was sixteen when she had me. She's forty-three now, though she tries to get away with saying thirty-five. If she used a date that made her thirty-nine, that actually shows emotional growth on her part." More likely, she'd lied about her age so often that she forgot what it actually was.

Elias held up both hands, which strangely enough stopped the whirl of conversation. "Let's start over."

The detective read from the file. "Her name is Elizabeth Jenkins."

"She goes by Lizzy."

"What about the Jenkins part?" Elias asked.

A fair question since Mom and I didn't share the same last name. She borrowed mine, the one I had before my marriage to Richmond—Lance—years ago from a male friend. The name on my birth certificate was one she'd made up and abandoned before I was in elementary school. "Jenkins comes from husband number four."

"She really does have more than one dead former husband?" Elias sounded fascinated by the idea.

I knew Richmond had tried to investigate my past to use it against me. Little did he know, the clueless bastard. He didn't get far because I'd lived in a patchwork of places and spent years trying not to create a paper trail.

My mom found me anyway.

"One husband was killed as part of a botched robbery when I was ten." That was a mom-created story and I never strayed from it. "Another died of a heart attack during sex with Mom. I was a teenager when that horror happened. One died after they split up. A car accident that my mom is convinced was staged by the guy's kids from his first wife in order to get his money. The last one, Arthur Jenkins, is very much alive, or he was a few weeks ago."

Elias nodded. "Which one is your father?"

I fought to keep my tone even. "None of them."

The detective took over again. "You met with Ms. Jenkins on at least—"

"Lizzy." Thinking of Mom as Ms. Jenkins was . . . well, I couldn't. She'd always been Lizzy in my head. She preferred I called her that so no one would think she had a twenty-seven-year-old kid. I called her Mom mostly out of spite.

The detective flipped through the pages in front of him. "We've seen the security video from the diner where you were at the time of Richmond's murder. You met this woman at the same location several times, in secret and away from your marital home."

Funny how the detective skipped over the main point. "We met in *public*. That's the exact opposite of *in secret*."

Elias cleared his throat. I took the noise as a warning to tread carefully.

"You gave her six thousand dollars in cash a week before Richmond was killed." The detective dropped that morsel as if the two items were related.

The timing did suck. "She told me on an earlier diner meetup her car died. She needed a new one for work."

"Where does she work?" Elias asked.

"A casino in Atlantic City." I couldn't remember the name because she'd switched jobs several times over the last two years. I kept an eye on her, usually from afar, to prevent her from sneaking up on me, though that strategy had failed more than once.

Detective Sessions made a humming sound. "Why did she meet you at the diner?"

"First, to ask for money. Then another time to collect it." No need to lie. That was the truth . . . mostly. "And that tells you all you need to know about my mom."

The detective didn't appear convinced. "You could have invited her to your house."

Oh, hell no. "Yeah, Richmond would have loved that."

"Had she met him?" The detective didn't wait for an answer. "Was she at your wedding? Has she been to your house?"

"No to all of those."

"I'm guessing I'm going to have trouble finding anyone in town who knows her."

I hoped that was true. "We aren't close."

"Yet you handed her thousands of dollars."

Because that's how emotional blackmail worked. Lizzy excelled in that area. "Do you have a mother, Detective?"

He leaned back in his chair and watched me. A minute passed before he treated us to his insight. "This is all very convenient, Mrs. Dougherty."

Talk about missing the point. "I assure you, Detective, there's nothing convenient about Lizzy Jenkins."

The questioning continued for another fifteen minutes. Elias batted away every insinuation and accusation. He also pointed out that the diner's security video confirmed my location at the time of the murder and that a mother and a daughter sharing a few meals wasn't a crime. The detective's theory about

Mom being my paid accomplice or contract killer, or whatever he thought, unraveled until Elias finally put an end to all the fishing.

After quick introductions between Mom and Elias and a bit of mindless small talk, Elias went to get the car, leaving me standing with Mom outside the police station. Just the two of us. A combination that never went well for me.

"You had one job, Addison." She smiled at the people who walked by, but her voice came out in a harsh whisper. "I don't understand how you could have messed this up so badly."

I didn't respond because she didn't want me to. This was the Lizzy Jenkins show, and my role was to act like an obedient, non-speaking side character.

She shook her head. "You're lucky I'm here to fix this Richmond mess."

Yeah, lucky. "I didn't kill him."

She snorted. "Even I don't believe that."

Chapter Thirty-Three

HER

Seven Months Earlier

A month before my twenty-seventh birthday my mom showed up at my office. The assistant job at the flooring center wasn't anything special. I answered phones, did the filing and ordering, and generally tried not to draw attention to myself. It was honest work for low pay.

I'd picked Dublin, a suburb of Columbus, Ohio, and home to golf clubs, parks, and a yearly Irish festival, because the small city struck me as a place my mother would never visit. Comfortable but not fancy or shiny enough for her. Looked like I was wrong.

Wearing a pretty green dress and heels so high they bordered on indecent, she entered the office and stared down at me. "You couldn't run from me forever, my dear daughter. You didn't think I'd track you down?"

A woman could hope.

"What are you doing here, Mom?" Near me. In the building's back office. In Ohio.

"Looking for you."

And just happened to stumble into Ohio? Don't think so. "Is your husband with you?"

"We are no longer together, a fact you would know if you stayed in touch."

That explained the timing of the visit. She was bored and when she got bored her thoughts turned to me and old schemes. Probably also meant she needed money. "If you're looking for something to do you could take up knitting."

"Don't act like you don't have a brain in your head. I raised you better than that."

No way was I touching that last part. "I'm working."

"You can take a break."

"Addison?"

Of course my boss picked that minute to stroll in. He'd been at lunch for two hours with some business friend he wanted to impress. Now he'd walked in, and I had a mess.

Mom shot him a big smile. "Hello. I'm Lizzy Jenkins. Call me Lizzy, please." She put one hand on her chest and rested the other on his arm. "I know you're a busy man but is it okay if I take Addison away from work for a few minutes? I promise I'll keep it quick."

He frowned but didn't grumble, which was a nice change. "Is everything okay?"

"We need to have a quick mother-daughter chat."

His eyes widened. "You're her mother? Can't be."

Here we go. Mom had his attention now.

She pulled a little closer to him, never breaking contact with his arm. "Well, aren't you sweet?"

The light in his eyes showed he'd been dazzled. "Addison didn't share that she had such a young and vibrant mother."

We were deep in it now.

"She told me all about you and what a good boss you are, but she forgot to tell me what a sweetheart you could be. Handsome, too." Mom stepped back and looked him up and down. Launched into full flirting mode. "Very impressive."

He laughed. "You're something. Aren't you, Lizzy?"

I was always stunned that this scam worked. The false flattery seemed obvious. Mom had developed schmoozing skills that she could snap on and off at will. My boss was her latest and most disturbing conquest.

"Addison, why have you been hiding this lovely man from me?"

Because I'd learned early to hide all boys, male teens, and men from her. Fake fawning was Mom's go-to move. Didn't matter if the guy was the mailman, our neighbor, her coworker's husband, or my high school math teacher. She attracted members of the opposite sex and basked in the attention they heaped on her.

My boss waved a dismissive hand in the air. "There's no problem. Take a half hour break."

He got angry when I took more than twenty minutes for lunch, but this was fine. Typical.

Mom squeezed his arm one last time before breaking contact. "It was lovely to meet you. Daniel, is it?"

"Call me Dan. And stop by any time, Lizzy."

She threw him a wink as he walked out the office door.

I had to hand it to her. The way she weaponized that charm was a thing to behold. I'd had a front row seat to this type of performance my whole life. Repetition didn't make the act any less astonishing. "Flirting with that guy? Really?"

She snorted. "It worked, didn't it?"

"I need this job, Mom."

"You have a job. Richmond Dougherty. It's past time you made contact."

The same name I'd heard for years. Mom's greatest prey. The golden goose she expected me to pluck. I'd done my own research on him and no thank you.

"Why go after him now?" The real question was why, after all this time, couldn't she let this go?

"You know why."

To get her revenge on Richmond. I was the pawn in her vengeance game.

"I asked you to step up years ago and instead of talking to me and working on a plan, you ran off," she said.

As fast as I could but clearly not as far as I needed to go. "That was a hint."

"Don't get fresh with me." Her sweet smile disappeared along with the lightness of her tone. "Others might appreciate your sarcasm. I don't."

She made me this way, but fine. I tried logic. "Richmond is a big deal. He has powerful friends and gobs of money. Getting into his circle will be close to impossible. I'd have to do surveillance for months to find a way in."

"Which is why you should have started this before his reputation became so entrenched." She toyed with the nameplate on my desk then sighed. "There's nothing we can do about your choices now. The delay probably is better anyway because he won't see you coming."

She ignored the fact Richmond reached hero status long ago and held on to that crown with a clenching grasp. "He might be untouchable."

"I didn't gift you that face and that body for you to talk like that."

That was as close as she'd ever come to a compliment. Of course, it was more of a reflection of her than a statement about me.

"You're going to make me say it." She walked around to my side of the desk and leaned against it. Closed the space between us. "You owe me."

Her favorite phrase. The source of her conditional love. She didn't care what her martyrdom cost me. Her only goal was to get her way. "Mom, please don't do this."

"I sacrificed my body and my youth to bring you into this world. I had opportunities and a life, and I gave up both for you." She kept sighing and shaking her head. Put on her full I'm-so-disappointed routine. "And how did you pay me back?"

"I'm sorry I was born." That was the only thing I hadn't apologized for before now.

"I cleaned up your mess because I wanted to. It was my job. But the risk is still out there. Anyone could figure out what you did, and what I had to do to save you. Think about what your life would turn into then."

My mind flashed to the blood and the knife. "That wasn't my fault."

"You had a choice that day."

When I closed my eyes I could see his body on the kitchen floor. "I was ten and terrified."

"And I stood up for you. At great loss to me, I might add. We had to move. I had to find another apartment, another school for you, another job. All because you overreacted."

The words hovered between us like a snarling beast. But she

wasn't totally wrong. Seventeen years ago, for a very brief period, she stepped up. She forfeited the life she'd picked for herself. She literally covered up a murder for me.

I acted in self-defense but Mom never bought that reality. Her first husband hadn't wanted kids. He'd made that clear. He hinted that it would be fine if she sent me somewhere or if I disappeared forever. I knew he wasn't kidding.

In her mind, that one act of protecting me—staging the dead body in an alley and making it look like a robbery gone wrong—showed her love for me. Maybe it did. Maybe that was all the genuine feeling she could muster for me or the sum total of what I deserved. I didn't have the energy to examine the situation too closely.

"This request isn't only about me. Richmond needs to pay for what he did. He killed my dreams."

By "her dreams" she meant Zach Bryant. The boy caught in the crossfire at school that day twenty-seven years ago. The one Richmond didn't plan to kill. Mom's teen obsession.

The father I never knew.

She clasped her hands together in front of her. The fake diamond band she wore caught the light. "I told you the night I moved the body for you that one day I would need you to do a little thing for me in return."

Sacrifice my future and risk my life for her quest. "It's not little."

She shrugged. "Big or small, your time is up. You're safe now but the police won't overlook a murder, even an old one, if they know about it."

Blackmail.

She leaned forward and smoothed a hand over my cheek.

The gesture, so close to loving and affectionate, always made me yearn for more. Made me regret that I couldn't be who and what she wanted. Reminded me that giving birth to me meant her dropping out of school and surviving a brutal beating by her stepdad.

"Addison." Her voice turned sweet with all evidence of our verbal sparring gone. "My beautiful daughter. It's time for you to fulfill your destiny."

I tried not to lean into her touch. I'd read enough self-help books about *breaking the cycle* to know this toxic relationship sucked the life out of me. That my loyalty to her wasn't reciprocated. Still, I craved her acceptance. The idea of experiencing just one day where she appreciated me without expecting something in return . . . well, that wasn't going to happen.

She wasn't going to let this go either. She'd been pushing me to act since high school.

I stopped mentally running and accepted my sick fate. There was no other way to move forward. I had to go through this to be free of her. "How am I supposed to pay my rent while I'm hunting down this destiny?"

"Consider that an incentive. The sooner you get to Richmond Dougherty, the sooner paying your bills won't be an issue."

Chapter Thirty-Four

HER

Present Day

Mom and I survived the first night together in a house in more than a decade. I'd left home as soon as possible, right after high school, and had been on the run from her, more or less, since then. I'd leave. She'd find me. Then the cycle would start again.

A few hours together and we fell back into old habits, which centered on me trying to please her and failing miserably. Ever since the threat-scribbled-on-the-wall night, I'd slept in a guest room down the hall. Mom eyed the primary suite when she arrived. The message on the wall was no longer readable but I couldn't risk her somehow deciphering it, so I gave her Richmond's old suite instead. Seemed like cosmic justice to put her in his space.

While I hoped she'd scurry back out of town after a night or two it was more likely she'd move in and start raffling off the furniture. She was accustomed to apartments and just getting by. This house, the property, the bank accounts, offered her a life she'd been craving since before she got pregnant with me.

We sat across from each other at the kitchen table. I pretended to scroll on my phone. She sipped her latte and hummed, which meant she was thinking. That was never good.

I had to ask.

"Where's the new car?" The used one I bought her after much begging.

"What car?"

Not an unexpected answer but still. "I gave you money for . . . You know what? Never mind."

Mom took a long sip of coffee. "I had other expenses, but now that you mention it my current car isn't safe. I will need a new one soon. Not a used one. A brand-new one with all the shiny extras."

At this rate I'd run through Richmond's stockpiled money in record time. "The estate hasn't been resolved."

"Why?"

"Because people think I killed Richmond." That wasn't the only reason. Richmond hadn't been dead that long and Elias was still settling all of the outstanding financial issues. I was fine because I had access to my account and the funds in other accounts where I'd been listed as a joint owner, but Mom didn't need that rundown. "Hell, even you think I killed him."

"The man was garbage. He deserved an unglamorous end." She shrugged. "But we're talking about you and your responsibilities. You always need to cover your tracks. Have a contingency plan. Not leave any loopholes his greedy family and friends can drive through."

Ping.

She frowned. "What's that noise?"

My cell. I'd specifically given the security app a special

ringtone because I couldn't afford to ignore it. Not when it seemed to chime a warning every five seconds.

"You'll quickly figure out that this house has a constant stream of unwanted visitors." I was including her in that group.

"You should install a moat."

She was full of good ideas this morning. "Tempting."

"Who thinks it's acceptable to stop by without an invitation?" She grabbed the cell out of my hand. "Oh, interesting. It's that handsome lawyer friend of yours."

I grabbed the phone back. "No. He's off-limits."

We'd been down this road many times. I didn't care who she flirted with or how, or who she slept with or even married, but she had to pick from a pool of men I didn't know. Like it or not, I knew Elias.

She threw me her patented *what's wrong with you* look. "That's ridiculous."

"I need him to stay focused on keeping me out of prison."

"He's perfectly capable of defending you while spending money on me." She let out what had to be a fake gasp. "Unless you're thinking that the two of you might get together and—"

"He's old enough to be my dad." An image of Mom and Elias kissing popped into my head. I blinked it out. "Stay away from him. I mean it."

Elias walked in the back door and stepped into the kitchen. "Ladies."

A smile lit up Mom's face. "It's good to see you again, Elias."

Elias didn't appear to notice Mom's rabid attention or the mother-daughter quibbling. He sat down at the table and set his cell in front of him. "I wanted to check on you both."

I didn't buy it. Mom was pretty and tempting and eager. Elias was a man with a wallet. This could go sideways fast. "I thought you were done doing house calls."

"Give the man some air, Addison." Mom put a hand on Elias's arm. "Would you like her to make you a latte? They're really quite good."

Time to put the brakes on this mess. "What's with the visit?"

Mom glared over my indelicate delivery, but Elias took the tone in stride. "I intended to talk about cellphone tracking, but we have a more pressing issue."

Days without a new problem or the threat of arrest? Zero. "I hate to ask."

"Someone leaked the information about your trip to the police station." He hesitated. If he was going for maximum dramatic impact he achieved it. "A story, citing confidential sources, will link your questioning to the change in Richmond's manner of death. The official finding is a basilar skull fracture due to blunt force trauma."

"That's a lot." And none of it sounded good for me.

"In other words, homicide. Specifics about a bat being the murder weapon won't appear. The police will hold that back to disclose at some later date, likely after their investigation is completed."

Kathryn. The detective. Lurking, well-hidden journalists in the police parking lot. One of those or a combination of them tattled on me. I'd bet Richmond's trust fund on it. "I guess it's a good thing I never leave the house these days."

"Absolutely not." Mom's coffee mug clanked against the table as she set it down. "That's not acceptable. She has an alibi."

"We all know that, including Detective Sessions. But it's clear he believes Addison killed Richmond with someone else's help."

There was no need to sugarcoat it. "He means you, Mom."

"Ridiculous. Why would I kill the wealthy doctor my daughter married? Mothers dream of that sort of lucrative matchmaking."

Dissecting that comment would get messy, so I skipped ahead. "Okay, what does this press attention mean for me?"

"For now, nothing except that many people who knew and admired Richmond will view you as the enemy," he said.

So, status quo. "Wasn't that already the case?"

"Did the detective leak this lie to hurt Addison? If so, we should sue him." Mom shook her head. "He could cost his department money with this slander."

"He's within his purview to apply pressure." Elias didn't sound impressed with Mom or the detective's antics. "My guess is he's being pushed by . . . others."

This time I only needed one guess. "Kathryn."

Mom snorted. "She should find a hobby."

Yeah, about that . . . "Annoying me is her hobby."

"Kathryn is just the start. Richmond was connected. He had powerful friends, including a member of congress and the governor. So, no trips off the property. No talking to anyone about Richmond or anything else. Keep the alarm on, the security up, and the doors locked." Elias ticked off his list. "Be vigilant."

"We need to go out and enjoy life. Why don't you stop all of this Richmond nonsense?" Mom asked.

Only Lizzy Jenkins would view a man's murder as a nuisance to her.

"Let's just be careful." Elias switched from serious lawyer mode to smiling. "Will you be staying here for a short time?"

"Addison clearly needs my help and support. I plan to move in. Yes."

She meant forever or until the money ran out. I pivoted to a less volatile topic even though I knew a showdown over money or stuff, or money *and* stuff, loomed in my future. "What about the cellphones? You said that was the original purpose of your visit."

"Right." Elias's smile faded. "Nick's next move is tracking. I wanted to double-check with you, Lizzy, about the location of your cellphone the night Richmond died. You and your cellphone and any places you may have visited. If you moved without it and, if so, how and where."

She glanced at me. "What is he talking about?"

"He often uses too many words when he constructs a sentence. It's a lawyer thing. You'll get used to it."

Elias sighed. "The police are going to use phone tracking data to determine where you both were in the days leading up to the murder and at the time of the murder. Addison told me she had her cellphone with her at the diner. That alibi matches the diner's security footage. I'm hoping your cell's data will show you also were nowhere near this house the day of the murder."

Mom snorted. "As if I'd be stupid enough to kill Richmond and bring a trackable cellphone along with me when I did it. That would be an amateur move."

She was going to get me arrested. "That response isn't disturbing at all, Mom."

"I was being honest."

"Maybe a little less honesty if you're talking to anyone outside of this room," Elias said.

Mom rolled her eyes. "I only know the two of you in this town."

"What Mom meant to say was that of course she didn't kill Richmond." It was a guess and one I hoped was true.

Elias shrugged. "Then we have nothing to worry about."

Easy for him to say. His freedom wasn't dependent on the whims of a woman whose self-focused lens never shifted to another person. And the idea of Mom killing Richmond now that I had the wedding ring and the money? Not hard to imagine at all.

For the thousandth time, I regretted killing Mom's first husband. He was a twisted bastard who would have killed me if I hadn't acted first, so he deserved to die. I just wish I hadn't been the one to do it because I'd been paying for that choice for more than a decade.

Chapter Thirty-Five

HER

Present Day

Ever since I opened the mailbox to find the threatening note slipped in there I'd skipped collecting the mail. I planned to continue that practice . . . then Mom moved in. It had been two days of nonstop contact and I needed some air, even if that meant going on a fake errand to the end of the driveway.

Leaving her unattended in the house had its disadvantages but there were limits on how much she could steal and hide in her car during the ten minutes I was out. Frankly, she could have whatever she wanted. Stockpiling possessions was her thing, not mine.

Before I headed out, I looked out the front window and across the expansive lawn. Information about Richmond's murder and my being questioned by the police hit the news this morning. I expected the media to descend soon. Better to take the quick walk and get back inside now. Stay one step ahead of the gawkers and haters.

"I'm going to get the mail." I yelled the comment and slipped out the front door before Mom could question me.

I wasn't looking to invite more conversation. Mom had been quite vocal about her rampant disappointment with what she viewed as my *Richmond failures*. In her mind, I was to get close to him—she didn't care how—then drain all of his money and publicly destroy him in a rain of fake crying. Play the aggrieved and duped woman. Pound his reputation into dust. Destroy him from the inside out then make it look like he skipped town in a cloud of corruption while she took care of what was left of him.

My premature widowhood messed up her revenge. Him being dead made the *exposing him* part tricky. At least for now. I planned to circle back and spill the truth, but the timing had to be right. That's why finding out more about Richmond's surgery games and the identity of his actual killer mattered. Until then, pointing out that he was a lying sack of shit would shine the murderer spotlight right at my head. I'd be viewed as the spurned, disappointed, and angry wife. An obvious killer.

So, I waited. And now I waited with Mom attached to my side, which was the worst kind of waiting.

Once out front, I inhaled, drawing the cleansing cool air deep into my lungs. Fall, with the shedding of the old and the fiery death of all that lingered, always appealed to me. The idea of starting over, of renewal, sounded promising. My life had been prearranged so that concepts like free will rang like a hollow joke.

A few minutes later I arrived at the mailbox. A quick scan showed a strange lack of press and absence of nosy neighbors on the quiet street. But a storm of angry Richmond minions headed this way. I could feel it. That's why I turned away without touching the mailbox. I could stay blessedly out of the know for a few more days about whatever hideous new threat might be waiting in there.

I turned back to the house and stopped. Something pulled at

me. A sense of being . . . off. I returned to the gate and tugged on it. Still locked, which was a relief. I looked at the hedges just outside the six-foot wall that outlined the property before glancing up at the security camera. The one usually aimed at the mailbox and the space by the entry pad on the other side of the gate. Now, the camera faced the sky.

A branch from the towering tree about five feet away lay on the ground. It looked like it had broken off and knocked the camera out of alignment. With the nasty throngs I assumed would show up soon, I needed the camera pointing in the right direction.

"Fuck me." Nothing was ever easy.

I opened the pedestrian gate, a door for foot traffic to the side of the larger driveway gate. I could unlock it manually from the inside but anyone who wanted to access it from the outside needed the code.

After all that had happened, I knew better than to step outside of the safe area, but the idea of calling Elias whenever I needed help sort of pissed me off. Balancing safety and smarts with the need to maintain a sliver of independence took a lot of energy.

One look at the camera from this side of the fence was all it took. I needed a ladder. Did I even own a ladder? Before I could mentally figure that one out I smelled . . . what the hell was that scent? Spicy with a note of tobacco.

The hedge moved.

No time to think or regret the rookie mistake of walking outside without a weapon. The branch. I glanced down, thinking to duck and grab it, but it was gone.

A hand clamped down on my shoulder from behind and

slammed me into the tree trunk. A strangled gasp of air whooshed out of my lungs. I tried to scream. But my body bounced against the trunk a second time and my head smacked against the wood, blurring my vision.

"No." I thought I yelled but my voice barely rose above a whisper.

I grabbed for anything. Material, slick like a raincoat, slipped through my fingers. I kicked back and hit a leg. Heard the sharp intake of breath other than mine.

Again. Hit this asshole again.

I tried to focus. To aim. To spin around and face my attacker. A scream raced up my throat right before pain crashed through me from behind. My back. My ribs. I gasped and fell to my knees. The muddy lawn squished beneath me, soaking my pants. The tree and the gate started to spin and the thud of footsteps echoed in my brain.

I lifted my head to catch a glimpse of the attacker and everything tilted. My body collapsed and my shoulder thudded against the damp ground. Pain vibrated through me, but I forced my eyes to stay open and rolled onto my back. Pillowy clouds filled the blue sky and the scent of wet earth wound around me.

Then the world went black.

Chapter Thirty-Six

HER

Present Day

I woke up on a startled scream. The sound broke through my consciousness and cut off the low mumble of voices around me.

"She's coming round," Mom said.

That was me screaming?

"Wait . . ." That's all I could choke out as I looked up through a hazy blur to see Elias and Mom staring at me with matching concerned frowns.

"Addison?" Elias's grim tone mirrored his expression.

"Call 911 again. Or the police." Mom grabbed Elias's arm. "Do something."

Instead of racing around, following her commands, Elias sat down. The cushions next to me dipped. The couch. I was on the couch in the television room. The area probably had some fancy-house designer name. I thought of it as the sacred space where I watched rich housewives from cities I'd never visited bicker on a big screen attached to the wall.

"What happened?" I touched the side of my head and immediately regretted the choice. The area around my temple pounded. Squinting blocked out most of the offending light but not all.

"That's our question." Elias studied my face, looking less happy with every second. "Why were you outside the gate?"

I'd ignored his warnings and advice and regretted that choice, but I'd been lured there . . . sort of. "The camera."

Mom let out a strangled sound. "You were taking photographs?"

"No, I—" Got up too fast and swear my bones rattled before I settled back into the stack of pillows behind my head. "Damn."

"An ambulance is on the way." Elias glanced at his watch. "I called when we were bringing you inside."

"A flashy vehicle with sirens is not what we need." I had enough unwanted attention, thank you very much. "Cancel it."

"No."

A typical Elias response.

Mom shook her head. "Elias is right. If the Rothmans hadn't come by and—"

"Who?" The name wasn't a bit familiar.

"Glenn and Kitty Rothman. Your neighbors." Mom waved a dismissive hand in the air. "They live directly across the street."

Those were their names?

"For some reason Kitty was wearing a designer dress in the middle of the afternoon. Ice blue and very pretty, almost like a cocktail dress, and not at all an appropriate match to her husband's buffoonish plaid golf outfit."

What the hell was Mom babbling about? "You mean Mrs. Nosypants and her silent husband? The two who are never outside except when terrible things happen to me?"

Elias sighed, as always. "Since they found you passed out on the lawn and used the intercom to call your mom for help we like them today."

The events that landed me here rushed into my head on fast-forward. The camera. The footsteps. The odd smell. Being thrown into a fucking tree—twice. "Did they see who hit me?"

Elias blinked a few times. "You were attacked?"

"Do you think I spontaneously fell down?" Now it seemed obvious. I probably was supposed to notice the tilted camera and go out there to investigate. I messed up the sequence, but the end was the same. Someone caught me off guard and got the upper hand. That was the last time I'd ignore or downplay a warning. "Apparently the notes weren't just for show."

"Notes?" Elias asked. "What are you talking about?"

He had one hand resting on the pillow near my head and one on the back of the couch cushion. The concerned fatherly act trapped me. Kept me from sitting up. That meant there was no way to call the words back now. Both Mom and Elias kept staring, making it very clear no one was going anywhere until I fessed up.

Fine. There was no reason to keep the mess a secret now. "There was a threat written on the wall of the primary suite in top-secret paint, though it's now more of a smear. Then I got a note in the mailbox. Those predated being slammed into a tree."

Mom held up three fingers. "How many do you see?"

"I'm not loopy." Well, I was but still.

"I knew I should have checked out that bedroom since you were so secretive about it. I'm going to look at this painting." Mom reached for her cell. "I'll take a photo, if that's possible, and be right back."

Elias waited until Mom left the room. "Why didn't you mention these threats before now?"

He seemed to know I wasn't making this up or embellishing, even though I excelled at doing the latter. This *you will pay* bullshit was all too real. No matter how I tried to laugh it off, ignore it, and work around it, the threat had grown until it sucked out the tiny bits of lightness in my day.

"I didn't think anyone would believe me." I also thought I could handle the pressure. Like so much of my life, the plan was to get through the worst with as little damage as possible. I hadn't counted on anyone moving security cameras and throwing me around like a rag doll.

Elias's shoulders stiffened as the dark tension swirling around him ratcheted up again. "Who would do this?"

Blame the dizziness or the unexpected wave of vulnerability, but I answered honestly. "As far as I know, only one person in this world wanted me dead. He told me every day of our marriage . . . except on the day someone shoved him down the stairs."

Richmond Fucking Dougherty.

Elias frowned. He'd been doing that nonstop for the last five minutes but this time showed more curiosity than concern. "Does not saying the words that day mean something?"

"I left the house and went to the diner because he was working, and I needed some air." But that wasn't all. There was the part I always left out of the story because I had to . . . until now. "And because his mood had changed. Overnight he switched from shitty to conciliatory. He made me coffee when I got up, which I didn't drink because I'm not a dumbass. Even talked about us going for a 'nice' drive and enjoying dinner out at a restaurant near the water."

"So?"

The potential for poisoning or drowning struck me as obvious, but the unexpected niceness was the true tip-off. All of a sudden the blackmail I had on him didn't seem to matter. He had no way to win the battle. Despite that, until the very end, the sick little narcissist looked for a way to work around the evidence I hid. He never believed he'd fail. He didn't think losing was a possible outcome for him. Ever.

On that last day something clicked in his warped brain. Between the rumors he'd planted and those "accidents" of his, he must have believed he'd flipped the advantage in his favor. He was wrong.

"Because I knew from the way he was acting that he planned to kill me and the countdown had started."

Chapter Thirty-Seven

HIM

Five Months Earlier

For an uneducated sewer rat, Addison could weave through the truth and issue warnings like a pro. She'd honed and targeted her skills, developing into a conniving monster in a very sexy wrapper. Long legs. Banging body. Knockout face that likely led more than one poor sap to his financial doom. Yeah, someone had trained her well.

Addison sat across from me in a dive bar in New Haven, Connecticut, about an hour outside Rye. The dark interior and scent of cheap beer fit her. Refusing to meet me alone, in private, showed her vulnerability. Behind all that tough talk lurked a woman—maybe five-six and sturdy—who jumped back and forth over a line she shouldn't cross.

She slid her finger over the rim of her glass. Water. Smart move. Keeping control of her mind and the drink at all times—even smarter.

"This is not a negotiation, Richmond. I don't care if you don't like my marriage terms." Her voice stayed steady. Clear. Forceful and commanding without yelling. "You only succeeded in selling your convoluted hero tale for this long because no one was alive to stop you."

So confident but her sarcastic bullshit would stop when I choked the life out of her. Watching the light leave her eyes would be the best day I'd had in a long time. But it was imperative I find her supposed trove of evidence first. Neutralize her, then make her disappear. That meant outsmarting her, which would happen. I just needed to find the right pressure point to squeeze.

She brought this on herself. She was to blame.

I tried one last time to give her an ending that left her alive and mostly breathing. "Be reasonable. No one is going to believe you."

"You do."

That damn map. Seeing it clouded everything. I'd watched Cooper burn it decades ago on the night before the world went wild. Unless he didn't really get rid of it because he wanted leverage. Not trusting me would have been out of character for Cooper. Wise, but not who he was, especially at the end when I had him turning in circles under a flurry of punishing verbal blows about Dad's unreasonable demands and Mom's refusal to forgive any slight.

I reached for the tone Kathryn once claimed to love because she said she'd found it reassuring. That was before she went to all those charity meetings and discovered the concept of gaslighting, a word she threw at me so often she acted like she'd invented it.

But the woman in front of me wasn't easy-to-satisfy Kathryn. Addison was a completely different type of beast. Still a woman and easy to train, so I steered her where I needed her to go. "There's a simple way out here, Addison. Let me help you find it."

She snorted. "Does that condescending crap work on other women?"

The fact she'd followed me for months, studied me, sent a

fresh bolt of rage burning through me. "Women like money. You like money. It's what motivates you."

"Money is your thing. That's what caused all of this. Your obsession with hoarding things and cash." Addison sighed. One of those long, exaggerated sighs aimed at causing maximum annoyance. "Your mommy and daddy were loaded but they didn't believe in handouts."

I would not do this. "Don't talk about my parents."

But she pushed on in that singsong voice. "They weren't impressed with your entitled behavior, so they cut you off. The plan was to teach you a lesson by making you get a job to cover your upcoming college expenses, even if that meant switching to what you considered to be a lesser school or attending part-time. Potentially, a huge embarrassment for you."

"You don't know what you're talking about."

"They wanted you to be something. Not just take."

"I am something." Better than her. Superior in every way.

"How long did you work on Cooper to get him to do your bidding?"

My whole life. I hadn't known what I was preparing for, but I was ready when the time came. "Do you like hearing yourself talk?"

"Everyone agreed your brother was the weaker of you two. Younger by one year and not as athletically or academically gifted. Following you around, trying to earn your approval."

"He took a lot of shit at school. I protected him." All true. Cooper was my job. Our parents coddled him, loosened the rules until they ceased to exist. I made Cooper a man.

She smiled. "You were the one with potential. You had lots of friends."

"Are those bad things?"

"No, but killing your parents for their money is."

The words sliced through years of carefully constructed ambivalence. After the shooting, I cried on cue for the cameras just like I'd practiced. I'd pulled off the unthinkable and was the only one left standing. I walked away with everything, putting the echoes of Dad's snide lectures and Mom's constant squealing about being a better person behind me. Cooper had been a loss but unavoidable collateral.

Faint regrets about being the sole survivor would well up now and then, mostly at the holidays, but even those moments proved fleeting. Being a national hero guaranteed an avalanche of invites over the years. Sporting events. Sitting with the First Lady at the State of the Union. So many admirers. With each new blessing and statement of gratitude for my quick thinking that day, the certainty that I'd forged the right path by becoming the only living Dougherty swelled.

Addison was the wild card now. Having her around as a daily reminder of all I tried to slough off could not happen. She was a threat to the future I'd picked, polished, and refined. If her scheming bought me a one-way ticket out of the marriage to Kathryn, then that might be worth the temporary hit to my reputation, but Addison's use ended there.

I glanced around our dark corner of the room. No one watched or leaned in. The bar manager pretended we didn't exist because I paid him not to notice us.

"One question," she said.

She would never limit herself to one. She didn't know when to stop.

"How hard was it to get Cooper to shoot your parents while they ate breakfast?"

Chapter Thirty-Eight

HIM

Five Months Earlier

Addison talked too much. I didn't discuss my parents. Couldn't think about them or family vacations or dinner conversations. I used my trauma cover story to shut down any questions and block out every memory from holiday celebrations to mundane afternoons.

Most people saw my practiced stark expression and their words sputtered out. They nodded or touched my shoulder in sympathy or used empty phrases to convey a sorrow they could not possibly fathom. A sorrow I'd stomped out of me.

In the beginning, I'd forced myself to replay every minute of that day, every gunshot, that kid who turned the corner at the wrong time and took a bullet, every echoing scream, all to mute the memories. Eventually, the visions clicked by like a series of events that happened to someone else. Detached and unreal, almost like an overwrought plot of a bad movie. I watched until the edges dulled and frayed. Until I forgot about that dead kid. Until I mentally walled off Cooper and my parents. Until I saw them as puppets dancing to my commands.

Addison cradled her glass between her hands. "Which one of

you shot poor in-the-wrong-place-at-the-wrong-time Zach Bryant?"

Right. That was the dead kid's name. A classmate of Cooper's and not on my radar.

"Did Cooper do all the shooting?" she asked.

Two guns. Two sons. A rain of bullets. Simple. Neat.

But I stuck to the story I'd created. "I was at school when Cooper shot Mom and Dad in our house. I went in early that day."

She nodded. "Over an hour early that morning. Then you made sure you were seen by your soccer coach and two other witnesses before slipping out of the building again. All before classes started."

"None of this is true." But it was and that pissed me off.

"You left the car your parents no longer believed you'd earned in the school parking lot to shore up your alibi, dodged security cameras, and ran home." She smiled. "I bet you had to practice that a few times to get the timing right."

Seven months. I repeated the steps in my mind, worked through every piece of my grand design and tinkered when the mental walk-through failed. The plan demanded a very public ending. If the police came to our house and found my parents' bodies I could have been implicated, and there was a strong possibility Cooper would have folded under pressure and confessed.

No, the police had to find Cooper away from home and see him as being on the run and panicking. He had to die. That meant tricking him and putting him in front of witnesses with the murder weapons in his hands while I rushed to dispose of my bloody clothes . . . but not his. I left his back on the floor near my mother's bloody head as further evidence of his culpability. In the post-killing frenzy Cooper didn't notice. He trusted me. Just as I suspected he would.

The timing had been perfect. Adding the school as the final location was the masterstroke. That Zach kid's death was unfortunate, sure, but the move put a target on Cooper as the aggressor and sole shooter and made me an avenging angel. I rushed in just in time. I begged Cooper to stop while everyone watched in horror. I killed him because I had no other choice. Thanks to my selflessness, I became a national hero, deserving a lifetime of admiration.

"The thing I regret not seeing sooner was how hopeless Cooper felt. He and Dad were fighting. Cooper snapped and shot . . . both of them . . . my parents . . ." The practiced sucking in of air at just the right time in the made-up retelling. The perfect crack of my voice. I'd mastered it all. "Then Cooper headed to the school, probably to kill more innocent people. We'll never know."

"You've told that story so many times I wonder if you believe it."

Her amused tone sealed her fate. "You think I want to relive that day?"

"Why not? The scheme is your greatest achievement." She kept her voice at an almost soundless whisper. "You and your brother killed your parents but you were in the clear. All the evidence implicated Cooper."

Cooper thought we were going to school to establish an alibi. That we'd be away from the house and seen by witnesses in the hallways and on security video before and after the killings. The school wouldn't be a crime scene. Once I had him wound up and ready to act, convincing him of the brilliance of my plan wasn't difficult. He believed I was protecting both of us, but I wasn't.

I'd read about a criminal case where the husband played with the house's thermostat to throw off the estimated time of death. An artificially hot environment could change a corpse's core temperature and skew calculations. I needed that buffer in case the police figured out I had time to return home, kill my parents, and get back to school.

So, I had Cooper change the thermostat. His fingerprints on it, not mine. His attempt to mess with the temperature, not mine. Either way I had cover, and his actions were in the spotlight.

But how the hell did she know any of the particulars? There was no way she spun a tale around that damn map that shouldn't exist and got this close to the truth.

"I have to hand it to you because this is where your devious nature really paid off. Pulling the fire alarm while your brother was on his way to dump the weapons left him alone and in full view as students and teachers ran out of their classrooms. Tackling him, making a huge scene where you begged him to stop and turn himself in, created an audience." She seemed to relish regurgitating the timeline. "But you didn't count on Zach being there."

I didn't. He walked in on the scene. Not my fault.

"Everyone watched, thinking you'd saved the school when what you were doing was eliminating a witness and the need to share your parents' money. You also got close enough to Cooper that no one would ever question the blood or gunpowder on you from your parents' murders."

Guesses. Had to be . . . but no one else had guessed. Who the fuck was she? "Why do you care about this? Take the cash I offered and go."

"A hundred grand is tempting but too easy for you." Her soul-crushing smile returned. "You need to feel a fraction of the suffocating terror your family felt as you picked them off one by one, you sick bastard."

I grabbed her wrist and dragged it onto my lap. Let her feel my strength as I clamped down on the fragile bones of her wrist. Medical school taught me how to heal, which inadvertently also taught me how to break. "If I'm a cold-blooded killer, why risk pissing me off?"

She didn't even wince as I tightened my hold. "Are you still trying to prove you're innocent?"

I matched her nerve with a load of my own. "I don't lose, Addison."

"You're going to lose everything you care about, leaving you a cracked and empty shell without a family or the pathetic string of mistresses you can no longer afford. Just another sad wannabe guy who led with his dick, cheated on his wife, and was forced to move into a small apartment to financially recover. Because you will be paying Kathryn and the kids. I'll leave you with enough money for that and only that."

"You think I'll let you take this life away from me?" She might know some things about me, but she underestimated my will. "I'll put you in the ground first."

"Do it and everything I have goes public, including . . . have I mentioned this? The tape."

The constant string of noise playing in my head cut off. "There's no tape."

"The one Cooper made of a conversation with you where you talk about disposing of the weapons. Touch me and everyone hears it."

"That tape doesn't exist." It couldn't. Not possible.

"It's almost as if your brother knew you were going to screw him and made a contingency plan. Guess he was smarter than you thought."

I dropped her hand. "You're a gold-digging whore."

"Every time you piss me off I add another zero to the amount you're going to lose." She flexed her wrist. The only sign the grab hurt her.

She should get used to my anger. "You can only push a man so far before he shoves back. Enjoy your win. It's temporary."

"But ruining you will be forever."

"Be careful what you wish for, Addison." If the fake marriage suited me, I'd let it happen. If I needed it to get closer to her to steal this alleged tape, I would do it because the move came with the side benefit of finally cleaving Kathryn from my side.

No one blamed men for dumping their older-model wives and trading up. The mistress soaked up most of the hate, which worked well here. That would take care of Kathryn.

Addison deserved a harsher ending.

One day very soon she would fall to her knees and beg for my mercy. Those would be the last words she ever said.

Chapter Thirty-Nine

HER

Present Day

Detective Sessions arrived a few minutes after the ambulance crew. Instead of surrendering to the sweet bliss of sleep and forgetting this day, which was my original plan, I fought through a barrage of annoying questions designed to determine the extent of my injuries.

Do you have a headache? What day is today? What's your address? What really happened out there? That last one came from the detective, complete with his usual scowling lack of charm.

After a half hour the ambulance crew left with my thanks and my adamant refusal to go to the hospital. I didn't trust the detective. He'd run tests or collect DNA, which would be a problem. I already had to hope my bat cleaning and general household subterfuge stopped that line of attack. I didn't want to make anything easier on him . . . or for him to find out my secrets.

With the medical personnel gone, that left Detective Sessions, me, Mom, and Elias. We squared off across from each other at the kitchen table.

Mom glared at the detective. "You owe my daughter an apology."

I could get to like this new, throw-up-the-barricades Mom.

This was all for show, of course. Part of her *I'm just here to help* scam but having her rush to my defense for a change ticked off an unexpected warmth inside me. This must be what kids who were loved and wanted by their parents felt like all the time.

The detective did not look impressed. "The same daughter who has a bedroom with a dent in the wall, a mess of strange paint on another wall, a hidden murder weapon in her greenhouse, and a motive to want her husband dead? That daughter?"

It did sound pretty grim when he lined the pieces up like that.

"You've falsely accused her of killing her dear husband. You leaked suggestive information about her. You've surrendered to Kathryn and her vindictiveness." Mom ticked off her own list while showing off pretty pink nails and a new manicure. "You've put a target on Addison's back and I want to know what you plan to do about that."

Detective Sessions sighed. "Your daughter didn't tell me about the threats."

Always my fault. This guy never wavered in placing the blame on me. "I wonder why."

Elias set down his coffee mug with a thud, grabbing the spotlight from the rest of the table. "Okay, let's keep this civil."

The detective kept staring at me. "Should you be in the hospital?"

Not happening. "I'm not leaving this house ever again."

"That would be smart," Elias said. "She has a sore back. She doesn't have any signs of a concussion, but we'll watch her for nausea, confusion, and the like."

Wait, was he moving in, too?

Elias kept going. "We're going to have a talk about hiring security."

"Yes." Mom nodded. "An excellent idea."

"I'm not inviting even *more* people into this house." If I felt better that might have sounded less targeted at Mom, but so what. My constant, futile search for peace kept getting derailed and everyone sitting at the table played a role in that.

"We have one letter and covert photos, which I will take back for testing. I doubt we'll find anything because I doubt any evidence has been preserved. And I can't tell what's under that slap of paint on the wall in the bedroom. I'm guessing heavy duty cleaning supplies took care of that." The detective hesitated for a few seconds. "Some people might think these alleged threats are a convenient way to throw the scent off you, Mrs. Dougherty."

This guy. "Do these people also think I threw myself into a tree?"

The attack did have a novice hint to it. If I had gotten to that tree limb first. If a car had come down the street. If I'd looked up a second earlier and could identify who hit me. There were so many ways the camera ruse could have gone wrong. I'd been unlucky but someone had gotten very lucky . . . so far.

"We're collecting security video from neighbors and checking Mrs. Dougherty's feed. If someone stepped onto the property or played with the cameras, we should see them."

The detective was tiresome and, frankly, a bit obvious. He'd pinned his hopes on me being the killer and drove to that conclusion no matter what the evidence said.

Mom's chair squeaked across the floor as she stood up. "I'm getting Addison something to drink."

"I've seen the news and heard the rumors, Nick. I know the pressure is building. You've got the governor's office all over you. You're dealing with a dead hero. People want answers now. There's talk about bringing in the BCI."

That was news to me. "'BCI' sounds official."

"The Bureau of Criminal Investigation. A division of the New York State Police. Think of them as state-level FBI." Elias kept his focus on the detective. "You need to rework your strategy here."

The detective's flat expression suggested he didn't care for that. "Don't tell me how to do my job."

"You have a widow who's been threatened and attacked." Elias pointed toward the window over the sink. "Now the press is outside her house."

"That's a good thing. That kind of presence should keep anyone else from sneaking up on her." Without taking a breath the detective shifted course. "Did you want Richmond dead?"

Yes. No question I did. The more I learned about him, the more dead I thought he should be.

Originally the plan was for me to ruin him and for Mom to swoop in and decide if he'd suffered enough. That was her thing. Then I lived with Richmond and his threats, saw what an evil jackass he was, and stopped wavering on the revenge part. Dead and ruined. Some people deserved both. Richmond certainly did.

I went with a shorter, more snide answer instead. "That's your question after finding out someone attacked me—"

Elias tried to talk over me. "Of course she didn't want him dead."

The defense didn't go far enough, so I outlined some truths the detective either didn't know or intentionally ignored. "Richmond has an angry ex-wife. He's upset some patients and there are questions about at least one of his surgeries. The father of one dead child is looking for answers, which has Richmond's former business partners panicked and potentially in trouble. Yet, your focus is only on me."

"You suddenly have a lot of theories about who killed your husband."

Not suddenly but the man didn't listen to reason. "And you only have one."

Elias cleared his throat. One of his big stop-talking cues. "That's enough."

The legal strategy here made no sense. This wasn't the time to scold me. I'd thrown out hints and Super Detective didn't even ask a follow-up question about Richmond's office mess. The detective might know about the Cullen family and the potential lawsuit, but the lack of mentions in the press suggested not. Detective Sessions had tunnel vision, which meant I was on my own.

"If someone kills me, will that convince you I'm not the villain in this?" I asked because I really wondered.

The detective's blank expression didn't change. "I think you're safe."

"And I think you're incompetent."

"Okay." Elias stood up. "Addison needs to rest."

The detective slowly rose to his feet and joined Elias. "I have more questions for your client to answer. I'll ask them when the rest of the forensics come back."

Whatever. "Find out who attacked me. That's who you need to question."

"We do seem to have a rash of violent people swinging bats

and tree branches in town. Never had those crimes until . . . when did you get here?" The detective shrugged. "Don't leave the area."

"I'm sure one of your covert sources would fill you in if I tried."

"That's right. Someone is always watching, Mrs. Dougherty. You'd be wise to remember that."

For once I hoped he was right because then there would be a witness to whatever happened next. I needed one of those because I didn't see any sign that the person who wanted me on edge and injured, maybe dead, planned to stop.

Chapter Forty

HER

Present Day

"I was serious. We need to talk about hiring a bodyguard for you."

The detective left and Mom ventured upstairs to look at the bedroom wall again. I expected Elias to launch into a "be more careful around Detective Sessions" lecture. Not this.

"Are you worried if something happens to me your bill won't get paid? Because you're the estate guy. I bet you can pay yourself."

Elias tensed. "I don't want you to get hurt and it's starting to feel like a distinct possibility."

Unexpected. Interesting. Genuine care for my well-being. Almost dad-like. Not the kind of thing I was used to at all. "You believe me about the camera and the tree?"

"Of course."

Not *of course*. I expected doubt. Pushback. Support scared the hell out of me because what did it mean? What would he demand in return?

Sarcasm stood as my usual go-to move in situations like this. Hide behind a thick wall of pretend indifference and barbed responses. I'd been taught not to show panic and punished for the one time I gave in to fear. That didn't leave a lot of healthy responses to counter danger.

But a curated response failed me. "I think the attacker was a man."

Not sure why I said it, but it was true. The detective barely asked. It might not be a bad idea for someone to know in case this nightmare scenario kept happening.

"Wyatt?"

"The body size was wrong." I understood Elias's question but couldn't see that answer. Wyatt personified *outraged young man* syndrome every time he stopped by the house, but he seemed equal parts confused and pissed. Still spouting the rah-rah party line about his dad and painting me as the homewrecker, which to Wyatt I was, but also struggling to make what he was told about me line up with what he saw.

I didn't know the kid and he might have learned diversion and lying tactics at his father's knee. He might be a rabid misogynist and all-around jackass. All possible. But under all the bluster Wyatt could just be a kid who'd been lied to and bullied in his own house and never taught any skills to deal with real world issues.

Another Dougherty family victim.

"That brings me back to the bodyguard idea," Elias said.

As usual, there was something Elias wasn't saying as he said something. I could hear the blank spaces. "Why?"

He studied me for a few seconds before speaking. "My investigator located August Christopher, the doctor implicated in Ben Cullen's surgery death."

The idea of Elias having an investigator on speed dial started my nerves spinning. "And?"

"August didn't leave the area. He doesn't have another job. It looks like he's been staying on property owned by his great-aunt in Fishkill, about an hour away."

So many questions. "Looks like?"

"My investigator hasn't seen him, but his backpack was there. His car is hidden under a tarp in an outbuilding."

I shifted in my seat, trying to find a more comfortable position in case bad news came next. "I feel like we're playing a strange game where I have to guess context and facts from your clues."

"The investigator is still working. There are some limits on what he can do, but he was able to track a vehicle that was parked on the Fishkill property earlier. Not August's car but another one registered to the great-aunt. That car has been in Rye. In your neighborhood."

"Your guy followed August?" And August was stalking me? That didn't make any sense. "How does August even know to come after me?"

"We'll ask him when we grab him, but now you know why I want someone with you at all times."

A mix of stray and fragmented memories bombarded my brain. I mentally searched for what this August guy looked like then gave up. Wading through every thought and every fear, I landed on an unrelated question. That seemed safer. "Did you have this investigator look into my past? I assume Richmond ordered that."

Elias just sat there.

So, yes. Not a surprise. I suspected it. I'd lived my entire life creating as little footprint as possible, which I hoped made things harder. Until recently, I didn't have a bank account. I paid for things in cash and didn't own anything. I lived my life at a sprint to make it harder for Mom to corner me. Those skills happened to hide the pieces of my life Richmond likely hoped to latch on to before we got married.

"Much to Richmond's annoyance, the investigator had some difficulty finding out the particulars about your past." Elias reached for his coffee mug then abandoned the move, letting his hand drop on the table. "He couldn't find a birth certificate to match Lance, the last name you used before Dougherty, but I stopped the work when Richmond died."

"Wouldn't it have been smarter to ramp up the surveillance, or whatever you were doing, in case I was a killer?"

"Richmond wanted to know who you were and why you were targeting him. Once I took over your representation I figured it was better that I not know." Elias smiled for the first time since I woke up after the attack. "Clients don't appreciate my looking into their backgrounds."

"Funny how that works." There wasn't anything amusing about any of this, but I was trying to hold it together.

Elias ran right over that. "Now that you know August is in the area be extra vigilant."

"No more jaunts to the mailbox. Got it."

Elias glanced into the hall. "Your mother. What do I need to know?"

I appreciated the expert lawyering that went into that innocuous question. I wasn't in the mood to watch my words, so I didn't try. The only concession I made to her being in the house was to lower my voice to a soft whisper. "Don't let the pretty face fool you."

"I can tell she's difficult."

"Toxic." And she was fine with turning me into roadkill.

He made a noise that sounded like humming. "Do you trust her? Will she protect you if this all goes to hell?"

He didn't write me off as dramatic. Another new sensation. "No."

"Any chance she attacked you at the mailbox? She was in this house."

"No." But the question had moved in and out of my head over the last hour. I wanted to believe no. The direction of the attack was wrong. She weighed less than I did. Unless she'd attended expert-level self-defense training she wouldn't have been able to keep me from seeing her face. But I wouldn't be surprised if she used my money to hire someone to keep me in line.

Elias sat back in his chair. "Seems like a lot of people want to hurt you."

"Weird, right? I'm lovely."

He picked up his mug again. "You're a survivor."

For days, sometimes weeks, I pretended to be. "I'm an escapee."

The mug stopped halfway to his mouth. "Is there a difference?"

A huge and, for me, insurmountable one. "I didn't survive. I ran. The problem with running is it's not permanent. Dodging and hiding become your whole existence because the escape is never final. The pain finds you and dumps you back in that dark place until you build enough resilience to run again."

Elias looked worried now. "That's how you view your life? Yourself?"

"That's who and what I am." I didn't see that changing.

Chapter Forty-One

HER

Present Day

Sitting at the kitchen island the next morning with a bag of frozen peas clasped to my sore ribs made me hate every television commercial filled with smiling families and steaming coffee. Fake PR bullshit. The over-the-counter medicine didn't do much for the pain or my mood. Watching Mom flit from the refrigerator to the stove as if she lived here didn't help either.

Neither did the text I received a few minutes ago. It came from Portia, which raised all sorts of questions about how she got the number and why anyone thought giving it to her was a good idea. She asked about my injury and said she was nearby and would like to stop in.

Kathryn's stink was all over this.

Knowing that a setup loomed, I should have said no. A thousand excuses to push Portia off popped into my head. I ignored all of them. No idea why except that Portia's obvious discomfort around her mom—in part because of the inevitable mother-daughter clash that came at her age and partly due to her grief over her dad—pricked at the *been there* memories I tried to suppress.

Fighting off empathy qualified as my superpower. I'd nurtured the skill for years. I could wrestle any form of caring into submission. *Thanks, Mom.* But spending so much time with her recently and reliving the memories of some of her greatest hits kicked my denial's ass.

Portia deserved better. She didn't know that or know me but maybe that bit of distance made it easier for her to try to connect. Or she was just like her parents and had me fooled. Not sure yet.

I texted back to alert her to the invading press and to let me know when she pulled up so I could let her in without waiting. Now the moment had arrived, and I had to tell Mom. The doorbell bonged before I could issue the warning.

Mom stopped in the middle of making a grilled cheese sandwich. "Why do people keep coming to this house?"

"I ask myself that question all the time. It's not as if I'm a good hostess." I'd had more visitors since Richmond died than I had my entire life before then. "This time it's Portia."

"Richmond's kid? Tell her to run back home to her bitchy mommy."

There was that lack of compassion I knew all too well. It kicked to the surface with ease. Back in school I had to attend these programs where the police would talk about safety and tell us to search for a law enforcement person if we needed help. If we didn't see one then reach out to a nearby woman. Knowing what my mom was like I always laughed at that suggestion.

I glanced at the security app video and saw Portia, head down, shifting her weight from foot to foot, with Kathryn hovering behind her. Just as expected.

Mom grabbed the phone out of my hand. "Is that—"

"The *bitchy mommy*. Kathryn." I threw the bag of peas on the counter.

"Do not let her in this house." Mom issued the command while waving a spatula around.

"Kathryn is not great with being told no."

"You have all the power here, Addison."

"Tell her." I could smell burning cheese. "You should flip that."

Mom made the same annoying *tsk-tsk* sound that played as the soundtrack to every memory I had from growing up. "This is disappointing."

"At least I'm consistent." But burning food and scolding would have to wait. I blocked both like I had to block so much relating to Mom. "You should go upstairs."

Mom's expression could only be described as chilling. "I am not hiding."

Yeah, great plan. "Kathryn shouldn't see you, or can she?"

There was so much I didn't know. Mom fed me information in pieces, not caring if any of those missing pieces destroyed me.

"She's lucky you're such a softie because I would leave her outside in the dirt." Mom waved the spatula at me a second time. "Let the dragon lady in."

"This should be fun."

I barely got the door open when Kathryn burst inside and headed for the kitchen. She got as far as the doorway, saw Mom, and slid to a stop.

Time for introductions. "Kathryn and Portia, this is my mother, Lizzy."

Kathryn's gaze roamed over Mom without any hint of recognition. Mom had dressed up to make her late breakfast, or early lunch, or whatever meal this was. The blue shirtdress and matching sandals didn't look as comfortable as my lounge pants and bunny slippers but were very pretty.

Had she put on makeup? Now I worried she'd asked Elias to stop by. The poor bastard.

"Your mother." Kathryn loaded a lot of disapproval into those two words.

I didn't have the mental strength for this today. "I assume you knew I had one."

"Richmond never mentioned relatives."

Mom finally lowered the spatula. "I doubt your ex discussed private family matters with you. He wanted you out of his life. That's why you were the ex."

Kathryn's mouth dropped open. "Excuse me?"

Oh, boy.

Portia moved beside me, dragging my attention away from the brewing brawl. "Are you okay? We heard you were attacked."

"Oh, please." Kathryn scoffed. "Is that rumor even true?"

I decided to answer Portia because her question sounded genuine. "I was in the wrong place at the wrong time, but I'm fine."

Portia glanced at the bottle of pain relievers. "Should you be in the hospital or—"

"No." For some reason I felt the need to console Portia. She had enough to worry about and work through without adding me to the list. "I really am okay. The ambulance people declared me well."

"Do you think the person who hit you was the same person who killed Dad?"

"Portia, stop." Kathryn's firm voice echoed through the kitchen.

"I don't know but I have security and my mom is visiting." I tried to lighten my voice and really sell that last part as a good thing, but Portia's frown told me she somehow understood.

"Is that why you're here? To check on Addison?" Mom asked Kathryn.

"Portia insisted and I wasn't about to let her come here alone." Kathryn shook her head. "The press is out there . . . now they've seen us. This is a disaster."

Portia sighed and rolled her eyes at the same time. "Mom. You promised."

The whole scene sucked. Sucked for Portia. For me. For all the daughters of messy mothers in the room. "I appreciate you came by to check. Thank you."

"What's the plan here, Addison? Are you looking for sympathy? Hoping to win people over? Because it's not going to happen. We all know exactly what you are," Kathryn said.

Mom abandoned her sandwich and braced her hands on the kitchen island. "You should shut your mouth."

Kathryn didn't look impressed. "Who do you think you're talking to?"

"Someone who wasn't invited but barged in anyway, using her daughter as bait."

Kathryn made a strangled sound that telegraphed how little she thought of Mom and her comments. "I see where your daughter learned her manners."

That was a mistake. Kathryn expected Mom to concede. Mom would burn the house down with all of us in it first.

"You want to fight me, Kathryn? I'm ready." Mom glanced at Kathryn's hair. Then to her perfectly pressed pantsuit that likely cost more than Mom's entire wardrobe. "I would enjoy messing you up a bit."

All because of Richmond. He wasn't worth the energy women expended when dealing with his memory.

I sighed to let everyone know I was done. "That's probably enough."

"Mom, we should go." Portia had shifted until she stood between Kathryn and the kitchen island, like a mom buffer. Her grip on the countertop turned her knuckles white.

"I see your daughter got all the common sense in the family," Mom said.

Kathryn pulled Portia against her side. "Don't talk about her."

Another eye roll. Portia had that move down. "Mom."

Kathryn grabbed her bag and wrapped an arm around Portia before glaring at me. "You and I aren't done."

She kept saying things like that. The Dougherty family really needed to tone down the theatrics. "It feels like we are."

Mom pointed toward the hallway. "The door is over there. Use it and don't come back."

"Not you, Portia." I had no idea why I put that out there, but the words kept coming. "You're welcome here any time."

Kathryn walked around the island, hugging her purse. I was so busy watching her I almost missed Portia pulling away from the island with a small black rectangle that looked like a USB drive in her hand. She practically threw it at me, pointed at her mom's back, then put a finger to her lips.

Kathryn spun around. "Let's go, Portia. Do not ask to return."

"Coming." Portia shot me a half smile then increased her pace to catch up with her mom.

I waited until the front door closed to open my hand.

Mom picked the item up and studied it. "Interesting. It's a listening device."

I wasn't an expert but it didn't look like one. "How do you know?"

"I've been married four times."

"And?"

"Men stray. You pick up some tricks to watch them."

I had no idea what to say to that. I was too stuck on the idea that Kathryn planted the thing. That explained her obsession with visiting. But when did she do it? Why? And why did Portia mess with her mom's plans? A few seconds later I got a text from Portia.

she put it there last time she thinks youre planning something

Thoughts jumbled in my head. I'd lost the ability to tell when I was being played and when someone was trying to save me, since the latter never happened.

I clenched the device in my hand then wrapped a kitchen towel around it because I had no idea how the thing worked or what the range was. "Portia came over to warn me."

"Maybe someone in that family is worth two cents after all."

I tightened my hold on the unexpected offering. "Despite your warning, Kathryn will be back when she realizes her device isn't working."

Mom smiled. "I hope so."

"Do not enjoy this."

Mom kept smiling. "All I'm saying is it's a good thing I brought a gun with me. Maybe I'll get to use it."

Chapter Forty-Two

HIM

Married, Day One

Elias had one job. His people needed to find specific information on Addison that would defang her blackmail attempts and send her running back to the streets. Languishing in a perpetual state of *who is she* was the one thing I could no longer tolerate, as I made clear in my instructions to Elias.

You need to dig up her past. Every trailer park. Every bar. Every strip joint. The men she's fucked. The ones she's blown. Hell, the women she hooked up with. Every piece of her life, including where she's ever lived, where she banks, anywhere she might store something she doesn't want anyone to find, and every person she trusts. Rip her life apart.

Acting unconcerned was not an option with that map and the tape I still doubted existed potentially floating around out there. Without any significant movement in unmasking Addison, the walls closed in. I'd spent two decades building an uncrackable puzzle box of stories. Wasted fake tears on unsavable sick children because the audience I played to demanded performative pain. Comforted weeping parents. Pretended to care while hitting and exceeding every career milestone.

All of it intensified my apathy. Conquering came too easy. The insatiable drive for *more,* as unidentifiable as that end goal was, was what pushed me forward. Get away with it once and you could do it again. That insight should have resulted in a sense of freedom, but it was confining. It set a bar I obsessed about jumping over.

Then Addison stormed into my life and destroyed the monotony. She had a goal and determination. I had a new target . . . one that remained a mystery.

Getting the marriage license had served both to stall and as subterfuge for gathering more intel. I'd hoped she'd produce a birth certificate as a means of identification but of course not. Just that damn Ohio driver's license, which I'd already photographed and given to Elias. The court clerk who gave us the marriage license asked for Addison's social security number. She provided one that I learned a few days ago wasn't hers.

The woman lied about everything, but her time was almost up.

Whatever this confidential, *you can trust him* detective Elias had on retainer intended to do, he better do it fast because today was my wedding day. Not a real one like my first wedding. There would never be a real one with Addison.

Today was the day I was going to teach Addison a harsh but necessary lesson. She liked to play games. This one was called *hire a fake officiant and make her think she'd won.* I needed her comfortable. Off-balance. Basking in the bright light of her impending failure and unable to see the trap waiting in front of her.

Elias and I stood in the family room of a guy who was supposed to be a minister. He worked at the church next door and agreed, for three hundred dollars, to play the role of minister and "borrow" the minister's house while he was away at a retreat. The guy clearly welcomed the extra cash. It was a small price to pay to maintain my freedom, and all it took was some *this little bitch is trying to trap me* bonding to win the man over. Problem solved. For now.

I wore a suit but only because I came straight from an office meeting. This mockery didn't deserve formal wear or a day off. It barely warranted an acknowledgment. But New York law required a witness and since Addison might have enough brains to check the rules, I dragged Elias along. He didn't know this setup was fake. He came to make sure the prenup got signed.

We did that song and dance earlier. Addison refused my version of the prenup, as expected. I signed her version because it didn't matter. Before I signed I wrote that we had to be married today for the document to apply. She agreed to the change.

But where was she? She'd been in the bathroom for ten minutes and, real or not, I wanted this nonsense completed and behind us. "I'll go check on her."

One knock and I opened the door. Addison sat on the bathroom counter in a straight black sheath that landed just above her knees. The cheap material matched the gaudy gold-plated watch she wore. The whole outfit summed up her bargain-store existence.

Well, she'd remember where she came from when I dumped her back there. That would teach her to take the money and run next time. A hundred thousand dollars would have changed her sad little life.

"What's the delay?" There wasn't a reason to sound anything other than frustrated because we both knew what a travesty this was.

She crossed her legs, showing no signs of standing up. "We need to wait."

"For what?" If she'd invited the kids to this abomination . . .

"The minister."

"Problem solved. He's in the other room." I gestured for her to move. "Let's go. You and that black dress. The dour color is a little much, don't you think?"

"I mean the real minister." She jumped down and stood in front of me, as if taunting me to take a swing at her.

Her grin set off a boiling rage inside me. A scalding heat that burned and destroyed all it touched.

"You didn't really think I'd let you pick the person who married us, did you? You're a known liar. Other people might not get that you can't be trusted, but I do."

I didn't say anything. Couldn't. The urge to strike her overwhelmed every other thought. The vision in my head of her bloody and gasping on the floor excited me more than anything had in a long time.

She brushed her hand over my jacket lapel, like she might with a real fiancé. "I checked out the so-called minister you picked. It took two calls to find out he was going away this week." She nodded in the direction of the closed door to the rest of the house. "I checked earlier and saw the guy sweating all over the couch out there. Not sure who he is but I hope you paid him well for his time."

"We came out today for you to make some ridiculous point? I'm a busy man, Addison."

"We're getting married today as planned." She had the audacity to smile at me. "I had to rip up your prenup and make you sign mine before the ceremony could start."

I saw the papers on the edge of the bathroom counter. That line about the marriage date had boomeranged on me. If we got married my only out would be her death. Now I had another reason to end her.

"Elias watched you sign." She sighed. "Calling the whole thing off now, without a good reason, would not work out for you. Face it. Your strategy backfired."

The cheap bitch winked. It took all of my control not to lunge.

She wouldn't shut up. "Before you try to grab the document and rip it up then rant about how Elias works for you, ask yourself if he'd risk lying in court for you. And, of course, I already took a photo of your signature and sent it to a trusted source."

Anger swept through me again, invading every cell, shifting and shaking through the foundations I'd built and shored up for decades. The praise, the devotion, every minute of standing in the spotlight and repeating my heartbreaking life story, crashed in on me.

"I'm going to kill you." It was a fucking promise.

"Yeah, that must be a hard habit for you to break. You disagree with someone then murder them." She shrugged. "There are other ways to handle conflict, you know."

I came within an inch of throwing her on the ground. The possible explanations ran through my head. She fell. She tripped. I could sell any of them to the men in the other room.

She didn't seem to realize she'd waded into peril because she wouldn't stop gloating. "You won't kill me because then everyone will know you also killed *them*. Zach. Your beloved family. The people who cared about you and never saw it coming."

"I'll come up with a way to get out of this." I always did. Nothing could touch me.

"You won't because you can't handle having the fucked-up layers of your life peeled back and your rotten core exposed." The doorbell rang but she ignored it and stayed in the bathroom. "All you have to do to make me happy is lose everything. Your family. Your reputation. Most of your money. Your freedom. The good news is we're almost there."

The rumble of conversation in the family room reached the bathroom. Someone entered the house. Someone who might actually bind me to this bitch.

"You're going to mess up one day soon."

She shook her head. "I'm actually not."

Her self-confidence pissed me off as much as the grating sound of her voice. Killing her would be a relief. Just like Dad. She acted like him. Two people who had a sarcastic comeback ready to fire at all times.

"The lie about being a hero is all you are, Richmond. Without it, you're a sad loser. Pathetic. Someone who should be locked up and forgotten. Thrown away like garbage." She patted my shoulder. "But enough foreplay. It's time to get married."

The way her tone changed with that last part. Amused, almost chirpy.

Strangling her. That was the answer.

A satisfying buzz came with imagining the moment she realized her pleading blew apart my decades-old *never again* vow. Circumstances had changed. Not my fault. She did this. She pushed and nagged. She wouldn't let go. She brought this on herself.

She straightened my tie. "Come on, darling. Time to get hitched and start that prenup rolling."

One more time. I'd have to kill one more time.

Chapter Forty-Three

HER

Present Day

Elias arrived at the house the next morning with two to-go coffee cups and chocolate croissants. If he was trying to win me over, he'd found the right combination. I didn't even care if he added the total café charge to my next legal bill.

"Why didn't your mom want anything?" Elias asked as he sat across from me at the kitchen table.

"She's getting her own coffee because, and I quote, *I can't stay locked up in this shithole forever.*" The first words she said before storming out today. The house had been blissfully quiet since. "Lizzy does not impress easily."

"She's been here for four days."

Was it only four? "An eternity."

"Are you okay?" He shook his head. "You really should have gone to the hospital."

"Sore and grumpy. Penned in and frustrated." I took a sip of coffee. "So, the usual."

"Well, I have good news for you."

"That would be a nice change."

"The DNA on the bat was compromised, and I think we know why. So does Nick." Elias shrugged out of his suit jacket and took a full minute hanging it on the back of the chair next to him before finishing his thought. "There's no proof you did anything, though it's clear you found a bat and cleaned it. Without getting fingerprints on it, which is interesting. Not a great look but not a theory they can make into a criminal charge without more." He slowed down to take a sip of coffee. "For the record, if you had left the bat as it was the police might have been able to find DNA from the actual killer."

"You think the person who used my bat to kill Richmond and planted it on my property for the sole purpose of framing me left their DNA?"

"Good point."

I had one every now and then.

"Between the lack of forensics, the house security camera footage from the day Richmond died, including you racing around calling the ambulance when you found him, and the information from the diner, Nick knows unless he can find an accomplice, he doesn't have a case against you."

That was a load of good news but nothing had been solved. I didn't feel an ounce of relief. Not after the last few days. "Does he have a case against anyone?"

"Not that I can tell."

Talk about perfect timing. I dropped the baggie with the listening device, or what Mom insisted was a listening device, on the table in front of Elias. "Maybe he should look harder at Kathryn."

He frowned but didn't touch it. "Where did this come from?"

"Apparently Kathryn planted the device in this very room on a previous visit. I'm assuming during her drop-in after the police searched the house."

"You're sure it was her? Why would she do that?"

Excellent question. "Ask her. She's your friend."

"She actually isn't." He studied the bag. "I'll turn this over to the investigator and see what he can figure out."

That felt anticlimactic. "I'm stuck in my house with my mother. It feels like we're not getting anywhere. For the record, I'm not enjoying these early newlywed-widow days."

"This might help. My investigator found our missing doctor, August Christopher."

That time a gentle wave of relief rolled over me. Not huge and not all-encompassing. More of a trickle. "You love to hold back information then drop it for dramatic effect."

Elias smiled but otherwise ignored the shot. "The man is in town. I spent an hour with him last night. He didn't say much except that he ran because he was afraid of Richmond. With Richmond dead, now he's afraid he'll be accused of murder. But he wants to talk with you. He's willing to answer questions about Ben Cullen's surgery but only to you."

Just like that the bit of relief I'd enjoyed vanished. If I trusted Detective Sessions I would have suggested August go to him, but that wasn't an option unless I wanted the doctor to run scared again. "When?"

"Now. He's at the gate behind the greenhouse."

"Remember what I said about you and drama? You thrive on it. Is that a lawyer thing?"

"I was giving him time to walk around to the gate. He's waiting with my investigator." Elias shrugged. "I worried August would get nervous and run, so I dragged him here and brought armed reinforcements."

The idea of meeting this guy and potentially hearing about a new, horrid thing Richmond had done should have had me jogging to meet him. Instead, excuses and reasons to stall jammed up in my head. "That entrance doesn't open."

"No, but there's a window in the door that we can unlatch from this side and talk through it. The barricade of sorts is safer for you anyway." Without warning, Elias stood up. "Ready?"

Abrupt. Serious. Quick. A restless agitation moved through me. Finding August had happened both too fast and too slow, but the reality of seeing him face-to-face hit me in a way that started alarm bells ringing in my head. I'd lived long enough and close enough to the edge—spent too many years ducking and hiding from Mom—not to listen to that incessant chiming.

Elias took off, and I was tired of waiting around for news, so fine. After a change from bunny slippers to sneakers, I followed Elias out the back door. We walked across the lawn in silence. There were a thousand questions I should have asked about this runaway-doctor guy and the investigator, about whatever topics Elias and August had discussed and why, but I couldn't call up the right words to spit out any of them.

After last night's brisk rain, the recently seeded grass sunk beneath my shoes. A slight wind blew across the yard, snapping off those last tenacious leaves and sending them dancing to the ground. We got within a few feet of the gate before I heard the low rumble of voices. Two men talking. Neither sounded familiar.

I inhaled, steeling my nerves for incoming news while Elias reached for the small window and cracked it open.

No! I put my hand over his and slammed the opening shut again. I backed away as the scent of tobacco hit me. Another sharp note seeped into my consciousness. One I couldn't identify but remembered.

Elias rushed to my side, keeping his voice to a low whisper. "What's wrong?"

"That smell." The memory of it haunted me.

"What are you talking about?" Elias glanced around. "The cologne? I think its's from—"

"August Christopher." That scent. The attack. "I smelled it right before I got thrown into the tree."

Chapter Forty-Four

HER

Present Day

Detective Sessions showed up when Elias called to report August and have him hauled away. The doctor yelled and flailed and insisted he'd been set up. None of it stopped the detective from loading him into a police car.

Now, six hours later, the detective had returned. I sat in my library, watching him pace back and forth in front of the big fireplace. Elias stood next to the couch and Mom claimed to be making dinner in the kitchen, but the woman hadn't cooked dinner . . . ever? More likely, she was hanging outside the room, trying to listen in while she pretended to let me handle this.

The detective started talking without any warning or preamble. "August Christopher insists he's never been near you before today and definitely never touched you. He admits he's driven by the house, as the GPS shows, but says he never left his car. Claims he was curious about you, which is not a convincing reason. At the least, it's clear he's been in the area and was parked nearby around the time of the attack out front. That gives us a place to start."

I liked a nice wrapped-up story as much as the next gal but

this one had *too easy* written all over it. “Why me? I don’t know the guy.”

“There’s no question he and Richmond had serious issues.” The detective hesitated. “It sounds as if your husband was playing a dangerous game.”

Not the usual mix of accusations and snide remarks that made everything my fault. It wasn’t clear what that meant. “What exactly did August tell you?”

“I know about Ben Cullen, if that’s what you mean. About his father’s accusations.”

I crossed my legs then uncrossed them. Getting comfortable proved impossible. “You’ve kept that little nugget of information well hidden.”

“Peter Cullen’s first stop after his son’s funeral was my office.” The detective shrugged. “I’ve been dealing with the man for months.”

The dismissive tone pissed me off. Peter Cullen, the grieving father. A man who deserved better. “You mean you’ve been ignoring any negative information about Richmond and focusing on me instead.”

Elias took a seat on the couch. “Let’s listen—”

The detective talked over Elias. “Mrs. Dougherty, I have two children. I can assure you I didn’t ignore Mr. Cullen’s pain.”

I barely thought of the detective as a functioning human let alone a dad. I’d worked the gossip angles, blending in while in town and listening, looking like a tourist and not attracting attention, in those days before I approached Richmond for the first time. My focus had stayed on my target, but an overview of the town’s inner workings might have been helpful before setting off on this wild misadventure.

Engaged and ready for whatever accusation the detective lobbed in my direction, I sat forward on the edge of the couch cushion. "Then you know Peter thinks Richmond didn't perform Ben's surgery."

"Yes."

Huh. This might be some new ploy to get me to talk. "And that August or Richmond's negligence, or some combination, killed Peter's son."

Elias frowned. "Hold on. That hasn't been established."

"Yes," the detective said at the same time.

I wrapped my fingers around the edge of the couch cushion and squeezed. "Then why have you been all over me?"

"Because if I learned that my supposedly perfect new husband—the one I clearly married for his prestige and bank account—was a fake, didn't have nearly the surgical skills he claimed and everyone in his practice pretended he had, and that his actions likely led to the death of a child, I'd be pissed. I might just kill that new husband for ruining everything."

The constant thrum of questions and rethinking stopped running through my head.

Elias whistled. "That's quite a hypothetical, Nick."

"You're agreeing that Richmond's reputation was based on a lie?" It was but I needed the detective to *say* it. I needed everyone to know it, and this was the way to begin that process.

"Overblown, according to August. Richmond's name brought a lot of attention to the medical practice and the hospital. There's a suggestion that being in the spotlight interested Richmond more than keeping his skills sharp, so the practice used him for PR."

"In other words, Richmond got lazy, to the extent he was even such a big expert to begin with, which I now question." Lazy. Negligent. Narcissistic. Dangerous. A jackass, in general, and a killer without doubt. Richmond wore a cloak of charisma he could throw off or cling to, depending on what he needed to be in the moment. His objective good looks covered the rest of the rot and decay underneath . . . until you got to know him.

Richmond both lived too long and died too soon. He deserved to wallow in the defeat of his crashing downfall. He also deserved to be dead, so in a way, things worked out fine.

"August says the rest of the team covered for Richmond to keep the accolades coming and the money rolling in," the detective said.

"Which means the good Dr. Thomas Linfield, head of that practice, knew the truth and is covering it up." I glanced at Elias. "A lot of your friends suck."

"He's not a friend or a client."

The detective nodded. "Good to know since he's the next person I'll be talking to."

"Peter didn't kill Richmond." I needed to say that. State the line as a fact and be clear. The man had been through enough. "There's no reason for Richmond to let him in this house. That leads to a new problem. Why would August want Richmond dead? To clear his own name, August needed Richmond alive."

"Careful, you might just discount all of the potential suspects except for you." The detective moved on, clearly not wanting a response to that comment. "You're sure about the scent during the attack?"

Elias winced. "It's distinctive."

"It was the amount. At the time of the attack, August had it slathered on like a high school senior looking to get laid at prom rather than a professional man who wanted to smell nice. This time was much more subtle, but it lingered."

The detective nodded, taking it all in. "Things are about to blow up and go public. Seems to me if you have anything to add about who Richmond really was, now's the time to do it."

"No. I'm good." Nice try but we weren't friends. The detective wasn't on my side. He needed Richmond's murder solved and it sounded like he had scattered theories about what might have happened and nothing to support any of it. No way was I getting sucked into that.

Detective Sessions didn't say anything else. He nodded to Elias and walked out, leaving my head spinning and the stack of possible murder suspects more jumbled than ever. A woman could get whiplash.

But there was one thing . . . "So now he believes I *didn't* kill Richmond?"

"Maybe we should give the detective a bit more credit for knowing how to do his job?" When I didn't respond, Elias sighed and switched topics. "The important thing is you're safe."

Am I? I thought about Mom in the kitchen. The Dougherty kids. Whatever Kathryn might cook up next . . . and whatever she'd planned to do with that listening device.

Elias was a smart guy, but he was wrong about this. I'd never been free, and nothing had changed about that. My usual inclination was to run. This time I was staying until I knew the ending.

Chapter Forty-Five

HER

Present Day

The news about Ben Cullen took two more days to break in public then it was everywhere. Photos of his face. Interviews with Peter. Sympathy and sorrow for him and for his wife, who hadn't left her bed since losing her son.

The stunned surprise that a national hero might turn out to be a doctor dud filled every comment section. The public had a habit of becoming hostile to people who accomplished too much, as if to say no one deserve unfettered acceptance. There was also a tendency to hate-jump—pile on and mix facts with fiction—when someone people believed in violated their trust. Either way, Richmond deserved the venomous shredding hopefully headed his way.

From what I could tell, Ben's death had been all over the news back when it happened. He grew up in nearby Scarsdale, so the devastating story had a *hometown boy* angle. The focus quickly had shifted to become the nonstop Richmond Show because he could not resist being a self-centered piece of shit.

I sat at the kitchen counter switching between news stories that suggested Richmond may have caved to pressure and overstated his credentials. That was the term one article used. *Over-*

stated his credentials. Even while being unmasked as a liar the guy got the benefit of a soft headline.

Mom stared out the window. "There are a few news trucks still out there but most left."

"I'd say life soon can get back to normal, but I have no idea what that means anymore."

Mom turned to me. "It's not normal because your work isn't done yet."

Here. We. Go.

The scent of *what have you done for me lately* filled the air as I readied for another round of mother-daughter battle. A lecture about all she'd sacrificed for me lingered on the horizon, waiting to launch.

"This whole exercise was about exposing Richmond and ruining his reputation. Telling everyone what he did back then. Avenging the dead. Revealing that Richmond killed Zach. Then killed Cooper and their parents in cold blood." Mom waved her hand in the air in dramatic fashion as she walked through her grievance. "I don't care about the surgery stuff. It's nice to see Richmond's professional life implode, of course, but that could cause additional problems. People could come after his money."

Money. Always money. "At least one child died thanks to Richmond's antics."

"That doesn't change the fact you're only halfway done with your job."

It should. Any number of factors should have stopped Mom's slow march vendetta. Forget about any pretense of her love for me because that was a huge question mark. Common sense and decency never penetrated her hard outer shell. She was guilty of omissions and outright lies. Her story shifted when she needed the facts to fit her narrative. She dragged me into this mess, used me as bait, and expected me to go along without question or complaint.

"Richmond's life is being dissected and analyzed. Soon that will include everything that happened on the day of the high school shooting. Once a liar, always a liar, and all that. People will question everything about him now." At least I hoped that was true.

"Question?" She sounded appalled. "That's not good enough. We need to strike while trust in him is at an all-time low."

I wrapped my fingers around my coffee mug and squeezed. "Richmond has kids."

"I don't care about them."

Not exactly a news flash. "Clearly."

"Distraught wife searches house and finds evidence of lying husband's murderous past." Her face lit up and excitement thrummed off her as she reeled off the fictional headline. "This August person and the dead kid set you up perfectly to show Richmond as a killer. Now you need to finish it off."

Nothing had changed with her. "Dead kid?"

Mom came over and sat on the kitchen stool next to mine. "We boxed Richmond in to minimize his ability to lie or, worse, to hire people to shut you up. The setup—that marriage—provided the means to work behind the scenes. He thought he could outsmart you with that fake wedding stunt but only ended up signing an agreement he never intended to sign. You didn't let him win, my smart girl."

Ah, yes. We'd entered the false flattery portion of this tired game. "He's actually dead, Mom. I think we took everything."

"I get that you couldn't rush in and spill his sick secrets right after he died because of the potential for blowback. And it looks like you didn't actually kill him, so being blamed would have been unfortunate."

Every response in my head ended with throwing her out of the house, so I just sat there.

She reached over and took my hand. "Now you need to deliver the deathblow. The kid's death gives you cover. Any wife would lose it and tear up the house after figuring out that every line of her husband's résumé was phony and every claim of him being a hero was a blatant lie."

She should at least act like she understood a kid died. "The deceased child's name is Ben."

"I don't care." She let go of my hand and slipped hers into her skirt pocket. She took out a thumb drive.

I didn't have to ask. The proof. The undercover recording of Richmond and Cooper talking about how to get rid of the weapons after killing their parents. Mom refused to tell me how she got the evidence, saying it was safer for me not to know. Whatever that meant. But I'd listened to it. It was real and explosive and had wrecked my life for decades.

Mom slid the drive over to me.

I didn't touch it.

"Finish this, Addison. Finish ruining Richmond Dougherty's reputation once and for all."

Chapter Forty-Six

HER

Married, Day Seventy-One

I picked up the espresso container right as the back door banged open. Everything happened at once—my yelp, the jump, the grounds spilling over my hand onto the kitchen counter then the floor.

"What the hell, Richmond?"

He stormed inside, his eyes wild and clothing torn. Blood trickled down his cheek and the smell of burning rubber followed him through the door.

"You fucking bitch."

"What is wrong with you?" He left to have lunch with Wyatt. I only knew that because I overheard Richmond's side of the phone call a half hour ago. And now this.

"I'm going to kill you." His voice shook with rage.

I ducked, but not in time. His hand wrapped around my throat. My back slammed against the edge of the sink as he loomed over me, using his height advantage to push his palm tight against my windpipe. Pain shot through me from behind and from the weight of him leaning on me. My gasp turned to a wheeze as he grinded and choked.

He shook me. "Did you think I'd let you go after me twice?"

I batted at his hand and fought and wiggled against his deadly hold. His fingers squeezed, cutting off my breath. A gagging sensation gave way to heaving as my lungs fought for air. In a frenetic race not to be too late, I reached out and slapped against the countertop. A pan crashed to the floor. A glass shattered. Shards crunched under my sneakers.

This fucker will not kill me.

Arms flailing and fists pounding, desperate to anchor my body and keep upright, I punched. Pulled back without aiming and let go. I hit skin on the first strike.

The fierce grip vanished in an instant, taking my balance with it. I clutched the counter to steady myself. Knowing I needed to run, I tried to concentrate and remember how close I was to the door. Blurry vision and muffled hearing had me stumbling. When I took a step, my body bent forward, and I sucked in air. The sound repeated like a death rattle through the kitchen.

I couldn't relax. Richmond was right there. Out of control. Homicidal.

Move! The order rang in my brain.

Harsh breaths and unsteady footsteps filled the kitchen. I shot straight up again and dodged to the left, hoping to land out of hitting range. My hand smacked against the coffeemaker and my hip jammed into an open drawer. Energy pinged and ricocheted around me. Equilibrium abandoned me while the kitchen whirled.

Backed up against the pantry door, my eyes finally focused again. Richmond stood a few feet away with a face alive with fury. He pressed his hand against his throat as he visibly swallowed. He looked wide-eyed and feral but frozen in place.

Punch landed. I hope it hurt like hell.

"You tried to kill me." His voice sounded scratchy and strained.

The alarm. I could set it off and the police would come. "What are you talking about? You stalked in here like a wild animal."

His hand dropped from his neck and his expression changed. Determined and unblinking. "Because you tampered with my car."

"That's ridiculous." The adrenaline continued its Olympic race through my body. "I've been right here."

He took a step toward me.

"Not this time." With no other choice, I grabbed a knife. Heard it slide out of the butcher's block. The overhead light bounced off the blade with a flash.

The handle fit in my palm. The sensation dumped me into an emotional hurricane. Confusion. Terror. Tightness stretched across my shoulders.

"Give me that." Richmond reached out.

The tip of the knife skimmed his forearm. He jumped back as a tiny thread of blood seeped out. Not a big slice but still shocking. For both of us.

"You cut me." His voice took on an otherworldly quality as he picked up a towel and held it to the minor wound.

"You were choking me. Then you threatened me." When he glanced at the knife, I tucked it in closer to my body. If he tried to tackle me, the blade would rip through flesh and plunge inside him. I would not hesitate. I'd fight through my revulsion to knives and kill him. "I will not hesitate to use this, so do not move."

"You're acting like the victim." He scoffed. "You poisoned me. You messed with my car."

"I'm not responsible for either of those events."

His heavy breathing calmed as he stared at me. "I don't believe you."

"I don't care." *Don't relax.* That refrain spun around in my head, forcing me to tighten my grip on the knife. "And next time I'll really stab you, so back up."

"Dad?"

The unexpected voice had me shifting as a new shot of panic wiped out the hold on my control. My nerves jumped and snapped as my gaze shifted from father to son.

"You never showed up . . ." Wyatt's voice trailed off as he looked at his dad and the bloody towel in his hands. "What happened?"

My focus stayed on Richmond. *Say it. Tell him your theory and I will spill everything I know about your twisted past.* I ached to issue the threat out loud.

"An accident." Richmond's mood shifted in a snap. His voice returned to normal, as if nothing had happened.

Fucking psychopath.

Wyatt didn't look convinced by his father's words. He hadn't stepped fully into the kitchen. He hovered in the doorway. "How?"

Richmond looked at me.

Do it yourself, asshole. No way was I fixing this.

"I came up behind Addison while she was cleaning and I scared her." He took a slow step toward me and slipped the knife out of my hand. He placed it on the counter. "Right?"

He sounded calm and logical. His tone had a *no big deal* edge to it as if he weren't lying his butt off.

I couldn't answer. I didn't trust my voice. Didn't want to do anything but yell and kick.

"Is everyone okay?" Wyatt finally walked into the room. "There's blood and—"

"It's a nick." Richmond threw the towel in the sink. "The bigger problem is my car. The brakes went out."

"What?" Wyatt's already anxious voice rose. "When?"

Richmond stared at me but answered Wyatt. "I went around the sharp corner over by the park and couldn't stop. I hit a tree but luckily I wasn't going very fast and didn't get hurt, so I walked back here to call the police."

This time I didn't stay quiet. "You didn't have your cell?"

"I forgot to charge it."

So fast. Richmond could lie on cue. He was a doctor. Not the type of man to get stuck somewhere without a phone, which meant this, whatever this was, was intentional.

The smell of coffee battled with the smell of what I now guessed to be burning tires. The tainted food. This new accident that he walked away from, looking like he rolled around on the ground for a few minutes. Wyatt right there, ready to act as a witness.

This was a setup. All of it. Richmond couldn't kill me outright, but he could suggest I was unhinged and after him. Make me the liar and claim self-defense. His plan unrolled in front of me. So clear and so obvious.

"Wyatt, I need you to drive me back to the scene." Richmond nodded toward the back door. "Go start your car."

Wyatt frowned. "Are you sure—"

"I'll be out in a second." Richmond didn't give his son a choice and waited until he left to continue. "This battle is not going to end the way you think it is, Addison."

Fake it. My insides trembled and my bones disintegrated to mush. He would never know what standing there cost me. "If you touch me or even look at me again, everything I have on you, about you, becomes public. I'm done playing with you, Richmond. Any more games and you won't be able to hold on to the scraps I'd planned to leave you."

"Empty threats."

"Then try this one. I could carve you into pieces then sit down in a puddle of your blood and eat a sandwich. That's how little you mean to me." I stepped away from the safety of the pantry door. "Consider that your last warning."

Chapter Forty-Seven

HER

Present Day

Wyatt asked to come over. He used the excuse of wanting to pick up more of his father's personal belongings. My mother said "absolutely not" so, of course, my *you can't tell me what to do* attitude kicked in and I said yes. But "him" turned out to be Wyatt and his mom, which was no surprise but still annoying.

I set the box Wyatt left last time and another filled with unwanted Richmond garbage in the entry hall for an easy in and out. The *you're not welcome here* hint didn't seem to bother Wyatt. He opened the box on top and looked at the contents before shutting it again.

Kathryn paced around, clearly wanting access to other parts of the house and huffing in frustration when my mom blocked the way to the kitchen. Kathryn finally stopped shifting and grunting and stood in the middle of the entry. Right under the crystal chandelier.

It was wrong to hope for a sudden earthquake, but I did anyway.

"We need to present a unified front," Kathryn said.

The woman's inability to read a room was astounding. "I don't know what you're talking about, but the answer is no."

I did know, of course. The Ben Cullen story had morphed from local to regional, and now had hit the national news. Richmond craved attention his entire life and he sure was getting it now. Rumors flew around town. Whispers turned into *he was always at the club and never at work* rumblings. His band of mistresses hadn't stepped forward yet, but that had to be coming. They had stories to tell and deserved to sell them and collect money for their trouble.

The hard-core pro-Richmond camp—the delusional majority—wrote the bad press off as jealous people wanting to cash in now that Richmond wasn't around to defend himself. The anti-Richmond group questioned every surgery and every death and asked what corners had been cut in deference to Richmond's past.

No one had taken a harder look at his hero origin story . . . yet.

"This assault on Richmond and his reputation is despicable." Kathryn was in full outrage mode with pent-up energy overflowing and hands flipping around in the air.

I could see Mom gearing up to start a scene, so I jumped in. "He deserves the scrutiny."

"How can you say that? He was a genius. He saved so many—"

My mom rolled her eyes. "Kathryn, stop."

I rushed in a second time because Mom could go anywhere after that. "If Richmond's surgical skills were bogus, and it looks like they were in part, that should be news because his medical practice has a lot to answer for."

Kathryn's lips flatlined and her voice rose in indignation.

"You were his wife. Do you understand what could happen? You could lose everything."

This sounded like projection mixed with some wishful thinking. "I'll be fine."

"Mom, we should go."

Poor Wyatt, always stuck in the middle of his parents' tirades. They seemed to drag the kid out whenever they needed cover, reinforcements, or a witness. He served as both security guard and accomplice. I was ready for him to go back to school. When was that happening?

Mom asked a question before I could ask mine. "Why did you bring your mother with you today? You have to know it's uncomfortable for Addison to have her here."

Wyatt shrugged. "She asked."

Mother loyalty. Kathryn insisted and Wyatt put aside his discomfort out of a warped sense of *I owe you*. He grew up in a household where parenthood was an unspoken tit-for-tat battle. I got it because I'd lived it, too.

Time for them to leave. "Doesn't matter. You can take these boxes, Wyatt."

Mom eyed up Kathryn. "We can send over whatever else you need. There's no reason for continued family visits."

Mom really was a ray of sunshine. She also wasn't wrong . . . about this. "For the record, Kathryn, I will not be putting out a statement of support for Richmond or saying anything to help his reputation. The public bashing appears to be deserved."

Kathryn gasped on cue. "You are the worst decision Richmond ever made."

"No. My daughter wasn't Richmond's biggest mistake." Mom

smiled in a way that gave off horror movie vibes. "I think we both know what that was."

The mood of minimal tolerance shattered. Every word ratcheted up the stark energy in the room. A seething anger, targeted, the kind that comes from a trail of broken promises and personal disappointments, choked the entryway. The conversation had shifted from an annoying game of one-upmanship to an epic standoff between two women with what sounded like a secret shared past and palpable anger that had festered for decades.

Tension clawed at the back of my throat as I attempted to swallow and breathe without gasping. My mother had little more than a passing acquaintance with the truth. I'd had that epiphany a long time ago as I watched her live her life and plan out mine. This was a whole other level of *what the fuck*.

Kathryn returned Mom's stare. "Lizzy. That's short for Elizabeth, right? Interesting because I once knew an Elizabeth. Horrid creature."

"Aren't you the charming socialite?"

"In my defense, some people come into your life who aren't worth remembering. Then they pop up again and the bad memories come flooding back. You have no choice but to deal with them."

The voice in my head that said *stop this* got outvoted by my curiosity. Neither of these women were built to back down, which meant this could end up in a verbal massacre.

"I'm trying to imagine you as a young girl, Lizzy." Kathryn's smile promised trouble. "Pathetic and craving attention. Flirting, hanging around where you weren't wanted. Generally being a nuisance as you begged for attention. Any kind of attention."

Mom shrugged. "It's better than being a spoiled little bitch with no personality or dreams. You know, the kind that might become a washed-up trophy wife who can't hold her man."

Oh, shit.

"What's happening?" Wyatt asked.

You don't want to know, kid.

"Your mother is talking, Wyatt. Let her speak." Mom's voice shifted to taunting. "Do you have something to ask me, Kathryn?"

If she didn't, I did. But Kathryn didn't say a word.

"I didn't think so." Mom shifted her gaze to Wyatt. She looked from him to the boxes stacked in front of him. "Lift with your knees."

Mom delivered her line as if she'd been practicing the dismissal for years. She headed for the stairs, leaving Kathryn staring after her and Wyatt juggling the boxes. No one said another word until I shut the front door after our unwanted guests left.

"Want to tell me what that was about?" I asked.

Mom stopped halfway up the grand staircase. "Women like Kathryn need to have the last word. I refused to give it to her."

The answer didn't have anything to do with my question. I knew a little about Mom's upbringing. The few bits she shared because they fit her agenda or furthered her you-owe-me narrative. Her submissive mom, out-of-the-picture dad, and distant stepfather. The volatile household exploded when her stepfather found the pregnancy test.

Getting kicked out of her house and bouncing around distant relatives' couches started the pattern that would repeat throughout her life—alone even when in a relationship and openly hostile to any form of affection. She expected rejection, almost welcomed it. She kept me at a distance, silently blaming me for the crashing of her dreams.

Then there was my dad. The boy who was gone from Mom's life long before she went into labor. The free ticket out of her unhappy existence who disappointed her in the end just like everyone else.

Very few of those stories mentioned Kathryn and even then only as an afterthought. "You worked at the Doughertys' country club."

"They didn't own it even though they acted like they did."

I refused to be derailed by semantics. "One of the rare times you talked about Kathryn was to tell me she never came to the club. She wasn't a member. Cooper and Richmond brought friends, but not her."

"That's what I said."

Talk about a dodge. "That exchange you just had sounded pretty personal, like the two of you knew each other and not just in passing. You conveniently left that part out of your life story."

"You're blowing a few comments out of proportion."

"You and Kathryn and whatever is between you directly impacts me." The omission kept me from seeing the entire game at play . . . just as Mom intended.

She didn't say anything for a few minutes. Just stood on the stairs, lording over the first floor as if she were lady of the house. "You dismantle the remainder of Richmond's reputation. I'll handle Kathryn."

Chapter Forty-Eight

HIM

Twenty-Seven Years Earlier

Twelve hours.

I tugged on my shorts, trying to pull the bottom edge closer to my knees. Every time bare skin touched the cool steel of the gun safe next to me second thoughts and stray memories of better times ran through my head. Mom laughing at breakfast this morning. The yearly vacation at the beach house. The holiday parties at the club where Dad would make us get dressed up and show us all off.

Those were things and replaceable. I would be able to buy whatever I wanted. Gain access. I'd meet women at college and enjoy the sound of their laughter. It would be enough.

The doubts would end tomorrow. I'd mentally walked through the plan so many times. I could speed it up or slow it down. Rewind and start over. Skip the part where the image got blurry and cut to the ending.

Mom and Dad. Dad and Mom.

The relentless lectures about wasting my potential. Their looks of disappointment. *No more partying. You need to get your priorities straight. What you do now impacts your future. One bad grade can destroy everything you've worked for. We won't always be here.*

You won't. I decided.

We've talked about it, and we need to make some changes.

They could never be happy and enjoy what they had. They put me in this position when they started going to "parenting classes" at that place in the strip mall. It sounded like a fucking cult. An adult playgroup where they earned praise for how miserable they could make their kids. Take the car away. Impose strict rules. Stop giving in. Stop saying yes. Be the boss.

These so-called friends took their money while preaching about the danger of giving kids too much. Mom said the theory was about living a simpler life. Complete bullshit but these new beliefs didn't show any sign of fading.

They'd run through the money eventually. Sell off all the cool stuff, maybe even the house itself. Let the club memberships lapse. Stop all vacations. No swimming. No tennis. Hell, they'd probably walk away from the business they'd built if their new overlords suggested it.

Where would that leave me? No money. No inheritance. Begging for the things I used to get without trouble. But this wasn't about me. Eight months of this garbage and still no relief in sight. They weren't *them* anymore. I didn't know these people. I didn't care about them. I wouldn't miss them.

My plan. Months of thinking and trying not to think. This was one of those times where I had to just act. Let my body walk through the scheme in my head. Take the gun and fire. Reload and fire. Run after them. Drag them back. Let them see my face so they would understand that their choices brought this on.

The safe combination was my mother's birth date. Easy to remember. Dad taught us to shoot, which was ironic. He loved guns, collected them, and would talk about the good life growing up on a farm in Virginia. Now those same guns would be the last things he saw. The guns and my face.

After it was over life could go back to normal. Not at first. There would be questions and interviews. That's why Cooper couldn't stay. He'd never be able to keep the secret. His commitment waffled. He wasn't strong enough. He couldn't hold on to his anger. He had to be reminded in exhausting detail how much life would suck if this went on.

I didn't need a reminder. I knew what I would lose if I didn't act.

Tomorrow morning would be the start of the life I deserved.

Chapter Forty-Nine

HER

Present Day

"Peter Cullen is on his way over." Another day, another visitor.

Being the most hated woman in town didn't stop the parade of people at my front door.

Peter had texted and turning him down seemed like a crappy move. The guy deserved some relief. With August in jail and talking, Peter might finally get answers about what happened to his son. He'd likely never find peace but maybe, at some distant point, grief wouldn't be his entire existence.

Dishes clanked as Mom dumped the remainder of her lunch in the sink. "I thought you weren't supposed to have guests. This is the second group in two days."

Mom's words to Kathryn continued to spin in my head. Mom refused to share details. She became hostile when questioned, so I tried to ferret out her secrets without her help. "You seemed to enjoy seeing Kathryn."

"Does anyone really enjoy spending time with that woman?"

A clear dead end. At least for now. "Peter said he appreciates that I listened to his accusations about Richmond."

The accepting gratitude thing made me twitchy. I didn't come to town to solve other people's problems. I came for one reason and that reason died before I could make Mom happy.

She turned to face me with her hands balanced on the sink edge behind her. "Honestly, Addison, I don't understand where your head is."

I didn't have the energy for this. Never did. "You've made that clear."

She treated me to her famous *tsk-tsk* sound. An oldie and not a goodie. The grating noise scraped across my last nerve. My control, already frayed, pulled to the point of snapping.

"I raised you to stand up for yourself. To put emotions aside and take what's yours."

Sound motherly advice. It spoke to independence and strength. A healthy battle cry passed from generation to generation. All fierce and worthy but so unrelated to my mother on every level. She knew the right words. She'd spout catchphrases and mantras then abandon them as soon as the audience cleared.

She didn't combat trauma. She created it, lashed it to my back, and forced me to carry it.

"When did this conversation become an indictment of my character?" Not that the sharp turn shocked me. Mom could upend almost any conversation to highlight her disappointment in who I was and how I'd failed her.

"You're so sensitive. I'm trying to help you."

There was not a sigh loud enough to wipe out the sound of her voice. "Mom, he's coming here to be nice."

"Oh, please. Peter Cullen expects something in return. Trust me. All men do." She pointed and nodded as she warmed to the topic. "You give something to get something."

"Your life motto." Except the "giving" part. She avoided that half.

My phone buzzed. A welcome break from Mom's unwanted lessons. A quick check showed a follow-up text from Peter announcing his arrival, just as I'd asked. Using the security app, I could see his car and confirm the license plate.

Elias had given me intel on everyone who might want to hurt me or Richmond or both, including photos and vehicle information. Very protective and fatherly of him. At the time it seemed like overkill. Now? *Thank you, Elias.*

Enough mom bonding time. I tucked my cell into my back jeans pocket. "I'm going to say hello, talk for a few minutes, then he'll go."

"Keep him out there. I'm tired of guests."

"Are you in charge of the house now?" Trying to sell this place was going to be a nightmare. Mom had become entrenched. Comfortable. Immovable. A bloodsucking leech.

Once outside, I shaded my eyes to get a better look at the car. The sun streamed through the trees, casting shadows on the windows as it approached. Instead of parking in the circular driveway, Peter continued down the extended lane that led to the separate three-car garage. The one next to the side porch I never used.

The garage was set back and tucked away in an attempt not to ruin the framing of the front of the grand house or take away from its mansion-like look. I couldn't blame Peter for his preference for privacy. He'd lost any ability to blend in once the Richmond surgery story hit the news. Everyone wanted to talk with Peter. People who treated his son's death as a terrible accident previously rushed to get the exclusive now.

Equally demanding, Richmond's fanboys squawked. They

blamed Peter for the destruction of Richmond's sterling reputation. Peter and me. Basically, anyone except Richmond. People gave him the benefit of the doubt even as the evidence against him mounted.

As the car came to a stop it hit me: How did Peter know about the extended driveway? He'd never been to the house . . . or had he?

A feeling of *not right* settled in my bones. A familiar and unwanted churning revved up inside me. My labored breathing pounded in my ears. My control, so clear and firm before I walked outside, faltered.

Inside. Go inside.

I shifted and my heel slammed into the bottom step to the porch. Pain ricocheted through my body as I bit back a squeal. My only thought was to bolt into the house and lock the doors. Call the police. Elias. Hell, I'd try everyone in my contacts list.

Thomas stepped out of the car. Not Peter. Thomas in Peter's car. Thomas who should be at the police station. Should be anywhere but here.

This was a very different version of Dr. Thomas Linfield than I'd seen before. The dapper, always-politicking professional in the expensive suit had been replaced by this guy. Harried and in a hurry. Fidgety and glaring as he dodged around the front of the car.

His uncombed gray hair stuck out from beneath a baseball cap he probably grabbed to disguise his appearance. He wore wrinkled chinos and a sweater. The whole look clashed with what I knew about him and his pampered existence.

And the gun. That was new.

"Thomas, I don't know—"

His wild eyes didn't blink. "We have unfinished business."

Chapter Fifty

HER

Present Day

Do not show fear.

I focused on the order to keep my brain from seizing in panic. A deep inhale and maybe I could push out intelligent words, something other than the gibberish rushing into my mind.

I looked to my right then left in search of a weapon. Anything to knock that gun out of his hands. "What exactly is the plan here, Thomas?"

"Get inside."

Not today. Not ever, actually. This was my house. My yard. I was in control . . . except for that gun. That was a huge fucking problem.

"You're a doctor, not an assassin. Do you think you can make me disappear?" He probably could but the point was to stall. I needed time. I really needed a mother who cared enough to check on me and look out the window then call the police, but that wasn't happening.

"I'm not going to tell you again, Addison."

Apparently we were on a first-name basis, which didn't fit with the weapon or the thick layer of desperation pulsing around him.

"I have thousands of dollars invested in security. I'm being watched by the whole damn town. There is no way for you to come on this property and not be noticed." Please have him be too far gone to notice the side of the house blocked any view nosy people loitering on the street might have.

His nervous squirming suggested his sole focus was on me. On breaking through and unleashing some twisted revenge for a sin he'd convinced himself I'd committed.

"I waited to come here until the press left," he said.

"How enterprising of you." The buzz of activity at the front gate had provided an unexpected level of protection. Not that I wanted the daily scrutiny back, but three acres stretched on forever when you needed someone to hear you scream. I could fight back but I couldn't outrun a bullet. "Where's Peter? That's his car, right?"

"He's in his garage."

"You confronted him?" That would kill any innocence claim on Thomas's part.

"I took his keys."

"You mean attacked him and stole them." Peter didn't hand them over. No way.

"I was careful. Came up from behind. He didn't see my face."

Sounded familiar.

"Curled up on the garage floor, he begged me not to go into the house. After all the big talk about taking me down and hiring lawyers, *he* pleaded with *me*. Then he passed out."

Thomas sounded unhinged in a way that differed from Richmond's murderous rages. Thomas lacked Richmond's narcissistic core. Where Richmond's ego blocked him from seeing his potential downfall, Thomas had clarity. He knew he had something to lose, which made him very dangerous.

"Peter probably thought you were robbing him and he was worried about his wife." I put my hands on my hips and tried to wriggle my fingers to touch my back pocket and slip out my cell. Elias liked to come running. This time I needed him to bring the entire police force with him. "She's struggling, Thomas. Her son died and—"

"Don't use that woman's pain to save yourself." He took another step, closing the gap between us.

My thumb hit the cell's screen. I'd read something about an emergency code. Buttons you should hit to call for help without actually making a sound. I dragged and pressed but I couldn't see to unlock it, so I had no idea what was happening. That left me with one choice—more talking while I worked out a solution.

Pots filled with red and orange mums lined the steps to the porch. Perfect for fall. Perfect to throw. Could I bend down and heave one before he fired off a shot? Didn't seem likely.

Words spilled out as I did a quick scan for a rake or a hammer or something with more heft than flowers. "Richmond's surgical abilities are being questioned. You'll be questioned."

"Are you a lawyer now?"

"No, but I think I could be. Doesn't seem that hard."

"This conversation is over." He pointed the gun at me then at the house. "Go."

Was the plan to shoot me in the kitchen? The house would muffle the sound, but the security video would highlight the rest. He wasn't hiding and didn't know how to dodge the cameras . . . unless he did. I had so many questions.

"You helped Richmond fake his credentials."

"Imagine having people tell you all your life that you're special. That you're better than everyone else. Combine that with real talent and a drive to be the best. That defined your husband." Thomas sycophantic tone and rushed words hinted at excitement. As if his hero worship survived Richmond's betrayal and the potential destruction of Thomas's livelihood.

I needed a replacement bat.

Thomas continued. "You knew him, or maybe you didn't. I can't get a read on you, but Richmond wasn't hard to assess. He enjoyed being a showman more than a surgical star. He preferred the lecture circuit to time in the operating room."

The people in Richmond's orbit never took responsibility. They pontificated while dancing around the sordid truth of their culpability. "You made it possible for his unchecked ego to continue. You covered for him by filling the room with other competent doctors and staff and pretending Richmond was the one doing all the work."

"You saw how people reacted to him. He was larger-than-life. He got the benefit of the doubt. We made concessions because he had achieved things other people couldn't dream of doing. When he acted like he was better than the rest of us, we accepted it because he was."

The whole defense of Richmond thing . . . I didn't get it. He cultivated this image and everyone went along. "He wasn't. That's the whole point."

"People believed what he said and gave his worst behavior a pass. With every lecture he'd embellish his abilities a little further." The more Thomas talked, the more enamored he became with his subject. "You let things slide once and then before you know it . . . they grow and . . ."

I didn't hear anything else because of Wyatt. He appeared in my yard. He jogged along the inside of the security wall, out of Thomas's direct line of vision. The *how* and *why* didn't make sense but Wyatt's presence renewed my hope of getting out of this conversation alive.

"Detective Sessions is a gigantic pain, but he'll figure out you're behind this. Is the plan to attack me then frame someone else?" Another familiar strategy. That was one coincidence too many. "Damn, it was you. At the gate. The tree branch."

"Why are you still talking?"

"You're the one who hit me. You set August up." My thoughts and words blended. Wyatt was right behind Thomas. Only feet away. For once I appreciated his trespassing. "Did you buy August's cologne and bathe in it so I wouldn't forget the scent? Because that's brilliant."

"Dr. Linfield." The only words Wyatt said.

An imperfect distraction but it worked. I grabbed the closest ceramic pot. It was heavier than expected and bulky. Not easy to throw, so I brought it up in an arc and slammed it into the side of Thomas's head. A vicious crack of ceramic against bone.

My hands shook and the pot fell. It tumbled to the ground, landing with a thud a second before Thomas's limp body dropped.

"The gun!" I reached for it and cradled it in both hands. Backed up and somehow stayed on my feet. Fought against the trembling running through me in case I needed to fire the weapon.

The steam ran out of my panic when Thomas didn't move. He was down. He wouldn't get back up for a while.

"You hit him." Wyatt sounded shocked as he checked for Thomas's pulse.

I also broke the pot. A split ran up its side.

"The police." My voice sounded so small and wobbly.

"Hey, it's okay." Wyatt stood up and touched my arm. He managed to look confused and concerned at the same time. "I tripped your alarm at the gate. The police should be on the way."

"Good thinking." I exhaled but the adrenaline burn wouldn't ease. A crash would come, but not yet. "Not to sound ungrateful but why are you here?"

"I was leaving the Rothmans. Your neighbors. I saw Dr. Linfield drive in and slipped in the gate before it closed." Wyatt winced. "I'd seen him here before when he wasn't supposed to be and—"

"When?"

"I thought the two of you might be working together. That's why I wanted the police here. It wasn't until I got closer to the house that I saw the gun."

This kid who should be at school was playing amateur detective and could have been hurt. "Your original goal was to catch me doing something wrong?"

"Yeah, you know, about that. I'm not sure Dad understood you."

Probably a compliment but not true. "That's where you're wrong, Wyatt. We understood each other just fine."

Chapter Fifty-One

HER

Present Day

Answers didn't bring relief. They raised more questions. The cascade of lies and secrets led to more damage. The ripple effect swallowed coconspirators and innocent bystanders and touched off new rounds of whispers and recriminations.

Never were the limits on what I'd learned so clear. There would be investigations and reviews of Richmond's other surgeries. None of that directly impacted me, except that Richmond's estate might need to compensate victims, depending on what games the insurance company played.

Thomas was in a hospital with a concussion. Safely handcuffed to his bed. His family locked down, refusing to talk to anyone. People in town were in an uproar. The press talked about conspiracies. Parents came forward, insisting Richmond and his team saved their children. Others, in pained voices, told horror stories about seeing their babies for the last time.

The unraveling should spill over and raise questions about Richmond's heroic teenage tale. If the armchair true crime detectives and police didn't step in, I would. But I was happy to let someone else uncover the truth and disclose it, cementing me in the role of the shocked and disgusted wife.

Mom hated that I wasn't taking a more active role in the downfall of Richmond's reputation, which is why I sat on the back patio, nursing a glass of iced tea and enjoying a minute of quiet. I welcomed the crisp air and soft whistle of wind. The confrontation with Thomas could have ended in bloodshed and death. The cacophonous crash and bang of *what ifs* and *could-have-beens* made it difficult to concentrate.

"If I didn't know better I'd say you were hiding." Elias sounded more relaxed than when he arrived at the house three days ago and watched Thomas get carted off in the ambulance.

"You do and I am."

Elias delivered a lecture during a call yesterday about listening to him and not inviting people to the house. I didn't know anything about having a dad but the mix of disappointment and relief in Elias's voice mirrored the dads I saw on television shows.

My positive mood bump vanished when Detective Sessions followed Elias out of the house and into my no-longer-safe space. I'd only expected one of them when Elias texted about a visit an hour ago. "Do you two ever get tired of rushing over here to talk with me?"

The detective nodded. "Yes."

"Definitely," Elias said at the same time. "But this trip brings good news."

"Where's your mother?" the detective asked.

"She's in her room. She's mad at me and, this is a paraphrase, needed to not see me for a few hours." She hadn't changed her fight exit line since I was a kid.

The detective frowned. "You two have an odd relationship."

Amen to that.

"August is no longer in custody, but dropping the assault charges won't save his medical career," Elias said.

"I'm not sure that's a bad thing." He'd marched along to orders he knew were wrong without saying a word. His poor decisions cost a family their child, which made it tough to root for him. "It's a fair punishment for getting wrapped up in Richmond's bullshit."

"Speaking of which, August is also telling everything he knows about Richmond and Thomas and the surgery deal." Elias exhaled. "In the ultimate fall from grace, Thomas has been removed from the medical practice he founded."

"That was quick. The poor bastard." I loaded that response with as much sarcasm as possible.

"And he could be looking at a murder charge," the detective said.

I nearly dropped my glass. "Peter Cullen is dead?"

"No, he's fine." The detective held up a hand as if to tell me to calm down. "I'm talking about Richmond. Thomas had a financial motive to keep Richmond quiet. People in the medical office said there was a lot of tension between the two of them ever since Richmond's divorce from Kathryn."

The detective's voice lacked its usual accusatory punch. Interesting since the divorce actually was my fault.

He continued. "Thomas also knew this house well and likely was someone Richmond would have welcomed inside on the day he died. Thomas not bringing a weapon with him and using something from the house suggests a spur-of-the-moment decision. Maybe an argument that blew out of proportion."

That meant Thomas knew about my bat and where I kept it. But how? Not from Richmond. He'd invested a lot of time in making me sound dangerous but would he admit to a colleague that his new wife hated him enough to keep a bat by her bed? Not sure.

"You're still investigating." I didn't phrase it as a question because the detective didn't say Thomas already had been arrested for murder.

"I'll keep Elias updated. Thomas is in a broken state. I'm hoping for a confession."

"Good luck with that." And I meant it.

The detective hesitated for a few seconds. "I'm assuming a man who would lie about something as serious as his commitment to sick children might have lied about other things in his life. It's up to you if you want to open that door."

With that, the detective walked away, leaving the usual emotional uproar in his wake.

"What the hell was that last part? You didn't tell him about—"

"No." Elias sat in the chair next to mine.

No lawyer lecture. A definitive no and I believed a genuine one.

That still left a lot of open questions. "Not sure I buy the theory about Thomas losing it and killing Richmond."

Elias relaxed in the chair. "Me either."

That was a massive problem I'd tackle another day. Right now, the subject I'd tried to ignore and dance around even though it was always on my mind poked at me. There was a reason I used disposable toothbrushes and cleaned out my brush and sink drain every day. Probably ineffective gestures but who knew.

"I have a client question."

Elias tensed but his voice didn't change. "I'm listening."

"What are the chances the police collected my DNA on one of their searches of the house?"

"Pretty good."

"That's not the answer I wanted." But it was the one I knew I'd get. Thinking about this issue was one of the many things that kept me up at night.

"I'm not sure how to advise you when you're still keeping secrets."

"The problem is not all of the secrets belong to me." The intimate details that locked me in a desperate conspiracy with my mother remained hers alone.

After a lifetime steeped in emotional blackmail and wrenching disappointment I merely existed. Trauma mixed with secrets until my mother's taunts became my belief system. She kept me alive, so I owed her. I could run but there would be a reckoning . . . and I was living that now.

The tragic part about escaping your past is that you never actually do. It's always there, in the background and in stark memories, waiting to pounce.

"I think part of you wants to tell me everything." Elias's voice was softer now, coaxing. "You deserve to unload some of that weight you carry."

I would have laughed at him if he'd delivered the line a few weeks ago. Now, I trusted him, or I trusted him as much as I was able to trust anyone. "I'm not a big sharer."

"And how's that working out for you?"

Happily widowed but nearly killed and still fighting and clawing to break free. "Not great."

"So . . ."

Time to jump in. "I need any collected DNA to disappear."

If the statement shocked him, he didn't show it. "You never told me where you grew up, or I guess I should say where your mother grew up."

Talk about an odd conversation turn. "Is that related to my DNA?"

"I think it might be." He sighed. "Maryland? Maybe in or around Annapolis, where the Naval Academy is?"

He was a smart man, but I wasn't ready to crack open that door. A nonanswer would have to suffice. "I've never begged anyone for anything in my life, Elias. I'm begging you to help me with the DNA."

He stared at me for a few seconds before nodding. "I'll do everything I can."

I believed him.

Chapter Fifty-Two

HIM

Married, Day Forty-One

Between Kathryn's incessant complaining and Addison's stranglehold on my life, I was done with women. They had a place. By my side, acting as my equal and my partner, was not it.

I'd married once out of necessity and once by accident. The first walk down the aisle completed the picture I wanted to present to the world. People equated marriage with stability. I became someone everyone could trust and should listen to. No longer a traumatized teen. A fully in control, successful man who beat the odds. A survivor.

A map and my dead brother, Cooper, caused the second marriage.

I'd hoped to thread the needle and pull off an extraordinary scam—get rid of one unwanted wife by pretending to marry a second one. The risk didn't pan out. It was a temporary setback and one I vowed to fix. That meant destroying Addison. She didn't think I could, which made me more determined to succeed.

Elias's investigator promised to find the fodder to send Addison running. That was only the start. After all her snide comments and that shit with the bat, she'd pay for her behavior. Her destruction would be my gift to every man who might have fallen under her spell or been subjected to her blackmail in the future.

Planning and gameplay were my strengths. I'd defeated stronger people. Older, wiser, wealthier people. Addison was nothing more than a nuisance, one that would barely register as a blip on the timeline of my life. It was time to start laying the groundwork for her erasure.

First, Kathryn. Every minute of her shrill fussing tested my patience. I'd been in our old house, sitting on the family room couch and tuning out her moaning for more than fifteen minutes.

Time to get to the point of my visit. "Addison is trying to kill me."

Kathryn stopped mid-whine. "What?"

"She's not stable." Kathryn spent the last half of our marriage droning on about "coded" words and phrases. From her frown, it looked like I'd hit one, so I tried again. "Addison is cunning. A master manipulator."

"*She* is?"

That grating tone. Kathryn enjoyed taking shots. Small, passive-aggressive hits as a reminder that she kept secrets that could ruin me. The marriage had neutralized her. The rushed divorce turned her into a potential problem.

Kathryn stopped fidgeting and sat down. She tended to be a ball of energy, always looking for some cause or errand to keep her busy. So much about her annoyed me. Idiosyncrasies and habits I tolerated for decades now made my temper spike.

"Why did she want to marry you in the first place?" she asked.

"Money. It's all that bitch cares about." Addison hadn't spent a dime yet, but the answer was good enough for Kathryn. I'd know more about Addison once someone on my payroll told me who the hell she was and how she fit into my past.

Kathryn was back to shifting around, playing with her necklace, as if she lacked restraint. "Do not put Addison's name on any of the assets."

An order? Kathryn had lost the ability to question me about money or anything else. She didn't recognize that, but I would remind her once I'd taken care of Addison. Dealing with one unwanted wife at a time was enough.

"The assets have been handled." My tone said *discussion over.*

Kathryn jumped to her feet again. "You promised none of this would happen. The marriage. Her in our lives." She grew more agitated the longer she spoke. "Your so-called wife should be paid off and gone by now. A hundred thousand dollars is a fortune for her. Please tell me you offered her the money like you promised."

Kathryn never contradicted me before we said our vows. She reeled me in with fake submission. Probably not the first bride in history to wait to show her backbone and unleash her argumentative nature until after the wedding reception bill had been paid.

She stared at me, as if waiting for a response. I had no idea what she'd said.

After a brief hesitation she wound up again. "I devoted my life to you. To our kids. I did everything you asked and ignored every slight. The other women." The sound of her sharp inhale bounced around the room. "Damn it, Richmond. How could you do this to me?"

In no universe was this situation about her. "You're getting hysterical."

"Gaslighting. Really?"

Her favorite word. "I was making an observation."

"Do you want to know what I see?"

Not even a little. "Addison's irrational behavior is the point. I have cameras and security everywhere in the house and on the grounds so I can spy on her."

Kathryn shook her head. "I want to believe you."

"Addison claims to know things."

"Yes, I get it. She's basically blackmailing you. But what exactly does she know? Why won't you answer that question?"

"Again, the specifics don't matter." Telling Kathryn might give her leverage, so she didn't need to know about the map and this supposed tape. It was sufficient for her to understand that Addison claimed to have proof and I believed her. "Until I figure out where Addison got her information and how much she really has, I need to play along."

"By being married to her."

I hated that part, too. I stretched my arm along the top of the couch cushions. Even Kathryn should see my lounging as a signal that I wasn't swayed by her outbursts. "It's a piece of paper that means nothing. A joke."

"Like our marriage was?"

The burst of strong will was the one downside of our divorce. That and losing a portion of my net worth, but I'd figure out how to get the money back. "Addison sleeps with a bat."

The air seemed to run out of Kathryn. She dropped back down on the couch, concern obvious in her eyes. "She could kill you."

Finally. "That's what I've been trying to tell you."

"You made a fool out of me. All because of her. This homicidal lunatic. And you've turned me into one of those forgotten first wives that you and your friends make fun of at the club."

That was more like it. I could handle her self-pity. "That's not true."

"Remember, Addison isn't the only one who knows about the things you've done."

I was about to put my hand on her knee. Show her some comfort, then that came out of her mouth. "Are you threatening me, Kathryn?"

"We're in this mess because of you."

Anger flared. Violent flames spilled out, burning through every promise I'd made to myself to maintain control. That need to reach out. To take her neck and squeeze . . . but I stayed calm. Clenched the couch material in my fist and rode out the wave of fury.

"I worked my ass off to give all of you everything you could want. I'm the one out there every day."

"You're being sued."

"I miscalculated with one surgery." I'd gotten complacent. A lawsuit loomed but I could talk my way out of that. Thomas couldn't afford to lose me. The blame would be shifted as far away from me as possible. "Do you have any idea how much time and energy I've dedicated to this family? To our financial security?"

All her squirming stopped. The hint of panic in her expression disappeared and her face went blank. "I know exactly what you've done to get where you are."

"And what *you* did." She could taunt but the facts condemned both of us.

"You're turning our lives upside down over some vague accusations from a woman no one would take seriously." Kathryn sprang up again. She rubbed her forehead as she walked back and forth in front of the fireplace. "I can't believe I let you talk me into any of this."

I tightened my hold on the couch material. "You seemed fine dividing our assets and taking the money."

"It was the first time you conceded to putting any asset in my name."

"Because I'm the one who earned it all."

My effort. My money. My dead parents.

"Don't do that." Her voice was softer now. Sweeter, as if she sensed she'd gone too far. "We're a team. We were supposed to continue being a team. You promised we'd separate long enough for you to remove Addison from our lives forever then we'd return to normal. You'd take the public hit for cheating on me, and I'd be graceful and take you back."

"That is still the plan." Not really.

"But Addison outmaneuvered you. Your guilt made you sloppy."

Every nerve jumped to attention, ready to strike. "Be careful about the words you throw around, honey."

I stood up as a signal the conversation was over. My work was done. I'd set the groundwork. Painted Addison as volatile and dangerous just as I'd done all over town. When the time came, people who barely knew her would line up to talk about her violent side. The rumors about how I'd married an unstable woman who lied about being pregnant would build. Whispers about how when I found out she tricked me and confronted her my mysterious "accidents" started.

That's when the power balance would shift in my favor. She'd need my help to avoid the police and the angry mobs. She'd panic. Her type always did when the money stream dried up. She'd hand over her supposed evidence to secure her freedom. I'd let her think she escaped the worst of my retribution. Then I'd get rid of her because I was not going through this bullshit again.

I had no choice but to kill her.

"Consider what we have as a death pact." I chose words calculated to produce the reaction I wanted.

Kathryn actually backed up. "I don't know what you're saying."

That was more like it. Her being afraid of me was new but not a bad thing. A little fear would keep her in line. "If I go down, you go down. We're in this together."

Some of the tightness eased from around Kathryn's mouth. "What if you can't beat Addison?"

Not an option. "I've never lost before. I won't lose this time."

Chapter Fifty-Three

HER

Present Day

The only good thing about Richmond being exposed for some of his gigantic faults was my newfound ability to go out for coffee. I had a clear lane, one that would likely close, but not before I got out for some air. The whole excursion took twenty minutes. I enjoyed every minute of it until I turned back onto my street.

Portia. Standing at the gate to the house. She wore another all-black outfit and pulled it off. The kid had style. But instead of her usual cool teenage detachment, she flitted around and repeatedly pressed the buzzer for the house intercom. She'd turned into a fiery ball of tension.

I pulled into the driveway and lowered the window on her side of the car. "What are you doing?"

She rushed over. "Is my mom with you?"

"The answer to that question will always be no." Kathryn. Always Kathryn. At the end of every problem, there she was.

Portia bit her bottom lip. "This is bad."

She had perfected the art of ignoring everything and everyone. Not today. Panic ran through every jerky movement and harsh breath. I could see her hands shaking.

"Hey, talk to me. What's wrong?"

"Mom saw the news and lost it. The thing with Dad's business partner. All the surgery stuff." Portia's gaze bounced around the yard and to the road. She was wound up and looked ready to pop. "Her cell kept ringing and she got more and more upset. Then she grabbed her keys and stormed out."

The more out of control Portia got, the calmer I became. One of us needed to stay in control. It sounded like Kathryn's tantrum meant she needed a few minutes alone to cool off. That seemed like a mom thing to do and not an emergency.

"Why do you think your mother came here?" I was the last person Kathryn would run to. She had friends. Charity people. Someone who wasn't me.

"She blames you for stuff."

Hard to argue with that.

In good news, the gate was locked. My alarm app wasn't pinging out a warning. No police in the driveway. No screaming.

I forced my mind to focus. Portia was my concern right now. The girl was near tears. She'd been dropped into this sucking vortex when her dad died and none of this was her fault.

Some of it was mine, so I unlocked the car door. "Get in."

Portia didn't argue. She plopped in the passenger seat and shut the door. Instead of talking, she fiddled with the window button.

Now what? "Can you call her? There are ways to track her phone. We could try that."

Portia shrugged. "She left her cell in the kitchen."

Of course she did. Not smart. Kind of annoying. Totally seemed like something Kathryn would do to piss me off . . . or she didn't want anyone to be able to track her.

I kept that concern to myself as I drove down the lane toward the house. Only my mom's car sat in the circular driveway. That didn't solve Portia's problem, but it solved mine. No run-in with Kathryn today. She was somewhere but not here.

"Her car isn't—"

Portia pointed. "I think that's it."

The side drive. The one that ran along the house, hidden from the road. The same one Thomas used. Time to rip the pavers out and bulldoze the whole thing to keep unwanted company from using it.

I pulled forward and there it was. A fancy black sedan. "Is that her license plate?"

"I don't know." But Portia's grim expression said she assumed yes. "She's in the house, isn't she?"

Stay calm. I thought the words then let them repeat in my head like a mantra. An angry Kathryn was a dangerous Kathryn. One of us in the car—unfortunately me—had to be the adult.

"She couldn't get inside." I made the comment more to reassure myself than Portia.

"Then where is she?"

Good question. If Kathryn was looking for a fight she could have rung the doorbell and . . . "My mom."

"What?"

Oh, shit. I threw off my seat belt. Every instinct told me to rush inside and break up the inevitable knock-down fight. The connection between Mom and Kathryn promised a bruising battle. Anything could happen. My money was on Mom to win, and she sucked at winning.

Lost in a nightmare about the showdown in my house, I forgot about Portia for a second. She sat in the passenger's seat all wide-eyed and tense. I probably shared the same look.

"Look, it's okay. I'll figure this out." I opened the car door. Portia reached for the handle on her side at the same time. "No. You stay here. Promise?"

She didn't answer right away. I waited for a nod then I took off. I didn't have time to weigh the possibility of her upholding her part of the deal. I needed to be in that house.

I rushed up the side steps. The thudding of my shoes warning the ladies about my impending arrival. Juggling keys and my bag, I opened the door and walked into the mudroom. I needed my hands free in case I had to break up a fight or something worse, so I dropped everything on the table.

Silence enveloped me. The only sound came from my harsh panting.

Momentum propelled me through empty rooms on the way to the front entry. Kathryn stood there looking uncharacteristically disheveled. Her purple wrap dress had pulled to one side and snagged high on her hip. The tie belt was about an inch from coming undone. She didn't have her usual expensive bag. Her arms hung at her sides. She kept grabbing fistfuls of material from the skirt part of the dress and letting go. Over and over.

Pale face. A glassy-eyed blank expression.

No sign of Mom.

I had a million questions. "How did you get in?"

"You ruined everything."

That voice, so distant and hollow. Not her usual racing words and overblown comments. She teetered on an invisible edge.

She shook her head. "You lied and bullied your way into our lives. Richmond is dead. People are talking about him. About me."

The hit to Richmond's reputation had threatened her social status and she was responding with a breakdown like I'd never seen. Portia needed to stay outside. Go home. Not see this. "Let's—"

"You don't get to talk!" Kathryn screamed the words.

Mom would come running any second and I needed Kathryn calm by then. Elias should conduct one of his drop-ins right now . . . and bring an ambulance. "Kathryn . . ."

"I offered you a deal, probably more money than you've ever seen, and you refused. Richmond and I both tried to pay you off, but you had to be greedy. You wouldn't leave."

Even while flailing she claimed ownership of everything she'd already lost. "Okay, I know you don't like—"

"You don't know anything." She moved closer. "You don't understand what I had to put up with from him. What I had to ignore and excuse from the beginning."

The twinge of sympathy and more than a little guilt surprised me. I'd written Kathryn off a long time ago. Seeing her now, I couldn't ignore that she bore the brunt of the divorce. I blackmailed him but her life was the one upended. Richmond might have been an asshole, but he was *her* asshole. He treated her like crap, but their lives were inextricably tied and losing that anchor had her floundering.

She kept moving, drawing closer. Her dress swished against her knees, showing off dark spots by the hem. They actually ran up to her waist and ended in a larger splotch. I'd missed the marks before but not now.

Blood.

The quiet house.

A dropping sensation, like being on a roller coaster during the downswing, started in my stomach. "Where's my mom?"

Kathryn's expression didn't change. "I brought my own bat."

Chapter Fifty-Four

HER

Present Day

Run.

Not caring where Kathryn was or what she was doing, I hit the stairs. Took them two at a time. Not jogging. Racing. The hammering of my heartbeat in my ears drowned out every other sound.

Scurrying. Frantic. Bolting up and down the hallway. Wild with fear. My chest rose and fell on labored breaths. My shoes thudded against the floor, squeaking when the soles met the hardwood.

I opened every door, letting each slam against an inside wall as I scanned the floor and furniture for my mom's sprawled body. Hating her. Loving her. The complicated reality of our relationship fell away in my desperate sprint to find her.

Mom alive. Kathryn out of my house for good. That was the plan.

I gripped the bannister and tried to wipe my mind clear. The booming screams of *you're too late* pounded against my temples. When I finally focused again I saw Kathryn. She stood there, still in the foyer below. Motionless and quiet.

I dashed down the stairs, not caring as my shoes slipped and my balanced faltered. I grabbed Kathryn by the shoulders and shook her. Her head bobbed back and forth. She didn't try to fight back or push me away.

"Where is she?" All the anger and frustration that had been simmering for months exploded. I morphed from worried to crusading avenger. A storm of regrets and demands pummeled me. The battle of the *what ifs* snuffed out by the pain I wanted to inflict on Kathryn.

"You're just like her. A manipulative little bitch, looking to make a quick buck and sleeping around to get it."

Her taunts challenged me. She wanted me to go after her, to be the one to lose it. Not happening.

I pushed her to the side. Mom had to be down here. Close by. "Mom!"

"She can't hear you."

The voice came from right behind me, as if Kathryn had whispered the chilling comment in my ear. That grating tone, usually so firm and condescending, turned haunting.

A shudder moved through me as I scrambled to check the rooms on this floor. I ran past the library door then doubled back. A shoe. Mom's shoe. Stepping inside I both wanted to see her face and dreaded finding her broken.

Slim blue jeans. Legs. "No, no, no."

I skidded inside and fell to my knees beside her slumped body. She sat on the floor in front of the couch with her hands palms up beside her thighs. Her head had rolled back onto the ivory cushion now stained red beneath her ear. I stared at her chest hoping to see air move in and out. Before I could check for a pulse, I heard footsteps.

"She deserved it." Kathryn's eerie voice cut through the silence.

I saw the bat first. Kathryn held it as she loomed over me. This bitch thought I was going to let her take a swing. As if I wasn't going to kick and scream this house down before she could touch me.

Wedged between the furniture and Mom's body, I didn't have many options. Looked like all the useless decorative stuff in the room finally had a purpose. The first coffee table book hit Kathryn's arm and she yelled in outrage. I threw the second one harder, aiming for her head but she ducked in time.

Next came the basket with those glass balls Richmond insisted were handcrafted and expensive. They looked like ornaments without the hooks. Perfect for fighting off a woman lost in her rage.

The first ball bounced off Kathryn and shattered on the floor. With the second, she turned her head in time for it to miss her face, but it cracked against the side of her head. She reeled back, stumbling and off-balance, which gave me a few seconds to climb over Mom and get up.

The fight lasted less than a minute. Then a new battle started. Kathryn let out an ear-piercing scream, part roar and filled with venom. She stalked toward me, her steps unsure and her body weaving. I beelined for the crystal lamp just as she raised the bat.

"Mom, stop!"

Chapter Fifty-Five

HER

Present Day

Portia. The second of relief gave way to a stab of *she shouldn't be here*. The blood. The bat. Her mother's unraveling. It was too much for me and I wasn't a teenager already lost in a hailstorm of grief over a dead parent.

"Portia?" Kathryn lowered her arms and stared at her daughter.

Kathryn sounded bewildered. Her face no longer twisted in a mask of fury.

I jumped on the tentative cooling of Kathryn's madness, hoping the break would give her a few minutes to wrestle back at least a portion of control over her disordered emotions. When Mom woke up she'd bring the hammer down, metaphorically and possibly literally, on Kathryn. No way was Mom going to let this go, but I couldn't think about that now. The immediate goal was to keep Kathryn focused on her daughter and not on the destruction of my mother.

"Portia was worried about you." My voice stayed steady despite my taut nerves.

"I do not need or want your help." Kathryn didn't snap. In contrast to her harried state and the weapon in her hand, she sounded like her normal, haughty self. "You found me, honey, and I'm fine."

The woman was not fine. Hell, I wasn't fine. It could be months before I could climb up to *fine* again.

"But . . ." Portia frowned as her gaze wandered over her mother then to mine. "She's hurt. What happened?"

How did anyone explain this rolling nightmare? The important thing was to get Mom help and get Portia to safety. The sight of blood splattered on the floor had haunted every one of my days for years. Portia didn't deserve that agony.

"Why don't you take your mom and go back home. I can handle this." I couldn't but what choice did I have?

"You are not her mother. I am." That time Kathryn did snap. Her voice had a pinched quality to it.

"Then act like it. Do you really want Portia in the middle of this?"

"No, really. She doesn't look okay. Does she need an ambulance?" Portia took a step toward Mom's slack body on the floor.

I tried to stop her, but Kathryn got there first. She stepped into Portia's path. "That woman attacked me, and I defended myself."

Bullshit. Forget unraveling; this was calculating. Kathryn planned this out and had her defense ready. Attack and lie. Blame me and my mom and take no responsibility.

Richmond had taught her well.

Portia tried to maneuver around her mother. "Why would she—"

"I'll call the ambulance." Anything to protect the kid I barely knew and didn't care about until a few weeks ago. She wouldn't end up like me. Broken and spinning. Caught between nightmarish visions of the past and her mother's unreasonable demands.

Kathryn smiled. "There's no need. Everything is fine."

Except for the bat hanging loose in Kathryn's hand and the revenge scheme running through her head. Sure, everything was just fine.

"Your mom was about to leave anyway." In case Kathryn hadn't picked up on my hint I drove it home. "You still can walk away. This is the time to turn back."

Portia didn't appear to be listening to me as she stared at her mother. "You were so angry when you left the house."

"I still am."

This woman. Even under duress and locked in a tsunami of anger she had to have the last word. "Kathryn, this isn't the right time."

"I appreciate the concern." Kathryn smoothed her free hand over Portia's hair. "I'll be home soon. I'm not done here."

Panic shot around the room and wrapped around Portia. "Addison?"

"Stop talking to her. Addison is not your friend. She destroyed our family." There wasn't any lightness to Kathryn's voice now. It boomed, cutting through the relative quiet of the house. "There are things you don't know about what she did to your dad. Other people are taking the blame, but she caused all of this."

Guilt weaponized. Words twisted and tainted. I recognized the motherly tricks all too well. "Don't do this to your daughter."

"No. You don't get to speak." Kathryn shook her head. "You took everything else. You can't have my children, too."

Mom's hand twitched. Maybe it was wishful thinking. My

glance lasted only seconds. Any longer would tip off Kathryn, but Mom's chest moved. She might not be awake, but she was breathing.

Relief made me light-headed. After all that had happened between us, all the words said and unsaid, I doubted I could still feel anything but there it was—actual concern. My side of the mother-daughter bond still kicked and screamed for air.

Mom needed medical attention and we were miles away from that happening with Kathryn on a rampage. "How are you going to get out of this? If this escalates even more . . ."

Portia looked at me then to her mom. "I don't understand."

Supportive hadn't worked. Time for an order. "Portia, leave. Now. I'm tired of this."

Portia's face crumpled. "Don't talk to me like that. I'm trying to help."

That's right. Turn on me. Be offended enough to leave and find safety. "You heard me."

"We'll be fine, honey." Kathryn guided Portia toward the door to the hall.

Portia didn't fight her mom's pull or touch. She walked without looking back. That stuck me alone with Kathryn, a woman whose boundaries and control were disintegrating by the minute.

"Your daughter isn't going to miraculously forget what she saw here." There was no easy road out of this for Kathryn. I didn't intend to help her find one. She'd gone too far. This would end with the police and criminal charges. "You're in my house. I'm not holding a weapon. We're defenseless."

"You're not innocent."

Not the word I used and there was a reason for that. "Portia is.

She's already grieving for her dad. You're putting her in the position of having to lie for you."

I'd lived it. Burying pain and pretending it didn't exist wouldn't destroy it.

"Did your mother make you lie about loving Richmond or were you a willing accomplice in her scam?"

Talk about an unexpected topic change. "I never said I loved Richmond."

"Do you love her?" Kathryn pointed the bat at Mom. "I wonder what you'll do to save her."

"Stop."

Kathryn touched Mom's arm with the end of the bat. "Why should I?"

Chapter Fifty-Six

HER

Present Day

Kathryn's perfect posture spoke to years of social training. The loose strands of hair around her face signaled she'd been in a battle. She hadn't unleashed her mocking tone, but it was only a matter of time. She came to do a job and it wasn't done.

My focus was on the younger Dougherty woman. The library sat at the front of the house with French doors to a patio on the side and a large picture window looking out onto the driveway. Turning slightly, standing almost even with Kathryn and only a few feet away put me too close to the bat but I could see Portia. Not clearly but enough to make out her movements.

She'd sprinted down the driveway to the pedestrian gate. After a few seconds of what looked like indecision, she picked up a rock from the landscaping. She struggled a bit with the weight of it before wedging it between the now open gate and the doorjamb.

Smart girl.

The alarm company would get a message about the open door. They'd call me for the password. Since I couldn't answer, the police should come to the house again. Portia also waved wildly at the security camera and punched the security pad. If the door issue didn't cause a warning light to go off, Portia's odd behavior would.

I couldn't tell what happened next. From this angle it looked like she ran to the neighbors' house. Getting a better look would warn Kathryn, so I stopped straining.

Kathryn no longer had the element of surprise on her side. But she had a weapon and I'd have to lunge for that lamp again or try to dart out of the room to win the next skirmish.

I should have tucked my cell in my pocket or held it when I stormed inside and started hunting. I'd dumped the thing in my bag when I got out of the car. That meant it sat at least three rooms away. Not helpful.

"Tell me what my mom did to you." I crouched down to take Mom's pulse and confirm that she was still breathing. The ballet move was a risk, but I got back up before Kathryn took a swing.

"She did it to all of us back then." Kathryn's I'm-better-than-you tone had returned.

Us. She threw out clues without knowing it. "You're going to have to be more specific."

Kathryn's eyes narrowed. "Do you think this is funny?"

"I haven't found a single moment in this town amusing."

"Not true. You enjoyed wrecking my marriage." Kathryn's hand tightened on the bat. "Richmond offered you a hundred thousand dollars to leave and you refused."

She'd referenced the offer before. The amount didn't register then. It did now. Both Kathryn and Richmond offered the same thing to get me to leave everything behind. On the outside, to the community and the kids, they pretended to squabble, but behind the scenes they sounded as in sync as ever.

"How do you know what Richmond offered me?"

"None of this was supposed to happen the way it did."

The money? The marriage? Unclear. But Kathryn knew the payoff amount. She knew to bring a bat to the house, my weapon of choice. It sounded like whatever bound Kathryn and Richmond together had survived their divorce and kept them talking.

Portia popped into view again. She stood just outside the main gate, talking on her cellphone. I couldn't hear mine ring or hear the alarm chirp. Maybe she was calling the police. Either way, alarm bells should be going off.

"You tried to kill him." Kathryn took a few steps until she stood next to Mom's feet. "I know about how you disabled his car. About the poisoned food. You lived with him. Only you. No one else had access."

I didn't do either, which meant Richmond setting me up was the only answer. Staging fake accidents would be easy for him compared to all his other schemes. "You don't think it's weird that he told you about those incidents? Wouldn't that have been humiliating for him?"

"He told me. I told the police."

Ah, yes. Detective Sessions. Kathryn ran to him whenever she wanted to plant a kernel of information for later use.

Portia was on the move again. She slipped through the pedestrian gate she'd propped open and walked toward the house. Away from safety and the police. Closer to danger and her mother's wrath.

Damn it. Portia needed a lesson in self-preservation. If I survived this, I'd teach her.

Watching both Dougherty women proved daunting. If I let my guard down Kathryn would pounce. If I didn't track Portia anything could happen.

Time for the only trick available to me. Stalling. "How do you know my mother?"

"I'm asking the questions." Kathryn followed my gaze then stared at the large window. "Why do you keep looking outside?"

Shit. "I'm not."

"Go to Richmond's office. Now."

Away from the big window where I could track Portia. I obeyed because Kathryn lifted the bat. Once in the other room, she lowered the shade and shut the curtains, blocking my view.

"I know who your mother is. The question is, who are you?"

For someone acting so irrationally, Kathryn sounded fine. That scared me more than the bat. "What does that mean?"

"It's a simple question," Kathryn said. "Are you Richmond's daughter?"

Chapter Fifty-Seven

HER

Nine Years Earlier

"You are not leaving this house, young lady."

Mom was in a mood. She knew about the graduation party, yet she hit me with that furious tone. She acted like I'd done something wrong when my day consisted of attending the ceremony and eating fast food takeout with her on the couch. I'd thrown stuff away. Cleaned up. Those completed chores should buy me a ticket out of the house for a few hours.

Mom had other ideas, but she missed one very important fact. I didn't have to listen to her anymore.

I held on to the doorknob so I could make a quick exit. Her temper had shifted from neutral to shrieking and it sounded like things were about to get worse. "I'm eighteen. I graduated from high school today."

Her hands went to her hips. "You act like something magical happened when you picked up your diploma."

Yeah, freedom. "I'm an adult now."

"That's good to know." Sarcasm flowed out of her, spilling across the floor and tainting everything in its path.

She couldn't let one hour just be about me. Every celebration, every conversation, had to link back to her and be on her terms.

During the few times the spotlight shifted, that I experienced a moment of triumph, she swooped in and trampled it.

That was the reality of our relationship. She tolerated me as long as I didn't overshadow her. If I towed the line, she didn't launch verbal grenades in my direction.

"Mom, come on." I'd stopped begging her for anything years ago but tonight mattered. I didn't have the money to leave home yet, but the day was coming.

"No, I heard you. You're an adult." She walked over to the basket on the kitchen table where she put the bills. "That means it's time you start paying half of the rent."

I didn't respond because doing so would only inflame the situation. With her anger building the only option was to stand there and take it.

"Are you prepared to do that, Addison? How about the utilities?"

She whipped an envelope at me. It landed at my feet. Reaching for it meant breaking eye contact, so it stayed where it was.

"The car insurance." She threw a second envelope.

I didn't move.

She gestured toward the refrigerator. "All the food you eat."

My job was to be grateful and silent. Any other day, sure, but this standoff had been simmering under the surface for weeks, waiting to explode.

"Why do you hate me so much?" The question I'd been wanting to ask since I turned ten.

Her expression didn't change. If the words shocked or offended her, she didn't show it. "I could have gotten rid of you. Abortion. Adoption. Everyone told me to pick one, but I didn't."

I'd heard this speech before. More guilt. Nothing about loving me.

"I'd already lost your father." She dropped the rest of the unpaid bills on the table. "His family had money. They could have taken care of us. We wouldn't have had to live like this, but I had to run to save us."

Zach Bryant. My dismal existence grew out of his premature death and the destruction of Mom's dreams. My job was to recognize her loss.

"This wasn't the plan." She gripped the back of the kitchen chair. "Working two jobs and scrounging for scraps? That's not how I saw my life. That's not why I sacrificed so much. Things should have gotten better when I got married the first time, but you destroyed that, too."

She never let me forget.

"But you can fix it. You can step up and clear that debt."

This was new. And scary as hell. "How?"

"I thought you were too young but, as you pointed out, you're an adult." Her voice sounded lighter.

I could barely hear her over the crashing sound in my head.

"You, my dearest daughter, are going to destroy Richmond Dougherty."

The guy she hated and taught me to hate. "I don't even know him."

"You will." She smiled. "You'll be my greatest weapon, and he won't see you coming."

I finally identified that crashing sound. It was my hope of breaking free from her shattering into pieces.

Chapter Fifty-Eight

HER

Present Day

"You really think Richmond married his own daughter?" I managed not to choke on the horrible words.

"I think he didn't know who you were when you tricked him into marriage." Kathryn switched the bat from one hand to the other but didn't put it down. "You and your mother are just sick enough, depraved enough, to try to get his money that way."

Saying anything risked all my mom's plans and both of our lives, so I just stood there, letting Kathryn spew and hoping she'd answer some of the questions I'd had for years about Mom's life in Annapolis.

"You supposedly know all this information about Richmond. You had a vendetta against him, and for what? You had intimate knowledge about how to weasel into his life. And your mother . . ." Kathryn's words came to a crashing halt. It took a good minute before she spoke again. "I don't think you have any idea of who she is or what she's done."

She wasn't wrong about that. Mom was a mystery. Before I could come up with a way to poke around in Kathryn's thinking her expression changed. She scanned the office and wariness replaced satisfaction.

Yeah, she'd made a mistake. She'd steered us into a confined area.

Watching that online video about turning household items into self-defense weapons had not been a waste of my time. There were plenty of lamps, desk supplies, and books to throw. The marble paperweight with the medical symbol on it would do just fine. The goal was to lull Kathryn into dropping her guard while I calculated the best way to aim and fire.

"Richmond wasn't my father." I said it with certainty. My mom was twisted but not quite that twisted. She had terrible secrets, some she'd only recently shared, but not this.

"Of course he wasn't. Why would you even say that?" Wyatt's voice boomed through the room as he moved into the doorway.

The whole damn family had shown up today. A visit from Detective Sessions would have been better. I listened for Mom. For police sirens. For any sort of help. Instead, I got Wyatt.

"What are you doing here?" Kathryn asked.

Wyatt eyed the bat. "Portia called. She's frantic. Now I see why."

I abandoned any form of subtlety. "Your sister needs to stay outside."

"Stop acting like you know anything about my children. You mean nothing to them." The last of Kathryn's usual refined veneer fell away as she lashed out. She didn't weigh her words. Her sole focus was on wreaking havoc on those who she believed wronged her.

Unlike my mom, Kathryn never blackmailed Portia and Wyatt into doing the unthinkable. In theory, Kathryn knew better. She had to understand that letting the kids see her like this, so out of control, would burden them in a way that changed how they viewed themselves and the world.

"Let's go find Portia." Wyatt put a hand under his mom's elbow.

Drowning in entitlement and too self-focused to see the destruction she left in her wake, Kathryn didn't give in. She gasped as if to say *how dare you*. "I'm not done here."

That ugly paperweight. I looked at it then at Kathryn. Aiming for the bat made sense. She could drop it, but I wouldn't be sad if I hit any part of her and stopped this madness.

"Mom, please."

Wyatt's caring tone appeared to incite her. She twisted her hands on the bat. "You don't understand what she is. She'll do and say anything to get her hands on our family money."

Wyatt gestured in my direction. "She's just standing there."

Still no reinforcements. I silently willed Portia to call the police since the alarm company seemed to be slow to act this time.

"I would point out you're all in my house." I took a step back, bringing me even with the edge of the desk. So close to that paperweight.

Kathryn ignored me. "What is it about this woman that makes you and your father listen to her and fall in line? You keep running over here like her pathetic lapdog."

She didn't slap him, but Wyatt winced as if she had. "I thanked her for paying for school. That's it."

"Why? Do you really not understand what she's done? How much damage she's caused? Your father is dead. Our money is in her hands. She is the villain, not me." Kathryn stilled. "Or are you sleeping with her, too?"

"Mom!"

"Kathryn, that's enough." She'd passed *enough* five minutes ago but now I'd end it.

"I wouldn't be surprised. She's even got Elias jumping to her commands. He used to listen to me, but not now." Kathryn practically spit the last part out.

Keeping calm grew harder by the second. "Look, Richmond is not my father. I am not having sex with your son or Elias. End of conversation. Leave."

Rushing to someone's defense was not my thing. I didn't have a martyr complex. I'd sloughed off the need to be liked long ago but bouts of unexpected empathy for the Dougherty children kept kicking my ass. Having both parents spin out of control and land in the public spotlight with their faults on vivid display promised a bleak future for the kids.

"She tried to kill your father. Have you forgotten that?" Kathryn fueled up on fury until she sounded manic. "Before she pushed your father down the stairs she tried to kill him with poison."

"That's not true." Wyatt shot back the denial.

The force of his defense surprised me. Could be he used the firm response to talk his mother off the emotional precipice, but nothing in our interactions to date suggested that he had that level of emotional maturity.

"Your father said so. He confided in me right before he died." She gripped the bat with enough force to turn her knuckles white.

Wyatt's gazed shifted around the room. "An accident at the deli. Then he had a car problem. No one's fault."

Wait . . . he looked up and to his left as he talked. That was his tell. I learned he had one the first time he let himself into this house after Richmond died.

Wyatt knew details. I wanted to know how but spilling what he knew now would only inflame an already hostile situation. De-escalation was key. "You should take your mom home and help—"

"Stop treating me like a child who needs to be handled. Richmond did that and I hated it. This time I'm the one handling things. For once, I decide."

Richmond. His fault. All of it. For being a piece of crap as a kid and for turning into a ruthless piece of crap adult. For a man who thought so highly of himself and soaked in every compliment, he sucked at being a father, a husband, and a doctor.

"Right before she killed him, your father warned me about her attacks. I thought he was lying to make me feel bad for him." Kathryn moved closer to me with her bat and her unblinking stare. "He miscalculated by marrying her and couldn't admit it. No, not the perfect Richmond Dougherty."

How did you stop someone from tripping and falling over an invisible edge? "Kathryn, don't do this in front of your son."

"Richmond was so manipulative. So sick. You don't even know." Kathryn's eyes looked glassy, as if she'd gotten lost in her own thoughts. "He hid so much."

Decision time.

She knew I'd discovered something about Richmond. That our marriage wasn't based on anything resembling love or attraction. But it didn't sound as if she knew specifics about my blackmail. It was possible she didn't even know Richmond's biggest lie, but I doubted it.

Some secrets begged to get out and this was one of them.

Rather than rushing in, I waded in nice and slow. "But I know. I know exactly who and what Richmond was."

Kathryn stared at me but, for once, stayed silent.

"Listen to what I'm saying." Could she even hear me in this state? "That's why he married me, Kathryn. Because I knew the truth about him and what he did. All of it."

"What are you talking about?" Wyatt's voice matched the crackling tension filling the room.

The minute you see your parents as separate from you, as real and flawed human beings, the world changes and you can't go back. The realization didn't even register as a bump to me. My mom skipped right over the *loving parent* stage, so there was nothing for me to miss or adjust to. Wyatt had a different upbringing. If the truth spilled out—every horrible detail—he might stumble and never get up again.

Kathryn shook her head. "She's trying to trick you. She's the one who tried to kill your—"

"I told you." Wyatt's voice cut through the end of her sentence. "Addison didn't poison Dad or wreck his car."

A strong and clear denial. He was telling the truth. He acted like he'd been locked down and near bursting with the need to spill all he knew about the incidents. That could only mean one thing and once he spoke the words he couldn't take them back.

I inched closer to the paperweight. "Wyatt, don't say anything else."

"But Mom is wrong about you. Dad was wrong, too."

His trying to comfort me was both unexpected and sweet but he needed to engage in self-preservation. In his mother's state anything could happen. Saving both of us from her rage might not be possible.

My hand covered the paperweight. The ugly thing had some heft.

"Listen to me." My chest ached. My head hurt. My mom could be dead and all I could think about was reassuring Wyatt. "It's over and it should stay that way."

Kathryn talked as if she hadn't heard the conversation going on around her. "Her diner story is a lie. She must have snuck back here and killed him. She had access to his food and his car."

I sucked at being a savior and Wyatt refused to save himself. All I could do was stand there and watch the ground crumble beneath his feet.

Kathryn shook her head. "She has to answer for—"

"It was me." Wyatt took a deep breath and blew it out again. "I poisoned Dad."

Chapter Fifty-Nine

HER

Present Day

This was a nightmare. A family nightmare. Technically not my family because I'd done everything to stay separate from this group, but I got sucked in. Clawing my way out proved impossible. I couldn't calm things down or stop the inevitable crash. Reckoning day finally had arrived. Richmond had dodged it and let it slam right into Wyatt.

The mood in the room kept changing. Fury morphed into confusion. I wasn't sure where we'd landed, so I palmed the paperweight, waiting for the right moment to go on the offensive.

"You're lying. You have to be." Kathryn gasped. Not one of those fake ones she used when she commented on my outfit or my slippers. This sound came from her soul, as if it had been ripped out of her. "I don't believe you."

"Dad came up with the plan."

Of course he did. Typical Richmond asshole behavior. Crowning a new accomplice in a new generation. This time, instead of his brother, Cooper, Wyatt played the role of assistant. More Dougherty roadkill.

I didn't think I could hate my dead husband more. I was wrong.

As the secrets seeped out, I couldn't save Wyatt or make this better. He'd made a choice. At his father's twisted request, yes, but Wyatt wasn't a child anymore. He needed to own his shit without anyone coming behind him to clean up the mess.

"Dad said Addison lied to him and that's why they got married. I thought she was the one who . . ." Wyatt shot me a quick glance. "He made it seem like he had no choice."

"That's right. She blackmailed him."

Kathryn's comment shattered any last pretense about her being estranged from Richmond. Even with the divorce acrimony and her insistence on fueling the *poor Kathryn* sympathy around town, their lives remained entangled. She knew exactly what was happening in my house and about Richmond's plans to cause chaos.

"He said he couldn't fake an allergic reaction and I had to help. I was nervous and added too much extract to the sauce on the sandwich." Wyatt hesitated but this didn't look like the usual twenty-something melodrama. He expected a big reaction to his news, probably shock or wailing.

I was too busy basking in a brief moment of *I knew it* satisfaction to feel anything else.

"He started eating the sandwich when he saw you coming back from your run. I thought he'd take one bite, but he ate half the thing. He was lecturing and got into it and . . ." Wyatt stopped to take in a huge gulping breath. "He was so pissed. I thought he was going to kill me."

"Knowing Richmond, probably." Being on the losing side of blackmail blew out Richmond's boundaries. Turning Wyatt into the latest Dougherty fatality wasn't inconceivable. If a plan allowed Richmond to slither away from trouble he'd do it, regardless of what that meant for anyone else.

Tension had Wyatt in a stranglehold. Disclosing the truth diffused some of the nervous energy radiating off him but not all. "Dad staged the thing with the car. I helped him after, but that was all him. He said he needed leverage against you. He wanted people to think you were unstable and dangerous."

Richmond's big plan. I could see all the pieces now. His goal was to put pressure on me so I wouldn't use the evidence I'd collected against him.

At seventeen he'd dreamed up a complex, diabolical masterpiece with moving parts, different locations, and an element of surprise. As an adult, he relied on shrimp extract delivered by his son. Quite the fall of the evil empire.

"He thought he'd run me out of town." I could almost hear Richmond's planned future threat. The grating sound of his gloating as he warned me about evidence he'd planted and the line of witnesses he'd cultivated to speak against me. He'd insist he won, and I *had* to make a new deal. My evidence in exchange for him not going to the police.

The bargaining wouldn't have worked, but he probably knew that, too, or he would have moved faster and not landed in that box.

"It was weird. He was, like, desperate. Furious but saying he had to be careful. That we couldn't mess up." Wyatt shrugged. "Then I screwed up the sauce."

"That's outrageous. He should never have asked you to help him. You are his son."

Well, look at that. Kathryn being a reasonable person and decent parent. I almost clapped. "Your mother and I don't agree on much, but we do on that point. If your father had a problem with me, he should have handled it and left you out of it."

"Okay." Kathryn seemed to shake off the horrid news. "Whatever Richmond did or didn't do doesn't change what needs to happen here. Today."

She meant me. Get rid of me. My hand tightened on the paperweight. "You insisted I tried to kill Richmond a few minutes ago. That was your whole reason for your being here, your excuse to come after me, and now it doesn't matter?"

"You did kill Richmond." Old Kathryn had returned. The perfect diction. The annoying self-satisfaction. "You came up behind him with that bat and hit him."

She tried to hold on to that story, but she'd said too much. Only one of us realized that. "It's funny how you knew about the bat. About the money Richmond offered. Hell, you knew the amount and offered the same. One hundred thousand dollars."

She waved off my point. "The part about the bat was in the news."

"It wasn't." I'd looked for any mention of the murder weapon. Elias told me the police would hold the information back and that's what happened.

"You're twisting the facts instead of facing them. That's what liars do," Kathryn said.

Dissembling. The performance wasn't one of her best. She said the words but couldn't sell them. She wove a narrative that absolved herself and kept her halo intact.

Watch me smash it to pieces. "You're saying everyone is a liar but you."

Wyatt frowned. "What bat?"

We were done. There was nowhere for this train to go. I bet on my instincts and went all in. "Is this how you want Wyatt to find out the truth about his father?"

That stopped Kathryn for a second. "He already knows about the surgery allegations. We haven't been able to avoid seeing and hearing them."

Nice try. "I mean Annapolis. The school. That map."

Kathryn's expression turned carefully blank. All anger and passion gone. "I don't know what you're talking about."

Poor Wyatt stood there, looking lost. The confusion showed on his face and echoed in his voice. "One of you please explain."

Kathryn's arm moved. The bat rose a fraction, not even an inch, but my brain shifted into gear. I lifted the paperweight and launched it. Aimed for the bat but hit Kathryn's arm. Probably more from surprise than pain, she yelped and let go.

The yelp turned into yelling. "You bitch."

She hissed when Wyatt touched her as if she might break into pieces. Her body rocked back and forth. She held her arm. Doubled over in pain, cradling it. She touched her wrist then her elbow.

Clearly Kathryn wasn't done with her time in the spotlight. Her ability to command a room remained unmatched. But in all the acting and whining she forgot what part of her arm was supposed to be in pain. I hit her forearm. Barely.

"Really?" My mom struggled with very real injuries. I needed to get to her, not wallow in this nonsense. "Don't you think . . ."

All the fake crying stopped. In a flash, Kathryn's knees bent and that supposedly injured arm reached down.

The bat. At her feet.

I dove for it.

Chapter Sixty

HER

Present Day

Kathryn and I hit the floor at the same time. Grunting and shoving. Kicking and punching. Wyatt stood over us, yelling for us to stop as legs flailed and our shoes clomped against the floor in the fight for leverage. My shoulder slammed into the hardwood when Kathryn climbed on top of me. That petite frame hid her determination to win. It gave her strength and made her mean.

The force of the adrenaline rushing through me touched off a round of dizziness. Energy pumped in my veins. All the disappointment and fear, all those moments of feeling powerless, welled up, fueling every twist.

I'd been born out of spite and raised in a bath of vengeance. My purpose—to live out my mother's anger—had been spelled out and drummed into me. No amount of begging, hoping, or running stopped her from sacrificing my life for hers. Jumping to her commands and submitting to her blackmail landed me here. Alone in a sea of dangerous, deceitful people.

That ended now. The days of doing her bidding and inhaling her fury were over. I fought for me.

I'd attended random classes here and there over the years. I never stayed long enough in one place to learn much more than the basics of any subject. The one exception—self-defense. I'd taken a series of classes in preparation for confronting Richmond. Those moves failed me during Thomas's attack, but they came in handy now.

Unsure where the paperweight went, I hugged the bat and rolled. My body covered it. The end pressed into my chest. All the aches and pains from my physical battle at the gate came roaring back, demanding attention. I ignored them and clenched until my muscles shook.

Kathryn reached around me and under me. Wyatt knelt down, trying to rip us apart. Odd noises filled the room and carried throughout the big house. Heavy breathing mixed with the sound of shuffling bodies as we rolled and fought for leverage. I banged my shin against a chair. The floor lamp toppled over.

Great results can be achieved with small forces.

My instructor repeated the mantra several times during the four-week self-defense class. The phrase stayed in my mind even though it sounded like bullshit. Big always trumped little. Strong defeated weak. Today, I needed determined to beat disturbed.

Kathryn draped her body over mine and dug her nails into my shoulder. A squeal built inside me. The pinching had me squirming. I slammed my elbow back as hard as I could. Right into her stomach. The result was instantaneous. Her labored breathing turned to a grunt as she rolled off me and onto the floor.

I scrambled to my feet, bat in hand. Still no sign of the paperweight. If I couldn't find it, she couldn't either.

Standing there, staring down at Wyatt and Kathryn's stunned

expressions, breaths hiccupped in my chest. Time blurred. The fight lasted a few minutes, maybe, but felt like four rounds in a boxing match. So many questions ran through my mind. How long had it been since I'd seen my mom? Where was Portia?

Kathryn stood up. She brushed her hands over her stained dress as her breathing slowed down and her composure returned. "You will not win. Not again."

Fine. Kathryn made her decision. My turn. "Wyatt, it's time you know the truth about your dad."

"What are you doing?" Agitated and fidgeting, Kathryn shifted around as her usual regal stance crumbled.

The secret begged to get out. Elias would warn me against this. Mom would be pissed because the reveal wasn't as big and dramatic as she wanted. Kathryn might lose it. Wyatt would be destroyed.

I hated the last part. Wyatt deserved better and dragging him further into this mess made me an unwanted accomplice in this tragedy. I'd wanted to spare him from this showdown, protect him, but that wasn't possible. Giving him partial information would be worse than arming him with the whole truth. There was nowhere for him to hide. He needed to be prepared and that couldn't happen if he only knew Kathryn's warped version of events.

"Your father was the one who planned the murders twenty-seven years ago. He killed your grandparents for money. He was the mastermind." Saying the words didn't bring any satisfaction.

"She's lying." Kathryn put a protective hand up in front of Wyatt as if her arm could block him from hearing the facts. "Stop this."

"Your father convinced your uncle to go along with his big plan." The words raced out of me between harsh breaths. "Cooper was younger and totally bought into everything your father said."

Kathryn grabbed Wyatt's hand. "Your father was a hero."

The bat was so heavy in my hand. Dropping it would touch off another skirmish. Using it would wreck what little decency I had left. But I had to focus on the past, not the present. "Your dad set himself up as the savior that day for the fame and the money. Cooper had no idea your dad intended to betray him."

"Don't listen to her. She is a petty con artist." Kathryn was seething. She abandoned any attempt to hide behind good manners and proper etiquette as she shifted and gestured and fought the words.

I wasn't done. "Your dad set up your uncle and massacred your grandparents. He lied to everyone, including you."

"That can't be true." Wyatt sounded tortured by the information being thrown at him.

No more games. No more pretending. No more hiding behind a fake marriage, regardless of the cost. "I have the proof. That's why your father married me, Wyatt."

"So, you did blackmail him?" The disappointment and hurt came through Wyatt's voice.

I debated dodging the question and ended up shading it. "It's the agreement we reached. We got married. Your dad lost control of his life and banks accounts and in return I stayed quiet."

My moment of triumph never came. The hoped-for catharsis fizzled. There was no payoff. Not even satisfaction at unmasking Richmond for the psychopath he was. The scene left me with the same emptiness I'd carried my whole life.

The two of them stood in front of me like a wall of outrage. In sync and against me. They looked ready to do battle, to join forces and take me down.

I still held the bat and one last emotional grenade. "What's worse, Wyatt, is that I wasn't the only one who stayed quiet. Your mother knew what your dad did."

Kathryn gasped. "How dare you."

"She knew before the killings happened and did nothing to stop him."

Chapter Sixty-One
HIM

Twenty-Seven Years Earlier

One week to go.

The countdown ticked in my head. I'd stopped concentrating in class. My notes consisted of drawings and maps. I destroyed both at the end of each day. No evidence left behind.

Screw homework. Screw Mr. Phillips and AP Calculus. The stakes were higher now. The school would cut me slack after the killings. No one would dare flunk the lone survivor and big school hero. I should get automatic top grades for my bravery. They'd all be grateful for being alive.

The plans were set. The last three components clicked into place. Gun safe. Car. School schedule. We'd timed out every minute and ran through the perfect scenario at least twenty times. Until it rolled without any hiccups.

Most practice sessions Cooper did well. He performed his assigned tasks. Figured out how to carry the guns and keep them hidden. He was an eager and willing assistant. He'd get into it and try to improvise. I stopped that shit fast. There could only be one leader, and that was me.

A few times after, when we were back home following a test run, usually after Mom's required family dinner, he'd question if we should go through with it. He'd talk about loving them. He'd ask who would take care of things and pay for stuff if they were gone. Every now and then he'd fixate on a good memory and want to forget the plan.

His back-and-forth answered my biggest question—what to do with Cooper? He lacked commitment, so I had no choice. He'd compromise everything. Feeling guilty one day, he'd tell the wrong person and we'd get caught. I couldn't take the risk of him unraveling my work.

"Are you bored or something?"

My mind snapped back to the present. In the back seat of my car. To the girl beside me with her shirt unbuttoned and her pink bra peeking out.

"No, babe. We're good."

She snorted. "Good?"

I hated that sound.

"Sorry. Family stuff." That wasn't exactly a lie.

"Do you want to talk about it?"

I did. I wanted to impress her with how I'd put the puzzle together. Gathering the pieces took months. Medical school would be a breeze compared to this.

Instead, I shrugged. "It's nothing."

"Then . . ." Her hand moved up my thigh.

I'd miss the sex. She let me touch her however I wanted. She was willing to try things. That's what made her so perfect. She did whatever I asked, and I forgot about her the second she was out of my sight.

The photo I convinced her to send me. That one time in the park. Dad was pissed I'd missed curfew, but it was worth it. And his opinion wouldn't matter soon.

People would be watching me after this was over, probably following me and trying to get a good look or a trauma-filled picture they could sell. I couldn't be seen laughing or sneaking around with her. This was serious. All tears and sadness. No fun. Perform so that people would say I was so mature and cheer for me.

Consistency was key. I would not get caught.

"Well?" She squeezed her body close, pressing up against me.

Why not? One more time. But hell, I would miss that mouth. She knew how to use it. She also listened and acted interested . . . and knew when to shut up.

Maybe I could keep her on the side and feed her some details. Share and enjoy some of the glory I'd have to pretend I didn't feel. Tempting. I couldn't trust her, but I could entertain her while she got me off.

She kissed my neck and her hand slipped into my jeans.

"Kathryn . . ."

Chapter Sixty-Two

HER

Present Day

"You can't be right . . . that's not . . . You got this all wrong." Wyatt hesitated over every word. His voice, anguished and thick with emotion, shook. He stumbled backward as if the weight of the truth proved too much to bear.

Seeing Wyatt reeling stirred up a violent mixture of doubt and guilt. Thoughts and memories battled in my mind. *Why didn't you wait? Give the kid a break.* I'd been thrown into a fire of family secrets. The scorching pain never subsided.

The dose of reality might be necessary but that didn't make the delivery satisfying. I mentally seesawed between shame and determination, landing on the justification that now was better than later. He had privacy in my house. The public didn't need a front row seat to his pain.

Soon, everyone who ever supported Richmond or cheered him on, those who didn't, and the few who never heard his heroic story would learn what really happened. The facts behind the shooting would seep out. Making that happen fell on me. Surviving the revelation fell on Wyatt.

He leaned against the bookshelves and seemed to regain his

balance. His physical balance. His emotional balance . . . no. "Dad killed them? His family and that other guy?"

The *other guy* deserved more than a footnote in Richmond's story. It would be nice if someone in the Dougherty family remembered that. "Zach Bryant."

Kathryn rushed to her son's side. She comforted him with touches and soothing words. "Of course he didn't. Your dad would never."

"You're so keen on exposing Wyatt to this conversation. You attacked me in my home. Then there's whatever the hell you did to my mom."

Wyatt frowned. "Wait. Where's your mom?"

"You don't know anything." Kathryn snapped at me but her efforts to calm Wyatt didn't stop. She fawned over him, hovered. Suffocated.

Wyatt didn't move.

"Richmond loved to hear himself talk. His ego demanded constant feeding. That was your job as his girlfriend, then his wife." He'd told her. He would have needed to tell her. Keeping the secret of his brilliant plan would have chipped away at him and denied him the curtain call he craved. And he wouldn't have waited.

"No. That's not true. I had my own life. I was a student and I . . . I . . ."

"You forfeited every ounce of decency to stand by your demented husband's side for decades." It was a guess but an educated one, and I grabbed on to it whenever sympathy flooded me. "You're in photos and mentioned in articles. Your job was to hang on his arm and help paint the picture of the grieving but stable all-American boy."

"Why would she do that?" Wyatt's flat voice barely rose above a whisper.

"Greed. Your grandparents' big pot of money." The obsession with hoarding money didn't register with me. I never had any and never dreamed of a life rolling around in it. "Now I have their money, and she hates that."

Kathryn visibly pulled herself together. She stood a little straighter and lifted her chin as if to say she would not be beaten. "That was a mistake that will be fixed."

Unbelievable . . . but not really. Even as the foundation crumbled beneath her, Kathryn's first allegiance was to recouping all she'd lost.

I refused to be derailed until I played my theory out to the end. "You and Richmond dated during college. You were always around him. In his circle. You knew what he did back then and you lived with it all these years."

"Wait a minute." Wyatt held up both hands. He looked like he wanted to stop the conversation zipping around him. Catch the horrible facts and pull them back for examination.

"She's vile." Old Kathryn had returned.

Forget the blood on her dress and my mother lying in the other room. Kathryn held court in the middle of Richmond's office. I tucked the bat closer to my leg just in case. "When I confronted Richmond with the evidence of what he did to his family, he ran to you. You both risked exposure if I wasn't handled."

"Mom?"

I vowed to talk until Wyatt believed me. "That's why you agreed to the quick divorce and settlement. You knew the evidence I had could implicate you. You couldn't afford that."

Kathryn rubbed Wyatt's shoulder probably the same way she'd been doing since he fell down as a toddler. "I was appalled by the affair and insisted on a divorce. I never dreamed Richmond would fail to get the life insurance he promised and put me in financial peril."

This woman held on to the fantasy of a happy marriage despite the barrage of evidence to the contrary. She was the only one in the room who believed in her vision. "He betrayed you. Over and over again and you never left him."

"Richmond humiliated me. He should never have done that."

The truth. Finally. "Because you had a deal, and that deal was held together by a secret so devastating it would destroy everything. You never thought he'd back out. You had leverage because you were the one person who could unmask him. Until I came along."

"Unlike yours, my marriage was real."

She had some fight left in her. Impressive, but her need to be the victim poked at me. She was not innocent in all of this. Richmond would have cut her loose long ago if she had been. She stayed by his side because he needed to have her there to watch over her and control what she said.

"You thought his fear of you squealing would bind him to you. Through the lies and the affairs, you had him caught and he could not leave you." Nothing else made sense. That had to be what happened.

Kathryn stood there with her hands fisted at her sides. Her gaze traveled to the bat then around the room before landing on me again. Her mouth pulled tight in the silence. "I should have waited and used that bat you kept beside the bed on you."

The whoosh of relief hit me that time. The truth. Sick and twisted and right in front of me all along. "But you did use it."

"Yes."

The last stubborn piece solved. The force of it stole my breath. Kathryn was at the bottom of all of this. "You're the one who killed Richmond."

Chapter Sixty-Three

HER

Present Day

Kathryn stood perfectly still until the second she didn't. She lunged for the desk next to me. Skipped the lamp and whatever else might have worked as a weapon. Knocked over a cup of pens and snatched the scissors.

"Mom! What the hell?" Wyatt jumped back, slamming into the bookcase with enough force to make it shake against the wall.

It's not a knife. Repeating the sentence didn't ease the panic running through me. Anything but a blade. The sight of it paralyzed me. I could feel my body and brain shut down.

The edge of the scissors flashed as it caught the light. Kathryn held them in her fist with the pointed end visible and her expression fierce. She flicked the blade around in the air. Taunting me. She couldn't know my fear or how anxiety flooded through every vein at the thought of the end slicing through my skin.

Only Mom knew what I'd done and she'd used that self-defense murder as fodder to make me dance at her command. She'd never tell Kathryn, but somehow Kathryn picked the weapon of my nightmares.

She didn't make a sound when she launched her strike. She

took racing steps toward me right as Wyatt pushed away from the bookcase. Their bodies slammed together only a few feet in front of me. Wyatt's block stopped Kathryn's momentum. She stumbled to the side, losing ground. Her thigh jammed against the corner of the desk. The haze never left her eyes.

Wyatt doubled over.

The air in the room stilled and walls seemed to close in around us, trapping us in a tight, suffocating space. Only seconds had passed during the shift from silence to the crescendo of harsh breaths and rustling clothing. My reaction was a beat too slow. I raised the bat but hadn't set my grip. I didn't know where to look—at Wyatt to make sure he was okay or at Kathryn to be on guard.

Kathryn didn't react to Wyatt's distress. She stalked toward me again, slower but equally determined. My muscles moved without any conscious signal from my brain. This time I raised the bat, ready to swing.

"Kathryn, stop."

Chapter Sixty-Four

HER

Present Day

Elias stood in the doorway. Another emergency visit. This time I welcomed it. At the sight of his grim expression and obvious fury the tension snapping across my nerves eased. If he was here, the police would be close behind. But I remained coiled, ready to spring.

A wail of pain cut through the uneasiness. Across the room, Wyatt cradled his arm. Thin ribbons of blood ran down to his hand then dripped onto the floor. The horror of what that could mean hit me.

"What happened?" I'd watched his mother's slow-motion wreck but missed this.

"Wyatt!" Kathryn ran to him.

"You stabbed me." Wyatt clamped his hand over the wound, but blood seeped through his fingers and his body listed to one side.

That shocked, almost breathless voice would haunt my nightmares. Wyatt took his hand away for a second and I regretted looking at his arm. A deep puncture, not a superficial cut or a light prick. Kathryn had nailed him.

"I didn't mean . . . it was her." The venom returned to Kathryn's voice. She pointed the scissors at me again. "Look what you made me do."

"Stop this." Elias stepped in front of me without an ounce of self-preservation. He held up both hands to confront one of the town's most prominent members as she careened into disaster. "Put the scissors down. Now."

Kathryn shook her head. "You don't understand what she did."

What was wrong with her? "Your son needs a hospital. My mom is injured."

Worrying about Mom broke my concentration more than once during the last half hour. The extent of her injuries could be severe. The slow drip of lies and years of deceit should have stomped out my ability to care. I craved the ability to be forever detached, or at least ambivalent. Despite every effort I failed.

I both hated her and loved her. The former clear with a list of reasons and explanations. The latter murky as it repeatedly knocked me down.

"Portia?" Elias called out. "Go outside and wait for the police."

"She's here?" I couldn't see her, but I heard footsteps behind me, getting too close to her mother's derailing. "Do it now, Portia."

My shout sent her running in the opposite direction. I didn't regret scaring her or pissing her off. I would have done anything to keep her out of the room. There was no way for her to walk into this scene and leave it unscathed. After this day she'd have enough horrible memories to wrestle with and digest without this one.

I owed her. Portia had called Wyatt and Elias and maybe the police. She'd subjected her relationship with her mom to a test it might not pass.

With one Dougherty child out of the fray, my attention switched to the other. Blood seeped out from under Wyatt's hand. Splashes landed on his shirt. On the floor.

Elias held his hand out to Wyatt. "Come toward me."

Kathryn grabbed her son's uninjured arm, stopping him. Pulling him close and clinging to him as he winced and struggled through the pain to push her away.

"Mom, please." Wyatt's voice sounded strained to the point of breaking.

"Don't you understand what needs to happen here?" Kathryn's unblinking eyes provided a window into the wild thoughts filling her mind. Somehow her voice stayed even. "We can still resolve this, put everything back together, but we have to move now."

The situation continued to devolve. She clearly had a plan in her head and intended for everyone in the room to jump to her command. Worse, she hadn't dropped the scissors.

Dread settled in my stomach and refused to leave. This mess could only have an unhappy ending. I threw Wyatt the blanket hanging over the back of one of the chairs. "Wrap it around your arm and keep it lifted."

That was the full extent of my first aid knowledge. The ambulance better show up soon.

Elias took a step in Kathryn's direction. "This is over. Give me the scissors."

"No. No, listen to me." Her now uneven tone bounced between pleading and ordering. "Addison has to die. It's the only way to get our lives back."

"Kathryn—"

She clearly wasn't in the mood for a lecture. "You're our attorney. You can't say anything unless we allow it. We'll explain that you walked in the room after Addison attacked us."

I couldn't control my rage. "You're going to claim self-defense against me in my own house? You can't be serious."

"Wyatt and Portia will understand once I explain all the sordid details to them." She tugged on Wyatt's arm. "You see what happened here, right? She provoked me."

"Mom killed Dad." Wyatt delivered the horrible sentence in a flat tone. She'd admitted her attack but hearing the stark words from Wyatt's mouth brought the tragedy fully into focus.

"I heard the part about the bat." Elias's deep voice mirrored the gravity of the situation.

Until that moment my mind had filled with stray thoughts and unanswered questions. I kept trying to weed out the clutter and concentrate. Elias had been outside the room when Kathryn exploded. He'd listened to every truth I insisted on unburying, spread out like a roadmap.

Now I heard the sirens. Faint, still in the distance, but headed this way as they had several times before. My exhausted body begged for the police to drive faster.

"Richmond was getting . . . complacent. Sloppy. Overconfident." Nervous energy wrapped around Kathryn. She stumbled over words and gulped in deep breaths. "He started to believe the persona we'd created."

We not *he*. She'd been in on all of it. A willing partner.

The witness Richmond left alive.

"I knew if . . . if there was a court case about the surgery someone could look into his past. There was so much at stake." She shook her head like she'd got lost in her panicked words. "I was on the verge of losing everything I'd worked for."

"So, you killed him." She did it and decided I should take the blame.

"We had a fight that last day about his strategy and how long his plan was taking. He could be so intimidating. That temper." She turned to Wyatt and continued to plead her case. "You know how he was. You all know."

"So, you picked up the bat." Elias said.

"He told me Addison threatened him with it." Kathryn moved toward the window. "He was so out of control. I . . . I needed to protect myself. I didn't have a choice."

"You did." Wyatt had wrapped his arm but his face remained pale and his voice shaky. "You could have done a thousand different things and Dad would still be alive."

The sirens grew louder. Closer.

"The police can't be here." Kathryn pulled back the curtain and peeked outside. Her fidgeting kicked up instead of winding down. "We're running out of time."

Before the police arrived and lawyers stepped in I wanted one last confession. She tried to shift the blame, but it landed squarely on her.

"How hard did you have to hit Richmond to make him fall like that?" Because it was intentional and preplanned. Richmond's murder was not a heat of the moment thing. Kathryn had been passionate in her fury when she targeted her ex. I'd bet my life on it.

Her mouth opened and closed. It took a few seconds for her to answer. "I didn't . . . You were supposed to be there. At the scene or close by. But that damn diner. I couldn't wait. You didn't see his face."

I'd seen his rage. I could imagine hers. All those years of serving him, fulfilling his needs, backed up on her. "And you knew you had to do something because he was capable of killing. He'd killed before."

Wyatt made a gagging sound as his body curled in on itself. "I'm going to be sick."

The room erupted in chaos. Everyone moved as if a whistle had been blown. Kathryn sprang from the window and raced toward me. The scissors aimed at my face, ready to plunge. Wyatt shouted as Elias pivoted to block the incoming attack.

Bang

The shocking noise made me drop. I squatted with my hands on the floor and my head low as adrenaline coursed through me, shaking my whole body.

"No!"

At the sound of Wyatt's scream, I looked up. Kathryn thumped against the wall. Her legs crumpled under her, and she started sliding. She landed in a sitting position that seemed to jolt through her whole body. Her eyes stayed open and filled with fear.

The stain on her dress grew. The drops turned into a splotch. More blood. This time hers.

My attention shot to the doorway, expecting to see the police pour in. One woman stood there—Mom. Tense shoulders and stiff arms. Blood matted in her hair and her shirt torn at the shoulder. She looked like she was two seconds from falling over but her eyes were bright and clear.

Mom lowered her gun. "I told her not to come here again."

Chapter Sixty-Five

HER

Present Day

Another first. I'd never been in a hospital before and didn't enjoy being in the middle of the sensory overload now. The halls had a distinctive chemical smell. The fluorescent lights buzzed. Machines pinged. Monitors and sensors went off every few minutes.

I sat in the waiting room in a too-small, uncomfortable plastic chair that dug into the underside of my thighs. A constant parade of people rushed by. Doctors and visitors. A few in tears.

Elias joined me with two cups of coffee. He sat down and handed me one. The rich smell tempted me, but I'd already heard someone complain about the harsh taste. I settled for cradling the cup, trying to force warmth into my chilled body.

I'd been checked out and declared fine. The word meant nothing because tremors still moved through my hands and my heartbeat refused to slow down. The fight with Kathryn aggravated the injuries from the fight with Thomas.

So many attacks. Thinking about the last few days turned my brain to mush.

"Any more from the doctor about your mom?" Elias looked every inch the concerned father. He wore what for him probably qualified as casual clothes. Dress pants and an oxford. He hadn't stopped frowning since he rushed into the house and stopped Kathryn from killing me.

"She has a minor skull fracture." Interestingly, a mild version of what killed Richmond. That likely meant Kathryn hit him harder than she hit Mom, and I had no idea how to interpret that. "It's a serious diagnosis but treatable."

The doctor said a severe break could have resulted in all sorts of horrible things, like brain bleed and fluid on the brain. The CT scan and MRI didn't show any of those potential issues, but she'd be in the hospital a few days for observation and treatment and then have whatever follow-up appointments the specialists recommended.

"I got worried when she started slurring her words." Elias sounded exhausted but refused to leave the hospital until we knew more about Mom's status.

I'd been so sure she was faking but then she started throwing up. "The doctor said we got lucky. With knocks to the head many people don't know they're injured until it's too late."

Elias made a humming sound. "She's going to be fine."

The word made my head pound. "She's like a vampire. Impossible to kill."

"Even vampires have a weakness."

"I've never found hers."

He stretched his legs out in front of him and let out a long exhale. "Normally I'd say you, her daughter, were her weakness."

"But you've spent some time with her and know that's ridiculous."

He laughed. "Basically."

He really was a smart man. He picked up on cues and cryptic

phrases meant to cautiously steer him in a certain direction. I liked him and I didn't like many people.

Detective Sessions walked into the quiet room. For once, I didn't dread seeing him. He had a bit of a swagger. Catching Thomas and Kathryn, and potentially blowing apart Richmond's decades-long hero story, made him look like a genius.

You're welcome.

He stopped in front of me. Not towering over me or using other amateur intimidation tactics this time. He genuinely looked concerned. He hadn't blamed me for anything or threatened to drag me in for questioning in days. Clearly we'd reached a turning point in our rocky relationship.

The detective didn't waste time with small talk. "Kathryn is still in surgery. She was shot in the lower chest. There's lung and spleen damage but the doctors are hopeful for a full recovery."

That was good news. Well, for Wyatt and Portia's sake it was.

"She needs to be in perfect shape to go to prison." She had a long list of criminal charges ahead of her. Her reputation in the community had plummeted. No one rushed in to defend her. She'd need to run through her bank accounts and other resources to clear her name. Lie, guilt-trip her kids into helping, and generally be a pain in the ass.

"I've informed the police in Annapolis. There will be a new investigation into the Dougherty family deaths," the detective said.

"She was careful not to specifically admit that she helped Richmond plan the murder decades ago." In the rush of danger, I thought she'd fessed up on that point, too, until Elias told me Portia stood in the hall outside of the study and recorded the entire conversation before he got there. Later, after the chaos died down, she played it for him. Kathryn had slithered her way into a hazy response that might not prove anything with regard to the older crimes.

Elias finished off his crappy coffee. "She was clear she killed Richmond. That's enough."

In self-defense. Even there she'd fudged the truth. "I bet she'll get away with it."

I had a longer speech about how rich people always weaseled out of stuff, but why bother. The press would run with stories about the murders then and now. True crime addicts would dig up details. Information about the tape and the map would leak out. Richmond would soon be known as the guy who suckered his younger-but-not-innocent brother and killed his entire family for money.

Job done.

"Did you know your mom had a gun in the house?" Detective Sessions asked.

The question sat there while I weighed the chances of this being some sort of trap. But Elias didn't step in, and the detective didn't seem to be plotting. "She mentioned it when Kathryn kept showing up at the house, but I honestly thought she was kidding."

"I gave Nick the listening device you found in your house," Elias said.

"To be clear, Portia found it and warned me." I had two sources of guilt and worry, and she was one. Her brother was the other. "Do you know how she is?"

"Both Wyatt and Portia are in shock. Family friends, your neighbors across the street, the Rothmans, stepped in to help."

The Rothmans. Again. I really needed to go over there and

introduce myself . . . or not. But I did have to admit the couple pitched in when needed and without being asked. They appeared to be decent. Maybe Richmond tainted my view of the town and my neighbors until I couldn't see that there was nothing wrong with the place. The area might be as pretty on the inside as it was on the outside. Not sure yet.

The detective continued. "Those kids have a long road ahead of them."

My job was to get out of the way and leave them alone. I'd unleashed enough shock and horror in their lives. But I couldn't stop thinking about them. "Their suffering and pain make me hate their parents even more."

"We have the evidence you turned over about Richmond and what happened to his family. Evidence you should have turned over as soon as you found it." This bit sounded like the old Detective Sessions. "When was that, by the way?"

"After Richmond died." Another lie but this one was necessary to protect my maze of convoluted secrets.

My butt had gone numb from the hard chair. I shifted around but couldn't find a comfortable position. The fidgeting after the lie was not my best timing.

When the detective stared at me instead of commenting, Elias did his usual legal song and dance. "She wouldn't have married Richmond if she knew the truth."

She shouldn't have married him at all. But that was a blowout fight I planned to have with my mother. As soon as she got out of the hospital and found a place to stay that wasn't mine.

"Of course." The detective looked around the room and checked behind him. "Is there anyone we can call for you and your mom?"

"No." Elias was the only person I had and how sad was that?

"I know your mom wasn't married to your dad but maybe he should be notified?" the detective asked.

The men watched me and appeared pretty invested in my response. They weren't going to get the details they wanted. I'd held the devastating truth in this long, even as it morphed and changed with my mother's delayed epiphanies, and I didn't plan to stop now.

"He's dead."

Chapter Sixty-Six

HER

Present Day

Elias arrived at the house two days later with Portia and Wyatt in tow even though their mom forbade them from seeing me. Only Kathryn would have the nerve to issue a command while under guard and handcuffed to a hospital bed and think anyone cared about her opinion.

The kids made their request through Elias instead of directly to me. I wasn't sure why they chose that route or why they wanted to see me but how could I say no? I'd set a bomb off in the middle of their routine lives. The ripples continued to blanket and destroy the world around them. They would forever be compared to their parents and judged by their actions. Portia and Wyatt were the children of ruthless killers.

The whole situation was unfair. Kids should be able to break free of their parents' reputations. Time would have to pass before it became clear if Wyatt and Portia had the strength to try and if the world would let them.

I buzzed them in at the gate and they soon walked into the kitchen. The specialty cleaners had come and once again eliminated the signs of the battles fought on the house's expensive hardwood floors.

Portia walked in without hesitating. Wyatt lingered in the doorway with Elias, looking ready to bolt if things turned upside down. I couldn't blame him. The ghosts of their parents' destructive decisions lingered. Any positive memory he might have of the place got swamped by the flood of terrible ones.

Elias broke the silence. "You were right. Portia pressed all the buttons on the security pad out front and hit it with a stone. That and the open pedestrian gate triggered the silent alarm."

Elias sounded a bit like a proud papa when bragging about Portia's ingenuity. The man should think about having children. His instincts were rock solid, and the kids would get used to his tendency to spout legalese. Eventually.

I didn't know any decent men. Except for him.

"You also went to the Rothmans to get help." I knew because Elias told me. Portia was the type of genuine hero her father had claimed to be. She could have lapsed into teen moodiness when I kicked her out, but she got the message and acted. I owed her and would honor that debt as soon as I figured out how. "Thank you. I don't know what would have happened without your quick thinking."

Portia stood by the kitchen island for a few seconds without saying anything then she launched her body across the room and thumped against my chest. She wrapped her arms around me in a suffocating bear hug. The sudden show of affection threw me off-balance. My instinct was to freeze but I didn't want to send the wrong message. It took a frown from Elias for me to get the hint and hug Portia back.

The uncharacteristic display of emotion ended as quickly as it started. Two seconds tops. When she pulled away her cheeks were bright red. She might be embarrassed but I was stunned. I also didn't want to ruin the moment or make her feel awkward, so I focused on Wyatt.

"Are you okay?"

A sling held his bandaged arm. Kathryn's stab had done some damage. He would need physical therapy once the pain subsided and the worst of the injury healed. The emotional scars would take longer to heal. If they ever did.

"Not really." Wyatt shrugged. "But that's not why we're here."

"Okay." I braced for verbal impact.

"I planted the notes." He visibly swallowed. "The one in your mailbox was easy. There's a blind spot with the security camera along the wall on the left side. I snuck in there."

Oh, shit. This kid.

I needed one more confirmation. "And the one on the wall in my bedroom?"

"You hadn't disabled my security code yet, so it was pretty easy for me to get in. I didn't think about it then but the alarm company probably has a record of my code being used." His rough tone spoke to how difficult it was for him to admit all of this. "Mom told me we needed to force you out. She planted a listening device to collect intel but then something happened to it."

Also Portia. The girl was a superstar.

"She hasn't admitted it, of course, but Kathryn hid the bat to frame you. She had it last and Wyatt didn't know about it," Elias said.

"But the notes . . . Mom kept begging me to do something and telling me that Dad would want me . . ." Wyatt paled. "Never mind. It doesn't matter."

His honesty did. "I appreciate your telling me the truth."

Richmond and Kathryn had used their son's loyalty and love against him. They'd weaponized him and baited him with lies. They caused damage and saddled him with mistrust that might take some expert therapist decades to unravel. I didn't want to add to that.

"Was the break-in you, too?" I asked.

"That was Thomas," Elias said. "After you visited Richmond's office, Thomas was convinced there was evidence that might implicate him at the house. He came looking for it, but the alarm stopped him."

"I was up in your bedroom writing on the wall. I watched him walk across the side yard and snuck out of the house before he could see me." Wyatt shrugged. "I thought he was meeting you. Figured you two were planning something. Then the alarm went off and I ran."

Nothing I could say would matter, so I didn't try.

"When Thomas found out he wasn't on the hook for murder he started confessing to everything else," Elias explained. "He's looking for a deal on the assault charges concerning what he did to you and wants to duck the hospital fraud issues. I doubt he'll be successful on either of those."

For a second I forgot I'd battled enemies on more than one front over the last few weeks. Many people in, and adjacent to, the Dougherty family had wanted me gone. They all failed.

Wyatt's stark expression didn't vanish. "I'm sorry. I should have—"

"You're forgiven." It was that simple. I didn't blame Wyatt. I blamed the people who created him and manipulated him. "I understand how hard it can be to say no to a reckless parent who is determined to burn the world down."

My reckless parent, Mom, came home tomorrow. Unfortunately, *home* meant to my crime scene of a house because she didn't have one of her own.

Wyatt looked confused now. "How can you forgive and forget something so shitty?"

Because his shitty acts didn't touch my mom's. At least he could apologize and when he did it was genuine. "Practice. And the forgiveness is real. We'll put everything behind us."

"There are a lot of arrangements to be worked out, but they're comfortable with the Rothmans for now. I know you have questions about them, but the Rothmans are good people. I think you'll find more people in this town are than are not." Elias used his usual careful wording to avoid saying harsh things in front of the kids.

By *arrangements* he meant all the questions surrounding the charges against Kathryn and if she would get bail. She was recovering but she'd be running through money and spending time saving her own ass soon enough.

Good luck with that.

"You two are welcome here. You both have my cell number. You can call or come over at any time." I wanted to give them new security codes for the alarm system, ones just for them, but I needed a bit more time to work up to that. Trust didn't come easy for me.

"We should go." Wyatt looked at his sister and nodded toward the back door.

Making empty promises wasn't my thing but I felt compelled to try. "You're going to be okay. It will take time, but . . ."

Wyatt frowned. "Maybe."

They left to walk across the street to their temporary home.

Elias stayed behind. He helped himself to coffee. Seemed fair since he basically lived here now.

"I never thanked you for running into the house when you did. You protected me and I appreciate it." I didn't understand why he did it, but I owed him.

"It's all part of the legal representation package."

"Really?"

He laughed. "Of course not."

"Look at you being funny." But he kept staring at me. Not in a weird way. More like studying me. All those things that were said during the blowout with Kathryn came rushing back. The admissions. The questions. I didn't know how much he'd heard or how much Portia had recorded while standing in that hallway, or if Kathryn's statements had planted a seed, but I could clarify one thing. "Kathryn was wrong. Richmond wasn't my father."

Elias slowly set his coffee mug down. "I know."

That was easier than I expected.

"He was your uncle."

Chapter Sixty-Seven

HER

Married, Day Four

The diner operated as my safe space. It was far enough from town and from Richmond that it offered a peaceful retreat from the new marriage nonsense. It was also cheap. Big fan of cheap food.

Only a visit from my mother could ruin the sanctity of this place. She sat across from me in the booth, sipping her coffee and frowning at my french fries as if they'd offended her.

"What was so important that you needed to see me right away?" Up until now she'd been satisfied with status reports via my burner phone about *The Richmond Situation*. Her phrase, not mine. Today she demanded a face-to-face.

Lucky me.

The meeting came with a lot of risk. Mom needed to stay invisible. And not just for this plan to work. I'd be fine if she did so permanently.

Richmond watched every move I made, likely because he thought I'd steal the silverware. The alarm system he'd installed with the cameras and the motion sensors and who knew what else had turned the house into an expensive prison. He vowed to find the evidence I'd stockpiled against him so it wouldn't be a surprise if he hired a private investigator to follow me around.

"You were supposed to tell me before you got married. Before the ceremony happened."

It had been four days. Four long days as the newest Mrs. Dougherty.

"I didn't have much of a choice. Richmond sprang the whole wedding setup on me. I barely had time to fix the mess he tried to make." I'd called her twice to clue her in but she didn't answer. Pointing that out would only piss her off, so I didn't bother.

Mom shook her head. "Only Richmond would scheme to fake a marriage."

"True. He's a very consistent jackass. You should see the crap he's pulling with the alarm." I ate a few fries, testing to see if she'd comment on my weight and the need to keep thin while pulling off this ruse. For all her faults, body shaming wasn't her thing, but she'd make an exception if she thought I threatened her end goal in any way.

Mom set her coffee mug down. Her fingers rubbed over the handle. Up and down as she stared into the distance. That's when I noticed the underlying jumpiness. She walked through the world with smooth detachment, always holding herself as if someone she needed to impress was watching. Her best clothes. Full makeup. Hair done. She was not the type to run to the grocery store in sweatpants.

When Mom didn't speak up I did. "The whole point was for me to marry the guy. Not give him wiggle room. Attack from the inside. I begged you to find another way and avoided you for years. Neither of those strategies worked to change your mind."

"I know how we got here."

I ate another french fry as I studied her. Definitely twitchy. But why? She'd dreamed up this con years ago and polished it to perfection. Forced me to help her by threatening to expose my crime. It wasn't lost on me that the scheming and underhanded planning mimicked Richmond's signature style. She'd lose control if I pointed out the similarities between her and the man she despised.

"I have some concerns." Forget offering nuance and details. Mom made the comment and stopped talking.

She had to be kidding. "Now you tell me. After I turned my life upside down and—"

"Not about my plan. My plan is brilliant."

More Richmond-ese speak. The shared personality traits jumped out at me now. "Just tell me what's going on."

"The sex."

"Excuse me?"

"Now that you're married." She talked in her regular voice, which was not quiet. "Sex with Richmond."

The double mention of sex grabbed the waitress's attention. She openly stared at us.

I dropped my voice to a whisper and hoped Mom picked up the hint. "Are you trying to give me *the talk* because it's a bit late for that. I think you were supposed to explain the birds and the bees when I was a kid or at any point up until when I first had sex, which was a decade ago."

Mom's hands dropped to the table. The harsh frown came a second later. "What are you talking about?"

"I actually have no idea. You're the one who brought up this topic."

She sighed at me. She always sighed at me.

"Have you slept with Richmond?"

She finally got there but where were we and why? I refused to believe she had remorse for shaping me into her weapon. That would never happen. This wasn't about sparing me or worrying about using me in any way. If she thought hot sex with Richmond would make her scam better she would have told me to do it. I would have ignored her, but she would have tried.

No, something unexpected and possibly diabolical ran around in her head. I couldn't think of anything scarier. "Why are you asking?"

"Fine. I'll say it. You should refrain from having sex with him. If you already did immediately stop."

I shoved the plate and the fries away from me and rested my elbows on the table. This wasn't a have-in-public kind of conversation, but she'd dragged us down this road. Unless she wanted us to meet here because she thought a public place would ensure I'd stay calm, which was a miscalculation. My heart rate revved up at the thought of what she might say next.

"Tell me why you're so concerned with my marital sleeping arrangements." The idea of sex with Richmond made me wince from the inside out. He was a killer. He killed my dad. Sure, I'd never known Zach but the least I could do was respect him enough not to have sex with the man who murdered him.

Mom was back to touching the mug handle. "There's something you should know."

I took the coffee away from her and put the cup on my side of the table. "Which is?"

The windup to her point had me squirming in the booth. The

world around us slowed to a stop and tension pressed against me from all sides. The other people and the noises in the diner cut off. She didn't live in a subtle world. When she wanted something, she said so. The verbal dancing terrified me.

"Zach Bryant."

Baby steps. "What about him?"

"I didn't know him. He came to the country club with Cooper Dougherty. They were friends, but I didn't date Zach."

"Wait. Are you saying you only slept with him once? Like, you met at a party and hooked up?" If so she'd really lost the baby lottery. And she'd been lying to me for years. She specifically told me they dated. Made it sound like he was her first love.

She made an odd noise. "I need to explain something about your father."

"More than what I already know? You started dating in secret and got pregnant, which he didn't know. He had a rich-parents problem, which you didn't see as a problem at all. Worst of all, he was in the wrong place at the wrong time when the Dougherty brothers walked into that school." That summed up what she'd told me—banged into me—through the years. "Which part needs explaining?"

I knew other details. Curiosity drove me to investigate and find a photo of Zach to check for any resemblance. Every bit of information told the same story. Athletic. Good student. Well-liked. Three brothers. Involved parents. I doubted his life was perfect, but it sounded idyllic compared to mine.

Teenaged me toyed with fantasies about going to live with my loving grandparents in their big house with plenty of everything and no Mom. Those fantasies fed me when Mom would have a tantrum. But then I grew up and realized the Bryants didn't need an unwanted reminder of all they'd lost. They were Zach's family. Technically, also my family but I didn't see the nonexistent relationship that way. I already had more family than I could handle.

Jumping into their lives and shouting, *I'm your surprise granddaughter,* might have been the dream at one point. Now it made me cringe. Me connecting with them meant connecting my mom with them. Let them celebrate and mourn their son as they knew him without all the baggage.

"I'm not talking about what Zach looked like or anything as mundane as that. This is much more serious," she said.

"You're being really dramatic. We're sitting here, in this diner and in this state, because of Zach." In reality, he'd become a footnote in her Richmond revenge story, or he had until today. "Thanks to you and your threats of siccing the police on me for what happened years ago, I'm already stuck in a marriage to a man who considers me expendable. The marriage is legal and if I'm not careful it could turn lethal. So, what do I need to know?"

"Fine."

"Great." *Get to it.*

"I never slept with him."

Wait . . .

"Zach Bryant isn't your father."

Chapter Sixty-Eight

HER

Present Day

"Cooper Dougherty was your father." Elias didn't say anything else after he delivered that stunner follow-up. Neither of us did for a solid two minutes.

I temporarily blacked out or maybe I hoped I did. The buzzing in my head drowned out any attempt at rational thinking. Answering Elias with the full, ugly truth was out of the question. An honest response would lead to a life explosion bigger than anything I'd experienced so far. That left me with the option of blathering on and hoping Mr. Lawyer would move to a new topic.

Keep the words neutral. That was the key. "Why would you think that?"

"All the worries you had about your DNA being analyzed by the police."

"There are potentially other reasons for that concern. Maybe I have a criminal record or need to hide my identity for some other reason." Most people in town assumed that, so why not lean into it?

He smiled. "Are either of those things true?"

"No."

"Exactly." Elias sat down on one of the kitchen barstools.

"The investigator I hired provided some interesting information about your family."

Oh, shit. "The one you promised was investigating August and not me. That investigator?"

"That was his task at the start, yes. When you told me your mom was a problem and couldn't be trusted, I had my guy look into her." Elias wrapped his fingers around the coffee mug but didn't pick it up. "Her past was much easier to uncover than yours."

I leaned back against the sink because I needed something to hold me up. "She lives her life wide open."

This was one secret I never wanted to spill. The secret Mom dumped on me *after* I'd already gotten tangled up with Richmond. The lie that tainted everything. The one lie I would never forgive. It sounded like Elias was about to ram up against it.

"Your mom grew up in Annapolis. She left school because she was pregnant with you. The public story was that she went to live with a relative in New York, but she never actually went to an aunt in New York."

"She doesn't have an aunt." That seemed safe to admit.

"The investigator didn't find anything to connect your mom with Zach. Zach had a girlfriend. People who knew him back then talked about her."

"It was a long time ago. Memories fade." That sounded somewhat logical. I hoped.

"For all of this to explode decades later, to go after Richmond, specifically, suggests a very personal and very targeted revenge. Your DNA worries made me wonder about how deep your connection to the Dougherty family went. That led me to ask the investigator to check into your mom's relationships back then.

She told at least one friend about sleeping with a boy from a wealthy family at the country club where she worked. Zach's family weren't members." Elias stopped to take a sip of coffee. "Richmond had Kathryn. Cooper was the quiet one. Easier to manipulate. He was your mom's way out of the life she didn't want."

I never made the connection before my mom spewed the family secret in the middle of my favorite diner. Never dreamed she could set me up for that sort of violation. What rational person would?

"I'm your lawyer but I'd also like to think we're friends. Reluctant at first and completely mismatched but still friends. You can tell me the truth. It stays between us."

Cooper Dougherty was my dad. The right words rolled around in my head and still didn't fit.

Friends were a luxury I avoided. Moving around, sidestepping emotions, keeping my past locked up, and not trusting anyone made genuine relationships impossible. I'd convinced myself I didn't want or need people. Complete bullshit. Making connections keeps you human. I'd been a hollowed-out husk for too long.

But if Elias and I were friends I needed to protect him while I protected myself. "If I married my uncle the marriage would be void. That means the money, the house, everything, would be up for grabs. The kids should get it all, but Portia is a minor and Kathryn is determined. And she's about to need a lot of money for expensive attorneys who aren't you."

"Well done." He actually looked proud. "Did you go to law school and not tell me?"

"It took a two-second internet search to figure out who wasn't allowed to get married in this state. Uncle-niece is specifically mentioned as forbidden, as it should be." The idea couldn't pass any *ick* test. "I also have common sense."

Mom's paternity bombshell after—conveniently for her not before—I got married caused me to look up a lot of things, including *how to break from your toxic mother forever.* That remained a work in progress.

"When we first started this journey you talked about how you couldn't know the location of my bat because you might have a legal or ethical obligation to disclose it . . . or something like that."

"Close enough," Elias said. "That was also a hypothetical conversation."

We seemed to excel at those. "Consider the question of my paternity equal to the question about the location of my bat."

He didn't say anything for a few seconds then nodded. "You're right. The marriage would be null and void."

"Hypothetically speaking, I didn't know when I married Richmond. I thought Zach was my dad, and that's why she wanted revenge. Mom sprang the family tree horror on me after. When it was too late."

It was important that Elias know this was all *her* idea and I got trapped in her mess. Mom lied for decades to stoke my bloodlust, spinning me round and round in the fatherhood sweepstakes before she landed on the answer that branded me a murderer's daughter.

"I'm surprised you didn't get violent when she told you the truth," Elias said.

"I came close." Picking the diner to deliver the news boxed me in. She didn't allow room for an outburst or throwing things or yelling. She maneuvered me into a benign outward reaction.

The private one included throwing up in the diner bathroom and crying in the stall until my mother came to fetch me. Later, we sat in my car while she pummeled me with excuses about how what she did wasn't a big deal.

The idea of marrying my uncle was so repulsive, so unthinkable and out of bounds, that I would have risked her divulging my part in her husband's death all those years ago to the police if she'd told me the truth before the wedding.

The initial horror gave way to a heavy numbness. She broke me that day. Finally and fully. She'd never been the usual mom but that day she became a monster. And I was the child of monsters.

"In this scenario, your mom was dating Cooper and that's how she got the evidence, including the map and the recording about the murders. Through him. When and how are questions, as is how deeply she was involved in the plot to kill the Doughertys. We're not going to examine those questions because doing so could raise the issue of her culpability, shine a spotlight on you, and potentially put your inheritance at risk."

I didn't need a fancy degree or weeks of research to come up with an answer. I blamed her. I always would.

"And if Kathryn and your mom knew each other back then it would explain why Kathryn came to this house to kill your mom."

Would it, though? That part remained murky. "So, how can we keep the police from testing for my DNA and unraveling all of this?"

"Nick."

"He's never the right answer."

"The DNA on the bat was corrupted, as you know. So, you're

clear there. My understanding is there's no other usable DNA on the items collected."

Luck rarely worked in my favor. Being saved by it now felt like a stretch. "How is that possible?"

"I'm repeating what Nick told me." Elias finished his drink and eyed the coffeemaker as if he intended to make another cup and stay for a while. "The blood evidence collected at the murder scene belonged to Richmond only."

The whole thing had an air of cover-up about it. Elias wasn't the type and the detective seemed like a straight shooter. Too obsessed with me being the bad guy but not someone who would make up or hide evidence. That would mean my superior cleaning skills destroyed all the DNA on the bat and in the house, and that wasn't believable either.

Nothing else came to me except for one thing. "I don't want to owe Detective Sessions a favor."

"Take that up with him." Elias started to make another coffee. "That leaves the issue of Portia and Wyatt. What now? Do you leave and cut them off or do you stay and have a relationship with them?"

Yes. No. Who the hell knew? The possibilities swirled around in my head. I hadn't landed on the clear winner yet. When it came to interacting with them—my newfound cousins, a fact that still left me reeling—the lines between too much time and not enough blurred. They'd remain hazy until all the criminal cases against Kathryn were resolved. Until then . . . "We'll work it out eventually."

"Hypothetically, you're related."

Weird but true. "No matter how hard I try to conquer it, I have a weakness for family."

Chapter Sixty-Nine

HER

Present Day

My mom and I didn't say a word to each other on the drive home from the hospital. The showdown would come in the house. My final goodbye.

I toyed with waiting a few more days for her to fully recuperate, but she didn't look frail or in pain. Her expression remained guarded as she watched me drive the car up to the house and stop at the security gate. I punched in the code and the gate swung open.

She turned to face me. Her intense stare dared me to fight her.

"Are you going to mope all day?" she asked.

I put the car in park and let the engine idle. This argument demanded my full attention and my hands free. "You're kidding, right?"

"I shot Kathryn for you. To rescue you." Mom returned to looking out the front window. Her frown resembled that of a petulant child who heard she couldn't have ice cream for dinner. "You should be grateful."

The unexpected comment knocked the words right out of me.

"I saved you." She emphasized each word.

If I assumed the role of aggressor she could, once again, slither away from any responsibility. The weight of her deceit and sick games would be lifted from her shoulders and piled onto mine. I would—in her mind and in every story she told about me going forward—be the one to blame for the demise of our relationship. Not her manipulation. Not the twisted plan to marry me off to my uncle. A fact that still made me heave. She would be absolved.

Fuck that.

I turned off the engine because this could take some time. "You lied to me my whole life."

She sighed. "Are we doing this again?"

We were in it now and I refused to back down. "You did the unthinkable when you put me in Richmond's firing line. He wanted me dead and all you cared about was killing the guy who stole your golden ticket all those years ago."

"You don't understand what I've done for you."

"I know what you did *to* me."

"Yes, of course. Poor little Addison." Mom shook her head and continued to look out the front window, avoiding eye contact. "You're not a child anymore, my darling. It's time for you to step up and take responsibility. You've had it too easy."

"How do you say stuff like that without laughing?" She acted like I was wasting her time by talking to her.

"I protected you from the truth because you were always so sensitive. I carried the burden alone." Her voice grew louder and firmer the longer she sat there.

"What truth are we talking about? Your version of the truth tends to be a moving target."

She faced me. Her expression spoke to her disapproval and absence of affection. "Kathryn was a whiny bitch in high school. Stuck-up. Thought she was better than everyone."

Finally, a tiny bit of conversation movement. "I get it. You hated her."

"We lived in the same town though we were miles apart in more than distance. She considered me garbage." Mom channeled her anger and frustration into the words, hitting the last one with force. "You should have seen her with Richmond. She'd hang on him and flirt with his friends to make him jealous."

That didn't make sense. "You said she never came into the country club. Where would you have seen this?"

"I studied her. I studied him."

"Wait, do you mean Cooper or Richmond?" My confusion kept building. Cooper should be the center of this conversation, not her teenaged jealousy over Kathryn, or whatever the hell this was.

"Richmond." Mom waved her hand in the air as if she could brush away her memories of him. "This is all your fault, you know. This . . . what you're doing right now. I tried to save you from this moment but you had to push and threaten. You opened this door."

My fault. Of course. Always, except this time I had no idea what I was being blamed for. She was talking in riddles and my patience expired. "What are you saying exactly?"

"Be very certain you want to know this before I give you the particulars."

More drivel. She was exhausting.

"Just say it, Mom." Whatever this juicy piece of information was it couldn't be worse than anything else that I'd heard over the last few months.

"Fine. I didn't get the evidence about the shooting and the school from Cooper. I barely knew Cooper." Her small smile came and went.

"Who . . . wait. How is that possible?" My mental and emotional connection to Cooper never passed the superficial level because all these years—right up until her admission in the diner—I viewed him as a minor player in this drama.

"I didn't have many options back then. I had the drive and determination. I had the will. I had certain assets." She never doubted the power of those. "I tried flirting with Cooper. He was pretty shy. He'd joke with friends and act all tough but then blush if I went near him."

I could imagine a younger version of her making a move. She'd wanted out of her house and into a different life. Nothing wrong with that . . . except for the deceptive method she used to get there.

"What's your point, Mom?"

"Cooper wasn't interested and there was no way he'd be able to handle confronting his parents with a pregnant girlfriend. He was too weak." Her words came out fast but clear. "But Richmond liked to fool around. He laughed about how squeamish Kathryn got when she touched him. She played hard to get. I didn't."

An invasive darkness washed over me, filling every pore. Dread seeped into my thoughts and my movements. It crushed down like a weight against my chest.

Was she saying . . . no, she couldn't be saying this. Even she wouldn't . . .

My thoughts stumbled over each other until they piled up in my mind. "Cooper was my father. You told me that bit of news recently. Remember me barfing in the diner?"

"I wasn't entirely truthful there either." Her expression lacked any emotion. "Richmond was your father."

Chapter Seventy

HER

Present Day

This had to be a joke. A vile, too-awful-to-contemplate joke. A new way for her to torture and control me. A game where the rules kept changing.

She droned on as if she hadn't dropped the ultimate bombshell. "We'd head out of town to get something to eat. I couldn't go back to his house because his parents knew Kathryn and what her role in Richmond's life was supposed to be. We'd use his car. We'd go to the movies. I'm not sure when he actually took Kathryn out because he'd come to me after practice."

No, no, no. Bile rushed up the back of my throat. "You said—"

"Richmond was going off to college. He had something to lose. He was the right Dougherty brother. I don't regret my pick in that sense."

My fingers fumbled with the car door handle. After a few tries I got it open and stumbled into the fresh air. A whooshing sound filled my ears until Mom's voice became a faint but persistent buzzing in my head. I heard a slam and realized she'd gotten out of her side and faced me over the hood.

"I figured he'd do the right thing but then the last time we were *together* he said Kathryn's name instead of mine. Actually whispered it twice during sex."

The ground fell out from under me. My knees actually buckled as the realization of what she was saying hit. Mom and Richmond. Not Zach. Not even Cooper.

"I can't believe this."

"I was curious about why he was so enamored with Kathryn, so I followed her. Slipped into her house, which was easy because it wasn't locked. People were more trusting back then." Mom shrugged as if her words didn't rip and tear at what little foundation she'd given me. "Anyway, I read her diary. Accidentally found the reference to the map then went hunting for it and uncovered the tape, too. She kept her top-secret stash behind boxes stacked in her closet. A good attempt at hiding but not good enough."

The pieces finally fit together. Kathryn hadn't known what evidence I claimed to possess and how it could turn their lives upside down. But then she met Mom and the memories came into focus. Kathryn finally understood Richmond's downfall would be her downfall.

"The map and the recording belonged to Kathryn." I had no idea what lie Kathryn told herself to make losing them all those years ago make sense. She probably thought Richmond stole them, but that didn't matter. Only Mom's actions mattered.

"She likely kept them as leverage against Richmond. Blackmail. Ironic, right? I'm betting she taped the conversation without him even knowing." Mom came around the front of the car to my side. "My plan was to go to Richmond and tell him he was going to be a daddy. I had the evidence of his plans for the shooting as a backup in case he didn't do the right thing."

The horror of what she just admitted hit me like a punch.

"You knew he was going to kill his whole family and did nothing to stop him." The same thing I'd accused Kathryn of doing.

"I didn't know the timing. I'd left a note for him to meet me the next afternoon. It turned out that was the day the of the killings, so he never showed up. The rumors flew around town about finding dead bodies in a house. I immediately knew what had happened and what it meant for my plans."

She stood a few feet away. Far too close. "You're telling this story like it's no big deal."

"You're the one who's so obsessed with the truth. Now you have it. You would have known years ago but you kept delaying."

The delay. That's what pissed her off.

Small inconsistencies now made sense. She didn't magically find the map and tape. She hunted them down and stole them. She didn't go to Zach's family for money because she couldn't. A DNA test would have proven she was a liar. She couldn't go to Richmond's parents because he'd killed them. She probably thought he'd kill her next to keep her quiet.

Threatening Richmond with what she knew wouldn't have helped anyway because, with his parents dead, his money situation was a question mark. That left her with few options and none of the planned-for financial support she needed. So, she waited and let the money pile up. She probably never thought the world would make him into a big hero and give him leverage, but that only delayed her plans. It didn't destroy them.

I hovered on the brink, teetering between throwing up and screaming the house down, reeling from the idea of Richmond as anything but my enemy. We shared a bloodline. We were fucking married. And all she cared about was her schedule and how I'd messed it up.

"What kind of sick person makes their daughter marry her own father?" We were outside and anyone could see or hear but I was too lost in a whirl of nausea and pain to care. "What if we would have slept together?"

"That would have been unfortunate but imagine Richmond's face when I told him what he'd done."

Unfortunate. That's the word she picked.

"You don't care about me at all." I'd danced around the realization for years. Thought it but fooled myself into thinking I was being too harsh. Not anymore.

"My plan wasn't about you, Addison. It was about me settling the score with Richmond by making him pay to get out of your marriage and to keep me quiet. Getting the money I should have gotten back then. But Kathryn killed him first and I didn't get to tell him who you were."

"To gloat."

She rolled her eyes. "Fine. Use that word."

"You're disgusting."

The amusement faded from her face and her tone. "Do not talk to me that way."

I walked back to the car and grabbed my bag. I'd been the only one who ever craved a bond between us and now I didn't want anything from her. Regardless of the pain shooting through me and the grinding sense of failure, I was done.

I'd sacrificed so much to please her. She'd sacrificed me. There was no way to forgive her for that, especially not when she insisted she didn't need forgiveness.

She watched every move. "What are you doing?"

Unable to see anything in front of me, I finally gave up and dumped the contents of my bag on the hood. More rummaging until I spotted the checkbook. The ink blurred as my pen scratched out her name. I would not cry over her ever again.

I ripped out the check and held it out to her. "This buys my permanent separation from you."

She took the check and frowned when she looked at it. "Do you honestly think I'd agree to walk away from Richmond's estate? That's millions of dollars. You're calling me names and spouting off in judgment, but you're the selfish one. You don't get to hoard all the winnings."

I was numb to her dismissal now. The check would clear out one of the accounts I made Richmond set up for me. The low six figures and the amount still wasn't high enough for her.

"I'm keeping part of the estate but giving the majority away. Trusts for Wyatt and Portia. Donations to charities. Peter Cullen will get a check. It won't bring back his son, but it will be something."

Her hand fell but she kept a tight grip on the check. "Absolutely not. You're not distributing my money to those people. I worked too hard for too long for you to hand out dollar bills on the street corner." She eyed the checkbook. Probably toyed with the idea of taking it. "You seem to forget I have leverage."

It took her long enough to drag that oldie out. The threat no longer carried a punch. It had turned into a whimper compared to what she'd done. "Use it. Turn me in. Go ahead. Implicating me implicates you, and I have money for attorney fees, thanks to Richmond. You still won't get one more cent."

The painful reality was that I let her use the defensive killing against me. She never could have turned me in and remained unscathed. I didn't do it consciously, but I ignored that fact because a part of me believed that if we had this tie between us, sick as it was, I still had a mother. Her venom tethered us, and I allowed it.

There wasn't enough therapy in the world to heal this wound.

Her tone changed. Softer. Calmer. "How could you do this to me? I just got out of the hospital. I need to stay here until I'm stronger."

Even fifteen minutes ago that emotional manipulation might have worked. "And I just found out that the sole purpose of my life was to make my homicidal asshole of a father give you money."

Despite all my running, over the years she'd cry out for food, money, or my time, and I'd race to her, heart and hands open because I'd confused being used with being loved. Breaking the lifetime habit and severing all ties would throw me into a hurricane of regret and remorse.

She wouldn't spend one second missing me.

She sighed at me the way she always did. The noise was her signal that it was time to move on. "I'm done fighting about this. I'm still your mother."

"In name only."

She moved so fast I didn't have time to block her. Her hand came up and she slapped me. I heard the crack a second before I felt the sting. She held her body stiff and straight. "You're angry now but you'll get over it. You always have these tantrums then calm down."

She depended on my acquiescence. Thrived on her ability to betray me and laughed at the way I ran back to her, begging for another round of insults and threats. Not one day more.

The rip that started with her lie about Cooper split open when she told me the truth about Richmond. The shredded relationship, already flimsy, now lay in tatters. Unfixable. Today a burning hole in my gut but, hopefully, one day a distant ache. Nothing more than a slight twinge of sadness.

"Actually, this time I won't." I handed her the car keys. "The SUV is yours. Richmond bought it. It's new. Let me know where you're staying. I'll send the rest of your things and the car title there."

No one warned me about the price of freedom. About how much emptiness and despair I'd have to wade through to find it . . . if I ever did.

I punched in numbers on the keypad and the gate opened. "I'll change the security codes and locks today."

"You're going to let those Dougherty kids come in and out, give them money and whatever else they need, but kick me to the street?"

"Yeah. They're family." Broken and messy but I might need them as much as they needed me. They couldn't know about our blood ties, but I could play the role of concerned stepmom. Put my body in front of theirs when it came to all the news that was about to break about their parents.

Found family. I'd stumbled over the term in those self-help books. Sometimes it was better to create a family than stay with the one that raised you. The concept suddenly made sense.

I stepped through the gate and closed it behind me. Mom kept up her complaints as I walked away. Her yelling echoed off the trees and through the yard. This time I didn't cave. I didn't give in to the fantasy of a loving mother or the gnawing pain at the loss of an ideal that didn't exist.

Nothing I tried was ever good enough. But I knew she'd cash the check.

Acknowledgments

In my previous professional life, I dealt with other people's divorces, custody battles, and family traumas on a daily basis. Honestly, it's easier (and way more enjoyable) to write fiction. The biggest benefit being that I can kill people and not get arrested. I'd been looking for the right book, the right characters, to combine my past and my present. To explore the reach and power of family dysfunction without losing the fast-paced, twisty turns of a thriller. I hope I delivered.

I'm sending out a huge thank-you to my editor, May Chen, for loving Addison and this thriller as much as I do. You make every book I write better. Publishing is a rough career and authors can be a little . . . needy (that's the nicest word I could come up with). Your support makes this bumpy ride bearable.

To everyone at team HarperCollins, thank you. I don't know how you all do what you do but I'm grateful for your dedication and expertise. My love for HarperCollins reaches across borders to all my international publishers, especially HarperCollins Canada. You have been amazing. One of these days I'm going to come up there and hug all of you. I promise to call first.

Writing is a solitary career. Surviving it isn't. I have a group of friends who keep me calm and rational (mostly) every day and I love you all. Also, when I've stressed about writerly things in the past, like getting book blurbs, a few amazing thriller writers stepped up and helped me out. Thank you to Samantha Downing,

Jessica Payne, Jamie Lynn Hendricks, Ashley Winstead, Megan Collins, Samantha Bailey, Carol Goodman, and Tessa Wegert for being welcoming and kind. You are all so talented. Please write faster.

Thanks to my agent, Laura Bradford, for doing all the non-writing work so that I can concentrate on the writing. A big thank-you to Katrina Escudero and everyone at Sugar23 for making the impossible possible.

To the Bookstagrammers and BookTokkers out there, thank you for getting the word out and supporting my books. My appreciation is immense.

To my readers, I honestly couldn't do this without you. I love you all.

My final thank-you is for my husband, James, who not only supplies the steady income and health insurance that make my career possible but also the love and support. You are the best decision I ever made.

About the Author

Darby Kane is a former trial attorney and #1 internationally bestselling author of domestic suspense. Her debut book, *Pretty Little Wife*, has been optioned by Amazon for a television series, starring Gabrielle Union. Darby's books have been featured in numerous venues, including *Cosmopolitan*, the *Washington Post*, the *Toronto Star*, and the *New York Times*. You can find out more at darbykane.com.